Does His Friend Think I'm Just Another Fortune Hunter?

The question came before Paula was even aware she was posing it to herself, and it made her sick at heart. Every time something like this happened, it intensified her feeling of helplessness about the relationship between Russ and herself, much as she loved him.

There were moments when she asked herself why she couldn't simply accept his wealth. Why she couldn't take it as much for granted as she did the fact that he had incredible green eyes and was one of the handsomest men she'd ever seen. But it didn't work that way.

Dear Reader:

Nora Roberts, Tracy Sinclair, Jeanne Stephens, Carole Halston, Linda Howard. Are these authors familiar to you? We hope so, because they are just a few of our most popular authors who publish with Silhouette Special Edition each and every month. And the Special Edition list is changing to include new writers with fresh stories. It has been said that discovering a new author is like making a new friend. So during these next few months, be sure to look for books by Sandi Shane, Dorothy Glenn and other authors who have just written their first and second Special Editions, stories we hope you enjoy.

Choosing which Special Editions to publish each month is a pleasurable task, but not an easy one. We look for stories that are sophisticated, sensuous, touching, and great love stories, as well. These are the elements that make Silhouette Special Editions more romantic...and unique.

So we hope you'll find this Silhouette Special Edition just that—*Special*—and that the story finds a special place in your heart.

The Editors at Silhouette

SERL-7/85

MAGGI
CHARLES
That Special
Sunday

Silhouette Special Edition

Published by Silhouette Books New York

America's Publisher of Contemporary Romance

For Phyllis Arruda, who shares with me the conviction that people are so much more important than things. With affection and a great, great deal of admiration.

SILHOUETTE BOOKS
300 E. 42nd St., New York, N.Y. 10017

Copyright © 1985 by KOEHLER ASSOCIATES, LTD.

Distributed by Pocket Books

ISBN: 0-373-09258-X

First Silhouette Books printing August, 1985

10 9 8 7 6 5 4 3 2 1

America's Publisher of Contemporary Romance

Printed in the U.S.A.

Books by Maggi Charles

Silhouette Romance
Magic Crescendo #134

Silhouette Intimate Moments
My Enemy, My Love #90

Silhouette Special Edition
Love's Golden Shadow #23
Love's Tender Trial #45
The Mirror Image #158
That Special Sunday #258

MAGGI CHARLES

is a confirmed traveler who readily admits that "people and places fascinate me." She is a prolific author, also known to her romance fans as Meg Hudson. Having studied the piano and harp, Ms Charles says that if she hadn't become a writer she would have been a musician. A native New Yorker, she is the mother of two sons and currently resides in Cape Cod, Massachusetts, with her husband.

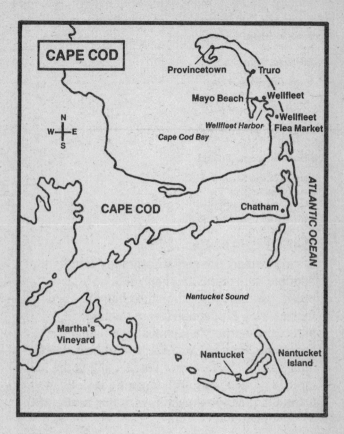

Chapter One

The fog drifted in from the bay that morning, swiftly wafting its way through the low-lying tree branches to blur the outlines of the big, drive-in theater parking lot.

Sea smoke, Paula had always called it, and she loved it. It was evocative of an earlier, easier time, when she'd spent untroubled childhood and adolescent summers here on Cape Cod in her grandmother's house. She could still smell the salt tang in the air, but then she'd only been back on the Cape three weeks. After a while she'd lose the ability to detect the saltiness. She'd become too used to it.

The dealer setting up folding tables in the space next to Paula's grinned across at her. A big, burly man, he looked more like a wrestler than a flea-market dealer.

"Hope this keeps up," he said, nodding toward the fog. "Won't be a beach day, then. We should make out like bandits."

Paula smiled back. She'd noticed that the big man's blue van had a Florida license, and she suspected he was a professional at this sort of thing, traveling from flea market to flea market with the season. A lot of the people setting up appeared to be in the same category. They were unpacking and placing their wares with the kind of expertise that comes only with practice. In contrast, Paula was a novice, and as she pulled the first of the two folding tables she'd brought with her from the back of her old station wagon she felt like she had ten thumbs.

The tables had been in the converted barn, now a garage, at the back of her grandmother's house. She dimly remembered their being used years ago for family picnics, and she doubted that they'd been touched in a decade. Rust had set in. The legs grated in their brackets and then stuck, and she couldn't budge them.

It was not yet seven o'clock, too early for the heat the weather bureau had predicted to have materialized. But already it was uncomfortably humid. As she wrestled with the uncooperative table, Paula could feel the perspiration beading her forehead and dampening the back of her neck.

"Damn!" she muttered aloud.

"Let me help you," a masculine voice suggested.

She stepped back willingly, assuming that this was her husky neighbor speaking, but then she stopped short. The man facing her was a very different type. Tall and broad-shouldered, he was wearing ivory slacks and a white shirt open just enough to give a tantalizing glimpse of curling dark tendrils nestled in the hollow of his throat. Smoky-lensed, oversized glasses camouflaged his face, but there was no secret about the rich ebony thickness of his hair. It was the kind of hair that made a woman ache to run her fingers through, and it was with an effort that Paula wrested her eyes away from it.

"May I help you?" he asked, a slim edge of irony overlaying his politeness.

"Yes . . . please," Paula said quickly.

A long, slender hand reached out to take the recalcitrant table she was holding away from her. She watched him bend over the table, assessing the position of its legs, and she found herself inadvertently assessing *his* position. He was very well put together. Slim, but not too slim. Tanned, he looked as if he spent a lot of time outdoors. And, well developed. She watched the muscles in his bronze arms tauten as he worked, and she noted that there was an easy coordination in the way he moved, and an economy to his movements, as if he believed that strength was something to be conserved. Paula suspected that he was a man who wasted neither motion nor words and, somewhat reluctantly, she admired this. Reluctantly, because she was so entirely the opposite. She tended to fly into things with an enthusiasm too often unbridled, and there were too many occasions when she was inclined to say far too much!

Her thoughts returned to this beautifully groomed, diffident stranger who was freeing the table legs with very little effort. He then yanked them outward, the locks that would keep them upright meshing easily.

He stood back, surveying what he'd done, still perfectly composed, still immaculate, and she wondered if he could possibly be as unflappable as he appeared to be. A cool customer, a very cool customer. He provoked her curiosity, bringing a certain impishness to the forefront. It might be an interesting experiment to try to ruffle him!

He glanced at her, his eyes hidden behind the big glasses, giving her the disconcerting impression that it was possible for him to see out, where other people were concerned, but impossible for other people to see in, where he was concerned.

"Do you have another table that doesn't work?" he

asked, a hint of a smile tugging at the corners of his mouth.

Paula nodded, and as she dragged the second table out of the station wagon she noted that there was even more rust on it than there'd been on the first one. Nevertheless, her volunteer helper unfolded it without difficulty, set it up, and then said, "That should do you. Despite the rust, they look sturdy enough."

"Thank you," Paula said. It sounded inadequate, so she said, "Thank you very much."

"Quite all right," he told her with a formality that was as out of keeping with the flea-market setting as he was. Then, with a wave of the hand, he left her to stride back across the lane that separated the dealer spaces.

So . . . though he didn't look the type at all, he was a dealer. This was confirmed as Paula watched him step behind two long tables covered with spotless white cloths that looked as if they must have been ironed only minutes before. An expensive cream-colored van that shone with factory newness was parked behind the tables. His, undoubtedly.

It was with an effort that Paula forced herself to stop watching the provocative stranger and to get down to tending to her own business. She draped two rather rumpled blue cloths over her tables, then lifted a couple of cartons out of the station wagon and began to unpack them. Glassware and china came to light, and as she set out the lovely old pieces, one by one, it was impossible to entirely swallow the lump that was developing in her throat.

Each item was so special to her, evoking its own set of memories. The small hand-painted Limoges pitcher had been her father's as a child, used to pour milk on his porridge. The shallow amethyst Tiffany-glass bowl had always stood on the sideboard in Gram's dining room. And Paula herself had often used the old commemorative china fishbone plate with a picture of Highland Light on it.

There were etched crystal vases and serving spoons

initialed with *D* for Danvers. There were Sandwich-glass candlesticks in a lovely shade of Vaseline yellow, an amberina punch cup, and a blue satin-glass rose bowl. One by one Paula carefully unpacked her treasures, and set them out on the display tables.

She'd spent two entire weeks cataloging her things, and then pricing them with the aid of antique price guides borrowed from the local library. She'd bought an account book into which she intended to list her sales, and she hoped that tomorrow morning she'd be taking a hefty amount to the bank, where she planned to open a separate account to be used only for the accumulation of money derived from her flea-market activities.

She needed money, quite a bit of money, if she was going to accomplish her purpose. But she was confident that she'd make it over the summer, selling her family heirlooms here in the flea market. Henceforth, she planned to be doing business on Wednesdays and Saturdays as well as on Sundays, and she found herself wondering if the tall man across the way would be here too.

She glanced toward him, and saw that he was setting out his own wares. From this distance it looked as if he, too, was offering a collection of antique glass and china. Was he unloading family heirlooms as she was? Paula wondered.

Again, she forced her gaze away from him, glancing, instead, toward the space next to her. She saw that the burly man had been joined by a very large woman. She had to be his wife, Paula decided whimsically. They looked as if they'd been made for each other.

The woman looked over at Paula and said laconically, "Sun's going to break through." She added, with no change of emphasis, "It's going to be hot as hell."

The sun was beginning to break through, a pale lemon disc swimming through the fog. As Paula set out a rose medallion cup and saucer she paused to wipe the back of her neck with a tissue. She wished she'd had the sense to put her hair up this morning. It was settling around her shoulders like a warm auburn cloud. The humidity brought out the natural curl in it and soft waves that were very becoming framed her face.

The day hadn't even started yet, and already her denim wraparound skirt was wrinkled, and her blue top was as damp as her neck. How *did* the man across the way keep so cool?

Paula was bending over a carton, tugging at an old Ironstone teapot, when a voice already familiar to her said, "That isn't Tiffany, you know."

She straightened slowly, wincing because all this bending and lifting was putting muscles into play that she didn't use all that often.

"I beg your pardon," she said, certain she couldn't have heard him correctly.

He'd added a Panama-type hat to his costume that could have just left Brooks Brothers, and it made him look as if he'd stepped from the pages of *The Great Gatsby*. His ivory slacks were still perfectly creased, and the crisp white shirt was crisper than ever. Good God, Paula marveled, didn't this perfect person standing in front of her ever sweat?

She was sweating. She felt sticky and miserable.

His camouflaged gaze swept her face, and he said quietly, "The lavender bowl isn't Tiffany."

"Amethyst," Paula corrected.

He shrugged. "Whatever. It isn't Tiffany, and that's what you've got it marked."

Paula stiffened. The bowl had been in her family ever since she could remember. She was almost sure Gram had said once that it had been a wedding present. And she distinctly remembered her grandmother cautioning, "Be careful of the amethyst bowl, dear," when Paula had been enlisted to dust the things on the dining room sideboard, occasionally, on a rainy summer afternoon. "It's Tiffany glass."

Now, fighting back her irritation—maybe he was simply misinformed—she said, "The bowl is a family piece and it's very definitely Tiffany. That's to say it was made by Louis Comfort Tiffany," she added, hoping that this bit of gratuitous information would make him realize she wasn't entirely ignorant about antiques.

He shook his head. "Neither Louis Tiffany nor anyone who ever worked with him had anything to do with making that bowl," he assured her. "It was made by the Imperial Glass Company in Bellaire, Ohio, probably about 1916. That's when they introduced their lustered art glass line, which they called Imperial Jewels. Most of the pieces were marked with a trademark in the form of a stylized cross."

As he spoke he reached over and plucked the bowl off the table, then turned it over, surveying the smooth bottom. "This one wasn't marked," he admitted, "but that doesn't alter the fact that it's a nice example of iridescent stretched glass, but definitely not Tiffany glass. You're doing yourself a disservice by mismarking it, and the price you've put on it is ridiculous! Three hundred and fifty dollars? A Tiffany piece of a comparable size might bring that, but your bowl isn't worth much more than fifty dollars, and I honestly doubt you'll get that much for it in a flea market. People come to places like this looking for bargains."

Paula clenched her fists, determined to contain her temper, which was beginning to sizzle. She said carefully, "I'm sure you mean well, Mr. . . . ."

"Russ Grayson," he supplied.

"I'm sure you mean well, Mr. Grayson," she repeated, "but this bowl belonged to my grandmother, and I think she knew more about it than anyone else. It was a wedding present. . . ."

Paula watched the edge of Russ Grayson's mouth curve into an expression too ironical to be called a smile. He said, "I don't doubt that the bowl was given to your grandmother as a wedding present. I'm merely saying that—"

"I know," she finished for him. "It's not Tiffany."

"Exactly," he agreed, "and unless you change the label you're going to make anyone who knows anything about antique glass and china suspicious of everything you have here. I'm sure you must realize that there are excellent reproductions being made these days which sometimes even fool the experts."

"I don't own any reproductions," Paula said wearily. The heat and humidity were getting to her. So was Russ Grayson, not because he was being almost insulting as much as because there was a ring of truth to what he was saying. If he was correct, if she'd mismarked any of her pieces unintentionally, she could be the loser.

She brushed back a lock of hair that kept falling over her damp forehead and said, "Everything I have on this table came out of my grandmother's house, Mr. Grayson. They're all things that have been in my family for a long time. Also, I've been doing my homework about them, and their value. I . . ."

The words trailed off. She couldn't tell a total stranger how important it was that she sell these things.

She saw Russ Grayson frown slightly, and he said, "Look, Miss . . ."

"Paula Danvers," she told him.

"Miss Danvers, I didn't mean to sound so accusatory," he said. "It's easy to make an honest mistake. Identifying antiques is trickier than most people realize, and there's so much chicanery in the field."

His smile became rueful. "There I go again," he admitted, his voice velvet-soft as he apologized. "I assure you I didn't intend to be insulting. I wanted to see what you had because I thought there might be a chance I'd be interested in making you an offer for some of your things."

Paula stared at him in disbelief. It was too quick a change of face to credit, and she watched him suspiciously as he picked up a small Bavarian china creamer painted with pink roses. He turned it around between his long fingers, then tilted it upside down so he could read the mark on the bottom.

Paula had always loved this particular creamer. It was a choice little piece and it had been used regularly in her grandmother's house. She began to wish she hadn't put it out for sale, and decided she'd remove it as soon as this disturbing man left her alone.

Disturbing? Yes, he was very disturbing. Watching him turning the pitcher this way and that, it was impossible not to recognize how beautiful his hands were. Slender, well-proportioned, they matched him. It was also impossible to find fault with the clean line of his jaw, the chiseled features, the rather high cheekbones. He had a strong chin and a mouth that was generously full yet had a firmness about it, as if he were used to keeping his emotions in check. Paula found herself wishing that he'd take off the dark glasses so she could see his eyes.

He seemed to be genuinely interested in the creamer, and so she intercepted any comment he might make to say, "That isn't for sale. I put it out by mistake."

He glanced up quickly, and Paula felt as if his eyes were assessing her through those dark glasses, and reading her much too correctly. He said, "Of course," and held the pitcher out to her. As she reached for it their fingers touched, and a quiver ran through Paula that was astonishingly powerful, and so tangibly sensual, her hand shook. If Russ Grayson hadn't been holding its handle, the little creamer would have crashed to the table.

"I'm s-sorry," Paula stammered, pulling herself together sufficiently to take the pitcher away from him. She held it, feeling very awkward.

"It's a nice piece," he commented. "You have a number of nice pieces. I do think you've overpriced them, though. What did you use as a price guide? You can't count in the sentimental value, you know."

Stung, she said, "I got copies of both the Kovel and the Warman guides out of the library."

He nodded. "They're excellent references. But they're not practical when you're hoping to sell your stuff in a flea market. And that *is* what you're trying to do, isn't it?"

Paula's hesitation gave her away. That, of course, was exactly what she was trying to do, but she wasn't about to discuss her financial needs with this man who was managing to irritate and attract her simultaneously, provoking an emotional tug of war that she didn't need just now.

She saw, to her distress, that he was watching her closely. Now he said quietly, "Look, I'm sorry. We've gotten off on the wrong foot, thanks to my bluntness, but I'd like to try to make amends. That's to say, I'd like to help you."

Paula hadn't thought she'd need help, not with this particular enterprise. The flea market in the Wellfleet Drive-In Theater was the biggest one on Cape Cod, patronized by thousands of people from early summer well into the fall. Taking dealer space in it had seemed the most expedient way of disposing of a quantity of her family heirlooms. She'd felt certain that she'd get more for them in individual sales than she would if she were to let an auctioneer unload them.

She'd done her homework carefully these past couple of weeks, carrying tomes on antique china, glass, silver, and bric-a-brac from the local library to the old family homestead she'd inherited from her grandmother.

She sighed. Evidently she hadn't studied long enough or hard enough. Glancing at her possessions sparkling in the sunlight that was filtering through the last of the morning mist, she was disheartened. It was going to be a blazingly hot and humid day, a beach day after all, and Paula had the sinking feeling that by late afternoon she might find herself packing up most of the things she'd just now unpacked and taking them home with her.

There'd be other chances, true. Even so, she'd counted on this first Sunday to set a pace, to give her the needed encouragement to keep on with the job she'd chosen for herself.

Something else this man had said echoed back.

"You mentioned you might want to make me an offer for some of my things," she reminded him. "Were you serious about that?"

"Possibly," he evaded. "But not at the prices you've put down, I'm afraid. This Royal Bavaria mustache cup, for example . . ."

Paula looked at the large china cup he was holding, flower-patterned with a cobalt-blue border, constructed with an inner rim, so that a man with a mustache could drink his morning coffee or tea without getting the mustache wet.

"These are very collectible," Russ told her solemnly, "but although this is good quality china, I doubt anyone would pay you the forty-five dollars you're asking for it. If you're interested in parting with it, though, I'd give you twenty-five."

"Twenty-five?" She shook her head. "No."

"I'm a dealer," he said flatly. And added, "What do you do ordinarily, Miss Danvers."

She hesitated. Then she said, "I'm a teacher."

There was nothing either ironic or rueful about the smile that curved his lips now. It was a full-blown smile, and it was disconcertingly attractive. Paula found her eyes drawn to his lips as if they exerted magnet force. It was impossible not to wonder what it would be like to feel those lips against hers. They would be warm and wonderful, tantalizing; they would be prologue to what could develop into a whole saga. Paula found her thoughts beginning to spin out of control and she slapped herself back to reality with the brute force of her total concentration.

She was letting this man affect her much too strongly. She was not behaving like herself at all. Her resistance to the opposite sex was usually exactly as good as she wanted it to be. She was not used to having a man put her at a disadvantage the way this one was doing, and she was annoyed at herself for having let him get under her skin so.

His lips curved even more fully to reveal even white teeth. He said, his deep velvet voice laced with light amusement, "I wouldn't have taken you for a teacher. A Gypsy singer, maybe, but not a teacher."

He was teasing her. Of course he was teasing her. Nevertheless, Paula could feel herself flushing.

He thrust out a hand, turned upward. "How about reading my palm?" he suggested.

"What?"

"My palm," he persisted. "I'd swear that you're a Gypsy even though your hair should be black instead of that glorious auburn. But all you'd need to convince me is golden hoop earrings and maybe a swinging red skirt with flounces on it. And all beautiful Gypsies read palms, you do know that, don't you?"

She found herself matching his smile, and he said, as if honestly relieved, "That's better. We were getting much too serious." He changed the subject abruptly. "Look," he asked, "do you have a hat?"

She nodded, "Yes."

"You should put it on, then. There's more heat to this sun than you may realize, though it's a fact that'll come home to you before much longer. It's going to be a scorcher, and you should protect your head. For that matter," he went on, eyeing her closely again, "you should have an umbrella or something. With that skin of yours—"

He broke off, and she prompted, "Yes?"

He smiled. "Your skin's so fair. If you stay out in the sun, you're apt to become a mass of freckles."

"I'm already a mass of freckles."

"No," he contradicted. "You've just the right number of freckles—"

He broke off, frowning slightly. Then, obviously intent on changing the subject, he asked abruptly, "You said these are family things?"

Paula's lips tightened. There was a note of caution in his voice she didn't like. She said somewhat defiantly,

"They're all family things, yes. They came with the house."

"The house?"

"My grandmother left me her house. It's here in Wellfleet. It's been in our family for two hundred years. I come from a long line of Cape Codders, Mr. Grayson." Her defiance was mounting. Right at the outset, when he'd questioned the amethyst bowl, he'd hinted that she might be something of a cheat, and this still nettled her. Did he think that she might be a thief as well? The idea hurt, and her chin quivered slightly as she said, "I come from people who went to sea in the China trade. They traveled the globe and brought back all kinds of things from far-off places to their wives and their daughters or their sisters, or their sweethearts. It's an old New England story." She paused. "But then, you're a New Englander yourself, aren't you?"

He *looked* like the epitome of a Boston Brahmin. But to her surprise he said, "No. No, I'm not. Not in the strict sense of the word, anyway."

The flea market had opened. People were beginning to saunter down the narrow lane that separated the tables. Russ Grayson said, "Well, I guess I'd better get down to business. I'll talk to you later."

Paula nodded, watching a woman in a bright blue dress pick up the Bavarian creamer and turn it over to examine the mark.

She found herself hoping the woman wouldn't buy it. Which wasn't getting into the spirit of things at all.

Glancing over the antiques he'd set out on his tables, the first object that caught Russ Grayson's eyes was a piece of Tiffany glass, a small iridescent golden bud vase that was exquisite.

He was tempted to take it across to Paula and to tell her that he'd exchange it for her Imperial Jewels bowl, but that would only be making a further fool of himself.

What must she think of him? Probably that he was a

pompous fool, he decided dismally, and he couldn't blame her. Why hadn't he kept his mouth shut about the blasted lavender bowl? Amethyst, he corrected himself.

He watched Paula rearranging some of her pieces, her head bared to the morning sun. So much for his words of caution! Her hair was an unusual color, deep and tawny like oak leaves in autumn. Her eyes reminded him of autumn, too. They were dark amber, large and very expressive. They'd warned Russ that he was nettling her, even though she'd been verbally polite. Nevertheless, it had been an innate honesty that had prompted him to speak to her as he had, though admittedly he could have been a hell of a lot more discreet.

Still, there were few things he disliked more than the dishonesty sometimes rampant among people dealing on the fringes of the antique business. Paula Danvers had become suspect in his mind the moment he'd spotted the Tiffany label. Now he was more than willing to admit that he'd been wrong about her. He only wished that he could start over again, with an entirely new opening gambit. He'd tried to placate her, but he was not at all sure he'd succeeded.

He found himself wondering how she'd react if he went across to her and suggested, once again, that she cover her head with something. Probably, rightfully, she'd tell him to mind his own business. But her skin was incredibly fair, she'd burn so easily.

As far as her freckles were concerned, he found them entrancing. Spattering her cheekbones and the bridge of her nose, they kept her from being a lily maid of Astolat and gave her a vital quality that he found very provocative.

She was tall. He'd noted that her head came just to his shoulders, and slim enough, and curved enough, and there was a zest about her that reached out to him because it was so foreign to him. Yes, she *could* be a Gypsy princess at that.

Russ had come here today as an experiment, and he tried to force himself to get back to business. But his gaze kept straying toward Paula Danvers and had it been a few hours later he would have said that his brain was becoming addled by the heat.

But it wasn't that hot, not yet. And anyway, it wasn't the weather that was bothering him. It was the woman across the way.

Russ had never been much of a believer in instant chemistry between two people. He was too much of a realist. But there was a quality to Paula Danvers that he found both impossible to define and very appealing. It was obvious that she knew little or nothing about antiques and he'd been sincere when he'd said he wanted to help her. But he'd already stepped on her feelings, and he knew he was going to have to be careful not to do so again.

Russell Grayson Parkhurst III, the sole owner of an internationally known antique shop and art gallery on New York's fashionable East Side, gave himself a sharp mental kick, then forced himself to answer questions about a Hummel figurine from a stout lady tourist in purple shorts and a flowered Hawaiian-print top.

Yes, the figurine was genuine Hummel. It had been made by Sister Marie herself. Yes, there were imitation Hummels on the market today. She collected the figurines? Well, then, of course she'd know that this was the real thing.

Flattered, the woman paid his price without quibbling, and Russ wrapped the figurine in newspaper, then stuffed it into a crumpled brown paper bag. But all the while his eyes were on the auburn-haired woman across the way, who'd dragged out a small folding chair, was sitting on it, and had finally, thank God, put on a floppy straw hat. She looked so forlorn that he wanted desperately to go over to her and pretend her damned Imperial Jewels was Tiffany glass after all.

Chapter Two

That Sunday inched along with agonizing slowness. By noon Paula felt that it should be time for the sun to be setting. She wanted that blazing yellow orb to disappear. She wanted the day to be over with. This experience had not been what she'd expected it would be. She'd made pitifully few sales, and then the only things she'd parted with had been trivia, a miscellany of odds and ends that she'd hesitated about before bringing out to the market at all.

She was intensely aware that, in contrast, Russ Grayson appeared to be doing very well. Time and again she saw him reach under his table and bring up a crumpled brown paper bag. Into it he'd thrust some item he'd just sold, wrapped in the telltale newspaper pages that were becoming synonymous with the flea market to Paula.

She shifted uncomfortably in the straight-backed

chair, wishing she'd brought suntan lotion along with her. She was getting a burn on her arms, and there was nothing much she could do about it. She could protect her legs by keeping them under the table, but her arms were fully exposed to the sun's glare.

As if he'd been able to read her mind, Russell Grayson strode across the lane that divided their spaces, and thrust out a tan bottle. "Coppertone," he said. "You need it."

She was not about to deny it. Again she glanced at his deep, even tan, and just now, hot and disheveled herself, she found his perfection irritating. He still looked remarkably cool, too, though she saw beads of moisture banding his forehead and edging his lips.

So, the man could sweat after all!

She was startled when he took off the oversize glasses, and she was unprepared for the first glimpse of his eyes. They were the most unusual—and also the most beautiful—eyes she'd ever seen. A deep, improbable green, clear as a pine-circled forest lake, fringed by thick black lashes.

He rubbed the area under one well-defined eyebrow. "A mosquito," he explained, "or something related to one."

A few insects had made Paula's acquaintance; she had her share of bites and had been trying not to scratch them. She sighed, and couldn't resist complaining, "It's so hot!"

He'd put the glasses back on again, and she wished she could ask him to take them off so she could be sure about his eyes. Could anyone's eyes really be that color? He said, "Didn't you bring a thermos of something to drink?"

She nodded. "Iced tea. I finished it hours ago."

"Paula—you don't mind if I call you Paula, do you?"

She shook her head.

"Well then, Paula, why don't you go over to the refreshment shack and get yourself something? It'd put you in the shade for a while."

She smiled ruefully. "I can't. There'd be no one to manage the store."

"I'll look after your tables."

He was standing with his back to his own tables, and Paula saw that there were three or four people browsing there. She said, "You have your own stock to look after. Matter of fact, I'm afraid you'll miss out on some business if you don't go back."

She didn't want him to go back, even though "back" was a distance of not more than ten feet. She wanted him to stay with her, to talk to her, to give her moral support. She'd never needed moral support more than she did right now.

He said gently, "Don't despair. It's slow today because it's so hot. People can't make up their minds in this kind of weather."

"Your things have been selling."

He shrugged. "I have some good values."

"And you think I don't?"

He smiled. "It's too hot to get into an argument about antique prices," he told her. He paused, and she knew that he had something else to say to her, something that he evidently was hesitant about broaching. She frowned. Had she mismarked something else?

She was staggered when, instead of pointing out another error to her, Russ Grayson said—a shade too casually—"Would you be free to have dinner with me tonight? We could talk about antique prices then, if you like."

Paula thought about going back to her grandmother's house and spending the evening alone, bemoaning her lack of success in the flea market while heating up a can of clam chowder. Any dinner invitation would have been tempting. This one was irresistible!

She tried to warn herself that she could be letting herself in for something. At twenty-six, Paula was usually cautious about taking a chance at letting herself in for anything where men were concerned. She'd run off and gotten married over her family's protests when she was eighteen years old, only to realize much too soon that they'd been right about Howard Fletcher. Howie had taken advantage of her in many ways. She had her share of emotional battle scars. But that was all behind her now. Long since, she'd picked up all the pieces and glued them together and, thanks at least in part to Gram, had gone on with her life.

She'd been careful about letting men into that life. She wasn't bitter or overly suspicious about men; it wasn't that. Rather, she wanted to be very sure before becoming serious for a second time, and thus far no man she'd met had really motivated her.

There was something different about Russ Grayson, and it wasn't just this tug of physical attraction she felt for him. She recognized and responded to the tug, the male charisma, but there was a mystery about this man that went beyond his obvious sex appeal. And it was that sense of inner mystery that intrigued her so much.

There could be danger in trying to solve such a mystery, though, she warned herself. Just one glimpse of his unbelievable jade eyes had unnerved her. How would she react if she were to spend an entire dinner hour across a table from him, staring directly into them?

I'd drown, probably, Paula told herself silently. And Russ accused, "You're smiling at some private joke. A while back you were laughing at some private joke. Is this a habit of yours?"

"No," Paula protested quickly.

"Will you have dinner with me, Paula?"

It wasn't her style to hedge. "I'd like that," she told him.

He had turned to watch two women who were assessing a tall cut-crystal vase on his table. "I'll be back," he promised, and she watched him cross to his space, liking the way he walked, liking everything about him—except his tendency to downgrade both her knowledge of antiques and the prices she'd put on the merchandise she was offering for sale.

She watched him greet his potential customers, and conceded that he could certainly turn on the charm when he wanted to. Even from this distance it was clear that he was mesmerizing the two women. She saw one of them reach into her wallet. Then money changed hands and there were smiles on all sides. The women turned away and Russ looked across at Paula, grinned, then raised one hand to form his fingers in a circle, making the international victory sign.

She grinned back at him, wondering what price he'd put on the vase he'd just sold. She had a similiar one on her table, though hers was smaller, and she hadn't had a nibble on it all day.

"What nice things!" Paula was shaken out of her reverie by a little gnome of a woman who peered up at her through inquisitive dark eyes.

"Thank you," she said.

"I'm Hilda Benson," the woman introduced herself. "I'm down at the end of the line near the refreshment stand."

"You're a dealer?" Paula thought with amusement that flea-market dealers did indeed come in all sizes, shapes, and ages.

"I've been in the business for forty years," she was told. Gnarled brown fingers were turning over dishes, cups and saucers, silver spoons, vases, small china boxes, and a miscellany of other things with a swift competency that verified the years of experience in this particular trade.

Hilda Benson nodded as if satisfied with what she was seeing and said, "Very nice, indeed. This your first time?"

Her eyes on Russ Grayson again, Paula wrested her attention back to the elderly dealer and said, "Yes." Then she added with a smile, "Does it show?"

"Maybe, a little bit," the answer came, a wisp of a smile taking the sting out of the words. "Don't mind if it's slow," Paula was advised. "Everyone's at the beach, and it's too hot for people to make up their minds about what they want anyway. A day like this addles the brain.''

Did it also addle the heart? Was that what was the matter with her? Had the tall man across the way addled her heart?

"Come visit me," Hilda Benson invited her, and then scurried off, darting along the line of tables to pause like a hummingbird along the way, hovering here and there.

She was a funny little woman, Paula decided. And saw Russ approaching, a thermos in hand.

"Lemonade," he said, holding the thermos out to her.

Paula's throat was parched. Still, she managed, "I don't want to take this away from you. You'll need it yourself before the day's over."

He shrugged. "No problem. If I get that thirsty, I'll patronize the refreshment shack. What did Jenny Wren want with you?"

"You're talking about Mrs. Benson?" The analogy was a perfect one. "She stopped by for a visit, that's all, and she was very nice. Also, she was complimentary about my things and she didn't say anything at all about my prices being too high. And she," Paula added with a spark of defiance, "has been in the business forty years."

"Before I was born?" he suggested.

"I would certainly think so."

He laughed. "I'm thirty-four," he volunteered. "So you have me there. Where do you live, Paula?"

"Off the road to Gull Pond."

"You'll have to be more precise than that if I'm to pick you up and take you to dinner," he teased her.

The thought of going to dinner with him was unexpectedly heady. Paula drew a deep breath and gave him the detailed instructions he'd need if he was to find Gram's place, which was off a dirt lane off a dirt road. When she'd finished, he said, "Will seven o'clock be all right?"

"Yes," she nodded.

Again, potential customers claimed his attention. And, as the afternoon progressed, Paula had a few customers of her own. A couple of times when she was offered less for a piece than she'd marked it, she yielded. She was here to sell these things, after all. But whenever this happened she cast a quick eye toward Russ Grayson, hoping he hadn't noticed that she was bartering. She didn't want him to think she was capitulating on her price policy all that easily.

He left before she did, packing up the remaining items on his tables and stashing them away in his van with an ease she found commendable. He crossed the space between them one last time to tell her briefly that he'd see her at seven. And as he pulled away in his van, she felt a sense of loss out of all proportion to reality.

She made a couple more minor sales, then started packing up. The flea market closed for business at four o'clock, and it was half past that hour by the time Paula had everything loaded in the back of the station wagon.

She was hot, tired, and she'd never felt stickier in her life. Once home, she decided to leave her things in the car for the night. She wasn't up to carrying them to the back room which she'd converted into a repository for her flea-market business. Not now. Monday morning would be time enough to cope with a lot of things, and to tally up how much she'd made today. She already knew it wasn't going to be much of a total. Not even a portion of what she'd hoped to make.

A shower helped. She washed her hair and toweled it partly dry. Then, garbed in a terry-cloth robe, she sat down on the edge of the bed with her hand dryer to finish the job, only to soon turn the dryer off, put her damp head down on the pillow, and promptly fall asleep.

It was a deep sleep, and Paula was disoriented when

she awakened. Glancing at the bedside clock, she saw that it was twenty minutes to seven, and she was horrified. She'd intended to take time with her dressing, wanting to look her very best for Russ Grayson. Instead, she hastily donned a full-skirted pink voile dress with a front-pleated bodice that hugged her curves, and an enchanting square neckline. A wide, matching sash emphasized her trim waist. She thrust her feet into slim white sandals, then quickly touched her lids with mauve shadow, her lips with pale pink gloss, and decided that would have to suffice for makeup.

She'd intended to do something special with her hair, but there was only time to brush it into a shimmering mass of waves and curls.

At the last minute she fastened on a pair of dangly earrings she'd found in one of the several boxes of jewelry Gram had amassed over a lifetime. They were gold, ornamented with pearl and rose-crystal drops, the rose bringing out both the pink in the dress and the slight flush in her cheeks.

Paula reached the front parlor with barely a minute to spare. As she crossed the room she heard a car motor, but it was not the cream-colored van she saw when she looked through the window. Tonight Russ Grayson was driving a sleek, low-slung black sports car that purred as he brought it to a stop in front of the house.

Two expensive vehicles. He was pretty affluent for a flea-market dealer!

Paula, spying upon him shamelessly from a vantage point at the side of the window, where she was hidden by the curtains, saw him climb out of the car and she caught her breath. Again, he was almost too perfect. Even from this distance she could see that the tailoring on his beautifully fitting camel jacket was exquisite, and his light tan slacks obviously had been made to order. The perfectly fitting clothes emphasized the fluidity of a body that moved with the graceful, yet very masculine, swing that had attracted her eye the first instant she'd seen him move at all. As he came up the bricked front walk, Paula's throat felt even drier than it had at the zenith of the hot afternoon, and this time she knew it would take more than iced tea or lemonade to quench her thirst.

As she went to open the door for him, she was trembling inside, and appalled by her reaction to this man.

My God, she told herself, *you're yearning for him . . . and you don't even know him!*

Nevertheless, as she opened the door for him, Paula had the crazy sense that her whole life was going to be turned upside down by Russ Grayson before this night was over.

Russ had been having second thoughts about this date with Paula as he spanned the distance between Truro—where he had a summer home—and the neighboring town of Wellfleet.

His high-powered car was too smooth, too efficient. He began to wish he'd run out of gas, or have a flat tire. Or that something not too monumental would happen to hold him up for a while, so that he could do a little more thinking.

His suggestion that Paula have dinner with him had been spur of the moment, yet surprisingly important to him. She'd looked so hot, so tired, and she was making a mess of things with the prices she'd put on her merchandise. He wanted to help her, with an intensity that surprised him. Usually, Russ confined his charitable impulses to writing large checks to organizations that, he hoped, spent their funds wisely in attempting to deal with the poverty and other problems of the less fortunate in the world.

In the monetary sense, Russ had never been unfortunate. He had been born to wealth, old wealth. Money was the last thing he'd ever had to think of. In another sense, he'd been extremely unfortunate. He had lived through some very black years, when he'd been too young to have had to face that kind of pain and reality. He liked to think that he'd overcome the bitterness, the anger, and the frustration that had been a part of those years, but he didn't delude himself. Sometimes vestiges of all those negative feelings that were part of his past rose to haunt him. And, sometimes, he was made to realize, forcibly, how little he really knew about people. He'd been isolated from people at a time in his life when he should have been learning about the interplay of relationships from personal experience. This left a big gap in his thinking, and in his ability to relate now.

He did well enough on the business level. He did *very* well on the business level. He'd even proved that at the flea market today and—as he took the turn to the left off the highway onto Gull Pond Road—Russ smiled at the thought. He could imagine his staff in New York seeing him out there today in the hot, dusty flea market, selling his wares like an itinerant peddler. But he'd gotten a kick out of it. In fact, he'd enjoyed the flea-market experience more than he'd enjoyed anything for a long time. He'd proved to himself that he *could* climb out of his ivory tower and deal with people on a one-to-one basis—something he'd been needing to prove.

Most of all, he'd enjoyed Paula Danvers. He'd watched her all day, averting his eyes only when he suspected that she was watching him.

He estimated that she must be in her mid-twenties, and she'd told him she was a teacher by profession. Most teachers had their heads on their shoulders; she was probably a lot more capable than she seemed to be, and didn't need his help at all.

On the other hand, unless she'd really thought she had a chance of rooking the world, the prices she'd put on her stuff were outrageous. She had some nice pieces; he'd been sincere when he'd said he was willing to make her offers on a number of them. But she'd been vastly misled by the price guides she'd been studying and it annoyed him to think he hadn't been able to convince her of that.

As he looked for the turnoff road Paula had described to him, Russ was trying to make himself believe that the only reason he'd asked Paula to dinner was so that he could demonstrate to her that she was starting out all wrong. If she really wanted to unload her family heirlooms, she was going to have to change her thinking.

But even as he tried to convince himself of his motive for seeing her again, Russ knew it was a blatant lie.

Paula had stirred feelings in him that had been dormant since, at the age of eighteen, he'd faced a terrible personal crisis. For the next few years, he'd gone through a mental and physical and emotional hell more devastating than he wanted to remember. Sex had been sidelined, there'd been no room for girls in his life, no room for anything except the single emphasis on survival. That, and that alone, had taken all of his energy. His capacity for love and laughter had gone down the drain in the effort just to hang on to life.

He'd beaten the odds, he'd been cured, he'd recovered completely. But the experience had done something to him. While he was still recouping from the greatest battle of his life, weak from the exhausting fight against the disease that had invaded his body, he'd plunged into the antique business to get his mind off his problems. Like Paula, he'd inherited a lot of family heirlooms. Unlike her, there'd been no need for him to think of selling them, but to pass the hours he'd started looking up information about the antiques he had, and one step led to another.

In addition to his world-famous New York antique business and art gallery, Russ now had interests in several other businesses—an importing company, and a glass manufactory that made wares from old formulas famous in their day. Every now and then he bought a new business, and each acquisition was rather like acquiring another toy. Ironically, because he didn't need to make any more money, the profits continued to mount.

For all of this, though, he'd been growing increasingly dissatisfied with himself. He'd been well for a long time, he'd had his share of women, but none of them had touched him deeply. For one thing, he was wary of women because he was never sure whether they were primarily interested in him . . . or in his money. He could not help but be aware that Russell Grayson Parkhurst III was considered a very good catch. And he had no intention of being caught!

He'd come to Truro this year feeling restless, frustrated, unfulfilled, and lonely. And his discontent with himself, his restlessness, had refused to be filed away and forgotten. The flea market had been a challenge of sorts. He'd needed to see how it would be to mix with the rest of the world on an anonymous level, how he'd be received, how he'd make out, and one day he'd seen the flea-market poster in a local store window and he'd decided it was exactly the right experiment site. The cellar in his Truro house had been full of boxes of antiques brought from a large house in Chatham he'd inherited from his uncle, and had sold three years ago.

Well, today he'd made out very well with the people who'd bought things from him. There'd been a rapport that he'd found very satisfactory.

And there'd been Paula.

Russ pulled up in front of her house, assessing it with a practised eye because he also was involved in a number of real estate holdings. It was a gem of a place, a real old Cape Codder, gray-shingled, the trim on windows, doors, and shutters painted a subdued blue. But it needed work. A new roof, for one thing. Reshingling, probably. Repainting, certainly. Money, in short.

Was that why Paula was selling her family heirlooms? How much did they mean to her? Had she priced them so high because, subconsciously, she'd never wanted to sell them at all?

How much did this house mean to her? It looked like a place that had been lived in, cherished. It wasn't merely a house, Russ thought. It had been—it was—a home.

Russ felt a stab of longing. His parents had been killed in a plane crash in Spain when he was ten, and he'd never known them very well, anyway. For all of his wealth, Russ had never had a family homestead like this one; he'd never had a family.

As he made his way up the brick walk to her front door, he found himself envying Paula Danvers and, simultaneously, wanting to know more about her. A lot more about her. Everything.

Chapter Three

Russ took Paula to dinner at an old inn that had once been a sea captain's house. He had made reservations, and they were led to a table in a secluded corner of a terrace that looked out upon the broad expanse of Cape Cod Bay.

"We've arrived just in time for the sunset," Russ observed as they were seated, and Paula could understand why the diners around them were so quiet. Everyone's attention was focused on the magnificent natural spectacle being enacted. The sun, slowly descending toward the long waterline on the distant horizon, was enveloped in a flaming orange-gold mantle.

"Looks like it'll make it," Russ said quietly. He explained, "Often, as you may have noticed, the sun disappears in a haze before it reaches the waterline, especially when there's been such a stretch of hot, humid weather. But I think we're going to see the whole show tonight."

He was right. Paula watched, mesmerized, as the sun touched the water and then, in a sizzling instant, disappeared over the edge of the earth. The sky was a mass of dazzling colors, radiating out in bands of amber and salmon, turquoise, gold, and a green almost as clear as Russ's eyes. Paler ribbons were cast out to dance across the water, catching the last glimmering rays as they streaked toward shore.

Tones of blue and charcoal and dark purple came to filter the sky and water, blending into a cool twilight that prefaced the coming of night, and Paula sighed deeply. The man sitting across from her, his chair half turned so that he, too, had been able to see the sun's spectacle, was statue-still. She sensed that he was as moved by intense beauty as she was, but she suspected that this was something he'd not be apt to reveal unless he knew someone very well.

She said simply, "That was wonderful. It's incredible," she added, when he didn't at once speak, "to think that it's something that happens every night and yet we pay so little attention to it."

He turned his chair to face her directly, and he smiled. But she wasn't to know if he intended to answer her because, just then, their waiter came to strike a match to a hurricane lamp centered by a thick white candle.

Russ's features were highlighted in the candle's soft glow, and Paula found it difficult to take her eyes off him. He was consulting with the waiter about the menu, so she was able to let herself look at him, and she knew that later she'd be able to etch his features from memory. His coloring was dramatic—that dark, dark hair and those unusual, intensely green eyes—but it was the planes of his face that she found especially interesting, the angles and the curves, the rugged masculinity that underlined his features. It was an aggressive face, in a sense. She suspected he'd be a formidable opponent. Also, there was an aloofness to it that telegraphed his being a person with a strong sense of privacy. But underlying all that, she saw a sensitivity that was not obvious; it was hidden deeply beneath the surface. Paula looked, and became aware of a vulnerability that was all too familiar to her. She was much too vulnerable a person herself, too easily hurt. It came as a surprise to discover that Russ, for all of his outward coolness and sophistication, and his casual, offhand manner, might be a kindred spirit.

He asked, "Do you like margaritas?" and she wrested her attention back to the moment. She nodded, and he placed their drink order.

There was a quiet assurance about him, a confidence to everything he did. Again, she noted the beautifully tailored jacket he was wearing, the beige shirt with the hand-stitched collar, and the tie, obviously silk, that combined camel and beige and burnt orange in a discreet pattern. His thick dark hair was cut perfectly, just long enough to be attractive, in style, and also in perfect taste. On a scale of one to ten points he would get the full ten points for grooming, she decided. Everything about him was meticulously correct, from his hair and his clothes to the blunt cut of his carefully manicured fingernails. Yet there was a latent fire in those green eyes. Banked, yes. But there. And the curve of Russ Grayson's mouth denoted passion. So did the slight flare of his nostrils.

He asked, his voice laced with amusement, "What is it, Paula? Do I have my tie on backward?"

"No, no," she said hastily, embarrassment stinging her cheeks with color. "I'm sorry. I was woolgathering."

He asked pleasantly, "Did the flea market live up to your expectations?"

"No," she said bluntly. "I haven't tallied up yet, but

I'm afraid I was a dismal failure." Before he could speak, she added, "I know. You're going to tell me my prices are too high. But honestly, Russ . . ."

It was the first time she'd called him by name. She realized this at once and knew she'd trip over her words if she said anything more until she'd recovered a composure much too easily lost with this man around.

Russ's smile was wry. "I'm not about to comment again about your prices unless you want me to," he informed her. "I already got off to a bad enough start with you, barging in as I did and accusing you of misrepresenting your Imperial Jewels bowl."

"Tiffany," Paula corrected, but she smiled as she said it. Then, troubled, she added, "It wasn't my intention to deliberately misrepresent anything."

"I'm sure of that," he said gravely.

The waiter placed their salt-frosted margarita glasses in front of them. A crooked smile tilted Russ's lips as he lifted his glass, and reached out to touch it to hers, saying, *"Salud."*

"Salud," she echoed. Then asked, "What's the rest of it? The toast, I mean."

"Dinero y amor," Russ said briefly. "Money and love."

He glanced up as he said this, and his eyes meshed with Paula's. She felt briefly as if she were being scorched by an emerald flame, then he said slowly, "You're very lovely tonight," and there was a huskiness in his voice that made her feel as if her own throat were tightening. In turn, this engendered a twist of emotion that made her want to reach across the table and touch Russ, and she gripped her cocktail glass more tightly.

Russ, as if forcing himself to get back on a more rational plane, said, "Speaking of your Imperial Jewels bowl . . ."

"Must we?" Paula asked him. She'd gotten a touch of the sun today, despite her floppy straw hat, and it gave a glow to face, which was now enhanced by the candlelight. Her pulse was thumping, and she wished that all the other diners on the terrace would vanish so that she and Russ could be alone with the candlelight and the night sky with its star-studded canopy over them, and the distant strains of music echoing the rhythms of her heart.

Russ's lips curved in that slight smile that reached out to Paula, further tugging at her heartstrings. "No," he said, "we don't necessarily have to talk about Imperial Jewels. Actually, I'd much rather talk about you."

She laughed softly. "That's my line," she told him. "I've been wanting to talk about *you.*"

"Oh?" Russ asked, a dark, perfectly shaped eyebrow arching.

"You're not really a flea-market dealer, are you?" Paula asked him.

His answering frown telegraphed something she'd already sensed about him. A kind of privacy. He was obviously reluctant to talk about himself, and she wondered why. The question she'd asked him hardly could be called personal.

He said rather hesitantly, "No. I'm not a *professional* flea-market dealer, if that's what you mean."

"Was this your first time today?"

He shook his head. "No. My third."

"I couldn't picture you as a regular dealer," she admitted, "but you seemed to know exactly what you were doing."

He smiled. "It isn't that difficult, Paula."

"I found it difficult. I guess I'm not much of a salesperson. When people came by my tables I just sat there and looked blank."

"I think you projected without being aware of it."

She shook her head. "No."

"You did to me," he said softly.

"What do you do most of the time, Russ?" she asked, sidestepping this. "Do you live here on the Cape?" She doubted it. He had too much of the city about him.

He said, "To answer your second question first—I

don't live on the Cape, no. I have a place in Truro I escape to whenever I can. As to what I do—I have an antique business in New York. I'm on vacation," he added.

"No wonder you're so sure of yourself, if you have your own business," Paula said. Then, curiously, she queried, "You say you're on vacation?"

He nodded. "Why so doubtful?" he asked her.

"Isn't it rather like carrying coals to Newcastle?" she queried. "Selling antiques in a flea market wouldn't be my idea of a holiday, if I were in the business."

"It's an entirely different sort of thing," he answered vaguely, and followed this up with a quick question of his own. "What about you? What made you decide to play at being a 'flea,' Paula?"

"My grandmother had been in a rest home for several years before she died," Paula said after a minute. "It pretty much drained her financially, but she managed to hang on to the house. She left me the house and all its contents, but very little cash to keep it going with. You saw for yourself that there's a lot of work that needs to be done, and there are taxes that need to be paid. It isn't that I want to sell any of the old family things," she added honestly. "I have to."

"And you decided the flea market was your best sales avenue?"

"I thought so, yes," Paula said unhappily. "After today, I'm afraid I may have been wrong. Obviously, people go to a flea market expecting to get a real bargain, not to pay a fair price." She saw his smile, and she said hastily, "I know. We weren't going to get into that again."

"Where do you usually live, Paula?"

"In Acton, not far from Boston," she said.

"With your parents?"

She shook her head. "My parents died within a year of each other when I was in my early teens," she said. "My father was a career army officer, so we always traveled a lot. But we came back to Gram's whenever we could, and I spent most of my summers with her. After Dad and Mom died I lived with Gram—except for about a year—but her health was failing by then." The sadness in the lovely amber eyes made Russ want to take Paula in his arms, to hold her close and console her.

"Gram put me through college," she continued. "I got a job in the Acton school system after I graduated, and it was Gram who put herself into a nursing home there. She said she could see me that way, without being a burden on me. That was four years ago. Gram died this past May," she concluded.

"We have a common bond," Russ said carefully. "I lost my parents when I was quite young myself, and my uncle brought me up."

"Where?" Paula asked him.

"Various places," he said evasively. "I went off to private school, sometimes we traveled during the vacation periods."

Again, she sensed that reluctance in him to say very much about himself, but she persisted. "Were you an only child?"

"Yes. Were you?"

"Yes," she told him. "Probably that's why my parents and I were so close."

"You were lucky," Russ said briefly. "I was never close to my parents. Matter of fact, I don't feel I ever really knew them."

The waiter was hovering discreetly and Russ beckoned to him, as if welcoming a diversion. They scanned the menu together, choosing flounder filets stuffed with lobster, a pilaf of wild rice, and a medley of vegetables flavored slightly with curry. Russ ordered an accompanying wine with an assurance that spoke for itself.

A succulent Caesar salad was set before them for a first course, and it became easy to turn their attention to the delicious food. Their enjoyment of it evoked an easy camaraderie that made it possible to talk about a variety of things without getting intense about any of them.

They discovered likes and dislikes, favorite vegetables and favorite flowers, the movies they liked or didn't like, the books they liked or didn't like. They learned that they were both mystery buffs, and that Boston's Robert Parker, with his detective hero, Spenser, produced page-turners they found impossible to put down.

They discovered that they both liked Beethoven symphonies, and some of the old Sinatra records, the early Beatle recordings—"I Want To Hold Your Hand," Russ said, with a suggestive grin—and jazz piano. They found that they both liked rainy, foggy days, and they liked to walk deserted beaches, off season, reveling in the cries of the sea gulls, the scent of the sand flats at low tide, the eternal lure of the shoreline, and the water, forever changing.

Paula said wistfully, "I think I could live on the Cape forever."

Russ looked at Paula, her lovely face highlighted by the candle's soft glow, and something twisted inside him, a pain that was at once bitter and sweet and so tantalizing, so provocative, he didn't know how to deal with it.

She'd said she'd like to live on Cape Cod forever and he wondered what it would be like to live anywhere forever, with someone like her. He couldn't envision it. He'd never truly shared himself with another person and, as he looked at her glowing face and heard the wistfulness in her voice, he wondered if he ever could break down his own barriers enough to let someone else into his life.

All of a sudden he wished he were clairvoyant. He wished very much that he were able to read Paula's thoughts, because he was certain they involved him. She'd been assessing him, taking his measure, even when he'd been consulting with the waiter over the wine list. There'd been an intensity about her doing so that had made him wonder if, somehow, she'd found out who he was. Who he was? That sounded pompous to his ears, yet the fact had to be recognized that ever since he could remember there'd been public interest in Russell Grayson Parkhurst III, spurred further by the media whenever reporters had the chance to get near him.

Fortunately, he was usually successful in dodging photographers and so his face was not nearly so familiar to most people as his name was. The abbreviation of his name that he'd given to Paula obviously hadn't meant anything to her and he couldn't imagine how she subsequently could have gotten any clue to his identity, unless it had been by a very long arm of coincidence. This was the third Sunday he'd gone to the flea market, and his anonymity there had been preserved without his even having to make any effort about it. So, unless Paula had come upon some magazine or newspaper story about him in the time between her return home today and seven o'clock, when he'd called for her, she'd been looking at him intently merely because . . . well, because, he supposed, she was as curious about him as he was about her.

She was lovely tonight, in her pink dress, and he liked her antique earrings. Her hair was gorgeous, a color feast, and he was glad she hadn't put it up. In the candlelight her eyes were a rich, luminous amber. Her nose had a delightful tilt to it, and her mouth, he decided, had been designed to be kissed.

Aware that he was staring at her, he turned his attention to the coffee the waiter was serving them, but it was a futile attempt as far as diversion was concerned. This woman appealed to him tremendously. He knew he could be as easily lured to her as a moth to a flame, but he didn't want her to discover his real identity, he didn't want any revelations being put on the board about anything until he knew her a lot better than he did now.

And he wanted to get to know her better, much better. This surprised him because he usually had a hard core of resistance when it came to even very alluring women. With the opposite sex Russ liked to be in a position of calling all the shots. But in addition to all the things she did to his male senses, he saw in Paula other qualities to further spark his interest. There was a determination, a spunkiness about her. She'd been miserable this afternoon at the flea market, hot and uncomfortable and disappointed, yet she'd seen it through. She'd stuck it out. Most of the women Russ had known would have packed up and gone home by the time the sun was high in the sky, if, that is, they would ever have mustered up enough initiative in the first place to pack their wares in cartons and make the trek to the market by seven o'clock in the morning in order to ensure getting a good space.

Yes, she was gutsy and beautiful and delightful to be with, but Russ also forced himself to recognize that she was inquisitive, and that he'd have to watch himself. As it was, he'd told her more about himself than he did most people. And he'd come dangerously close to telling her too much when he'd confessed that he'd been brought up by an uncle, with whom he'd sometimes traveled during school vacations.

During those vacations, he remembered now, his uncle had always combined alleged pleasure with business. Sometimes it was more than his own business with which he'd been concerned. George Parkhurst had been called upon to represent government interests, dealing with international monetary funds on a very high level. He had been an astute financier—and as cold as ice, a highly sophisticated man who'd had little time for his skinny, bewildered nephew.

They'd never achieved a real rapport, though they'd been closest to it after Russ's illness had been diagnosed, this coming as a real shock to his uncle. Mostly, though, Russ remembered holidays spent alone in his uncle's somber Sutton Place apartment. Summers had been divided between the house in Chatham and a boy's camp in New Hampshire. . . .

Paula interrupted his memory trek with a question. "What's the going rate for thoughts?" she asked him.

For a moment Russ didn't know what she was talking about, and she elaborated with a slight smile, "A quarter? Fifty cents? A dollar? Certainly no longer a penny. How much would you take for yours?"

Ah, but she was discerning. Too discerning. Russ forced himself to reply lightly, saying, "Nothing, really. Matter of fact, the things I was thinking really weren't worth much more than a counterfeit nickel."

There was a lopsided moon in the sky as they walked across the parking lot to Russ's car. Paula, glancing up, traced the course of the dipper and then said, with satisfaction, "There! That's north."

"An astronomer?" Russ asked her.

"No, but the stars have always fascinated me. When I was little I used to think I'd like to discover my own comet. Maria Mitchell did, years and years ago. She lived out on Nantucket and her father made her a little observatory on the roof of their house, with her own telescope." She laughed. "I also wanted to be the reincarnation of Cleopatra so I could float down the Nile on a flower-filled barge," she confessed.

"With Mark Antony by your side?"

"Of course. Then I wanted to be the first woman in space, but I'm afraid I've lost my chance for that."

They had come to a stop at his car, and Paula was standing very close to him. Russ, his mind wandering abstractedly, noted again that her head came just to his shoulder, and he found himself wanting to experience the feel of her head against his shoulder. He wanted to run his fingers through the mass of her glorious auburn hair; he wanted to savor her, to let his nostrils become filled with her sweet scent. Her fragrance was a combination that evoked neither flowers nor spice but, perhaps due to Paula's own chemistry, was uniquely her own.

Bewildered by his own inchoate longings, Russ knew only that he wanted to savor her, to know every inch of her. He wanted her!

He stared down at the top of her head with a longing that jolted him. Paula was special, so special that it frightened him, because he wanted to be very sure that he wasn't going to make any mistakes with her. There was so much to learn about her, and this desire simply to know her and be near her was like nothing he'd ever experienced before. Underlying it was that sexual message older than time, true. But never before had he felt this blend of sensuality mixed with so many other things. It was a potent combination.

Paula's face was averted from him. She was staring up at the sky again, star-watching. He touched her, tentatively, on the shoulder. Then, as she turned toward him, he moved his hand upward to cup her chin in it. The feel of her flesh was tantalizingly soft and wonderful.

Her eyes widened as she looked up at him. "Russ . . ." she began.

Her beautiful full lips moved as she spoke his name, and Russ's longing became converted into an undeniable force. He drew her into the circle of his arms, his lips covering hers so that anything else she may have been about to say was blotted out. Her lips were velvet, pulsating with life, and as his mouth moved over them, claiming them, Russ's emotions became kaleidoscopic, and threatened to whirl out of control. He saw her startled expression, saw her begin to draw back as if moved by an age-old instinct. But as his pliant mouth moved on hers, demanding her response, the tug between them almost becoming tangible, Russ felt as if his emotions and hers had crystallized into a single force. Their kiss became the essence of a delight edged with a brand of torture, because as their mouths merged, as their lips parted to invite a mutual exploration by tongues that penetrated and encircled, they evoked an ecstasy that was almost unbearable. The need for fulfillment—its pain mixing with their pleasure —cried out to both of them.

Their kiss was terminated only because both of them were overwhelmed. Paula drew back and Russ could feel her trembling, and the realization of what he was much too close to doing swept over him like a cold wave.

With an effort he forced himself to gain back control, to fight down this enormous surge of desire. Almost abruptly, he reached across her to open the door of his car for her. The invitation was clear, and he saw that she was plainly bewildered as she responded to it, getting into the car and sinking down in the low bucket seat.

His lips were tight as he turned the key in the ignition switch and heard the engine's deep-throated purr, and he didn't dare look at her. He was still far too aroused, and there was a limit to even his self-control. But before he could put the car into motion she said sharply, "Stop!"

He caught the vehemence in her voice and turned toward her, surprised by it. But before he could speak she said, her hand already on the door handle, "Come to think of it, I'll walk, thank you."

A streetlight just behind them cast a silvered band across the front seat of the car. In its swath Paula was fully visible to him and he saw that her eyes were wide and angry, her face pale and tense.

Suiting action to words, she clicked the door handle down, and in an instant Russ leaned over, clasping his hand over hers, his grip firm and strong.

"What are you talking about?" he demanded.

"I'd rather walk, that's all," she insisted stubbornly, and despite himself Russ grinned.

"Little spitfire," he accused tenderly. "Do you think I'm rejecting you?"

The amber eyes blazed. "I'd rather not discuss it," she said coldly.

"Stop acting like a teenager," he advised gently, still smiling, still holding her hand tightly.

Before she could sputter an answer, he leaned across the gap between the bucket seats and found her lips unerringly, and his kiss was sweet, tender, far more poignant than he'd ever imagined a kiss could be.

He said, rocking a little from the effect the kiss was having on him, "I forced myself to stop because I wanted to go on . . . and on and on, Paula. So very much further." Then he added frankly, "It's too soon for that. Also, I want something so much better for you. The right time, the right place." He ran a hand through his hair distractedly, rumpling its smoothness. "What the hell am I saying?" he asked, posing the question to the night and the stars and the sliver of a moon.

"The truth," Paula said wryly, after a moment, her voice very small. "It is too soon."

The restaurant was only a few miles from Paula's house and she wished the distance were longer, because they traveled it much too quickly.

Briefly, as he'd run his hand through his hair and had asked the moon and the stars what the hell he was saying, Russ had come out from behind that invisible wall that usually protected him, and he'd let her see him with his guard down, his handsome face very, very vulnerable.

She'd damned cars with bucket seats. She'd wanted to bridge the physical distance between them, to touch him, to hold him, to murmur little assurances into his ear. And it was impossible to get that close in a car like his—unless she catapulted herself directly into his lap, something she couldn't bring herself to do.

She *had* felt rejected when he'd suddenly opened the car door for her, terminating their embrace as if it had been programmed that he do so. By then, it had been a good thing that he was holding her because her knees had felt as if they'd become brittle twigs and could not possibly support her. The emotional impact of his kiss had been close to devastating. Paula had melted, literally and figuratively, and so it had been a shock to look at him and see that his face had become set in lines she could describe only as rigid. His mouth, compressed, had been thin, and she couldn't believe it was the same mouth that had assaulted hers with such unbridled passion only seconds before.

Yes, she'd felt hurt, rejected, and her temper had sparked as a result. She'd been more than ready to trudge home—and then Russ had let her have a glimpse of his own deep feelings, and it had taken very little explanation on his part to make her know he was right. They'd been close to an emotional edge neither of them was ready for. It *was* too soon. But she'd needed a little more time than this brief cross-Cape drive to pull her act together, and to face him with the kind of equanimity she wanted to present to him.

They pulled up in front of the old double-Cape. Paula had forgotten to leave a light on, and the house looked dark and forlorn, so very much alone.

She was ambivalent about her feelings toward asking Russ to come in for a nightcap, or for a cup of coffee. It was an invitation she wanted to issue, yet she drew back. They'd touched some very deep bases and she knew that she, personally, needed her own space in which to regroup. She also knew that to attempt to maintain an idle conversation with him over a drink or a cup of coffee would be far too anticlimactic. They both had other things on their minds.

He forestalled her having to make a decision by saying, "I'll wait till you turn some lights on."

"That's all right."

"No," he insisted quietly. "I'll wait."

Paula nodded, then escaped out of the car, hurried up the walk, and switched on the lamp in the tiny entrance hall. She went back to stand in the doorway, a feeling of incompleteness sweeping over her that made her wish she'd asked Russ to come in—regardless of the consequences.

She heard him call out, "Everything okay?" and made the automatic response, "Yes."

"Then I'll phone you in the morning," he told her, and was driving off before she had the chance to shout back that she didn't have a telephone.

Chapter Four

It was a long night. The old house seemed to close in on Paula. There were too many memories connected with it to handle just now, too many things concerning it to worry about. Paula got up in the pre-dawn hours and made herself a cup of hot milk, but even that time-proven remedy failed to lull her back to a restful slumber.

When, finally, she stumbled out of bed, groggy from lack of sleep, she was sure she would see deep, dark circles under her eyes when she looked in the mirror. Instead, there was a healthy glow to her face, thanks to having spent most of yesterday outdoors at the flea market. The dark circles were there, though, she thought wryly. They were psychological, rather than physical, that was all.

As she made her bed and straightened up the house,

Paula was fatigued and dejected, and annoyed at herself for allowing such negative forces to take possession of her. She was determined to get over this unpleasant sense of depression. Nevertheless, once she'd gone over her inventory of the things she'd taken to the flea market yesterday and deleted the things she'd sold, it became impossible to put on a cheerful face, no matter how hard she tried. The financial results were dismal.

Russ Grayson had been right. She had to admit it. She *had* overpriced her merchandise. Maybe, she admitted, this was at least in part because, subconsciously, she'd wished she didn't have to sell them at all. These pieces of china and glass and silver were the only tangible evidence she had left of her family. For that reason, rather than because of their monetary worth, they were very valuable to her. Yet the decision to be made was a clear-cut one. Either she was going to own a houseful of antiques with no house to put them in, or a house relatively clear of debts, but with a lot fewer family heirlooms in it. Provided, that is, that if she lowered her prices her things would sell.

She had covered her dining room table with a variety of her treasures and was marking down the prices on them when the doorbell pealed. Paula nearly dropped the cranberry crackle-glass vase she had just picked up when she heard it. Her heart began to thud. Maybe this was premonition, maybe it was just plain wishful thinking but, she told herself, it had to be Russ at the door.

It was.

He was wearing jeans this morning—strictly the designer type, she noted—and a green T-shirt that brought out the amazing color of his eyes. But even in such casual clothing he was as perfectly groomed as ever.

Paula, by contrast, also had on jeans, but she'd bought hers in a discount department store. She, also, was wearing a T-shirt, a yellow one, but she'd smudged it in the process of lifting a couple of dusty cartons, and in trying to rub off the smudge, had transferred a part of it to her cheek.

Her old running shoes had holes in the toes. Russ's looked as if they'd come off the shelf in a sports shop no later than the day before yesterday.

We're different, Paula opined unhappily. *Maybe too different.*

Brooding about this, she held the door open, staring up at Russ, and after a moment his lips twisted into that tilted smile she found so appealing and he asked, "Are you going to let me in? Or are you deliberately blocking my path of progress?"

She stepped aside hastily. "I'm sorry," she said, falling over the words, and nearly falling over her feet as well. This man had the *strangest* effect on her.

"I apologize for barging in like this," Russ said smoothly, "but I didn't want to wait till Wednesday to see you again."

"Wednesday?"

"Aren't you going to the flea market Wednesday?"

She was trying not to stare at his mouth, trying not to remember how it had felt last night, warm and pliant, his kiss passionate, her response equally so. She said, forcing her whirling thoughts into a narrow funnel, "Yes. Yes, I do plan to go to the flea market Wednesday."

They'd moved into the little center hallway and he glanced toward the dining room to their left.

"Working already, I see," he commented.

"Just . . . pricing some things," Paula told him. She made a rueful face. "I'm marking them down," she confessed.

To her surprise, he said, "Don't be too hasty about it, or you'll be apt to go from one extreme to the other. You don't want to give your stuff away, Paula. There's a happy medium."

"I'm sure there is," she agreed, leading him into the dining room. "The problem is in finding it."

"I'd be glad to help," he offered. "I don't want to

push my way in, that's all." He added, "I appreciate your feelings about your possessions. You have some very nice pieces and it's much harder to put something up for sale when it has a sentimental as well as an intrinsic value."

She was surprised at his perception. Surprised and touched, as well. Most of the men she'd known hadn't been that understanding. Certainly, her ex-husband hadn't been.

She was conscious of Russ watching her closely. He asked gently, "Do you want me to help you price your things, Paula?"

"I'd appreciate it very much," Paula said almost humbly. "I admit I don't know nearly enough about what I'm doing despite all the books I've been studying. I have a lot to learn."

He nodded. "There's a lot to learn, when it comes to antiques," he admitted. "It's a matter of touch, of feel, almost as much as it is of sight."

Paula was watching his hands as he picked up a couple of small objects and ran his fingers over their surfaces. She felt her mouth go dry. She almost envied these inanimate objects.

It was with an effort that she concentrated on what he was telling her when, looking over a blue Canton covered ginger jar she'd just put a new price on, he shook his head and said, "You *have* gone overboard. You should be able to get at least fifty dollars for this, and you've put only twenty-five on it. Try fifty, and I'll buy it," he added.

Paula tensed. She had a terrible suspicion that he was going to offer to buy a number of her things this morning—at prices that were probably still too high for them—and she didn't want this. She was far too interested in Russ Grayson to let herself become obligated to him. She wanted to be free to explore the relationship she felt brimming between the two of them, without any barriers in her way.

Determined to set the issue straight between them,

she said, "Russ, I wouldn't think of selling the ginger jar to you."

"Why discriminate against *me?*" he asked her.

"Because you're a dealer, for one reason," she said. "I *do* know enough to realize that in order to make a decent profit you'd have to put the price on the jar so high you'd probably never be able to sell it."

To her surprise, Russ burst out laughing. "You *are* learning fast," he said. "As it happens, though, I don't want to sell it."

"You collect Canton?" she asked him.

"No. But I like this particular piece, I'd like to keep it."

She considered this. Then she said, "All right. In that case, I'll give it to you."

Russ frowned. "Don't be ridiculous, Paula," he told her. He put the ginger jar back on the table. "You won't make much money if you start giving away some of your best pieces," he chided. His smile took the sting out of the statement. "Now, suppose we pull up a couple of chairs and start going over your prices," he suggested.

Much later, Paula made coffee and brought in two brimming mugs for them. She sat down at the dining room table, fully in control of herself until Russ pushed his chair next to hers. Then she felt as if every muscle in her body were straining in the effort to avoid a visible reaction to him. He smelled of soap and fresh air and sunshine and a faint lemon after-shave, and it was a scent that turned into an elixir as it filled her nostrils. She sniffed deeply, and the effect was potent. How, she asked herself, could she possibly concentrate on pricing antiques with this man at her side?

She was vibrantly aware of everything about him. His thick dark hair. The tanned skin. Little laugh wrinkles at the corners of his eyes. A certain mobility to his mouth—his mouth had a language all its own. When he reached out to pick up a Moon and Star pressed-glass toothpick holder, his hand brushed the back of

Paula's hand, and she became a self-contained forest that he'd just set afire. She drew a deep breath, needing oxygen, needing space from him if she was to function normally, and the drawn breath came out as a gasp.

Russ turned to her swiftly. "Something wrong?" he asked her.

"No," she said. Then she fibbed, "I . . . just got a stitch in my side."

"You're sure you're all right?"

"Yes," she said hastily. Nodding at the toothpick holder he was still holding, she said, "I wonder why that didn't sell. It's a nice one."

Russ grinned. "You may hate me for this," he said, "but it's not an original."

Her eyes narrowed. "You're telling me it's a reproduction?"

He nodded. "Yes. But it's still a nice piece, Paula. It's overpriced, that's all. Because it's a reproduction doesn't mean that it's not desirable, collectible in fact. Look, I can *feel* your edginess. Cool it, will you?"

He spoke gently. She couldn't take offense at what he was saying, and after a moment she managed a rather tremulous smile. "I'm sorry, Russ," she murmured. "Sometimes I get carried away."

His eyes were lingering on her face, and he said dryly, "So I've noticed. I should think you would have developed a tougher hide, teaching bunches of today's kids, as you do."

"My kids are still young," she told him. "I teach fourth graders. I don't know myself how I'd relate to teenagers. They can be hard to handle, but personally I think that's mainly because so many of them are so mixed up. I was mixed up myself when I was a teenager, weren't you?"

It was as if a veil drifted suddenly over those green eyes. He said cautiously, "Yes. I was . . . quite mixed up." And Paula became conscious, again, of the way he tended to hold back when something came up that involved him personally.

The question sprang impulsively, as so many of Paula's questions did. "Have you ever been married, Russ?"

"What brought that up?" he asked curiously.

"I don't know. I was just wondering."

"No, I've never been married," he told her. "What about you?"

"Yes," she said. She knew he was waiting for her to continue and after a moment she went on slowly. "I was married just out of high school."

Russ asked quietly, "Want to tell me about it?"

"Not particularly," she said frankly. "As I've said, I was just out of high school. This was in Arlington, right outside of Boston, where Gram was living then. I ran off with Howie which, of course, hurt Gram very much. She couldn't believe I'd do something so drastic behind her back. But when I came creeping around to her a year or so later, she was wonderful. She helped me get through college and into teaching."

Russ digested this. Then he asked, "What about your husband?"

"What about him?" Paula countered.

"Was it your idea to get a divorce or was it his? Or am I being too inquisitive?"

"I brought the subject up," Paula said rather grimly, "so you're not being too inquisitive. Howie and I had a high school romance that should have ended with graduation. We were just a couple of kids, absolutely different in every way I can think of."

"Except that you must have shared a certain . . . physical affinity?" Russ suggested.

She flushed at this. "Yes. Yes, we did in the beginning. But . . ." She looked at this man sitting next to her and hated raking up the sordid details of her marriage to Howie. Once they'd actually gotten married she'd become a possession as far as Howie was concerned. And he'd used her.

She said, "We had nothing in common, and the physical bond wore very thin." She added steadily,

"Howie liked variety. I was not willing to go along with that."

"I see," Russ said, looking at her as if she'd put a distance of a thousand miles between them.

"I'm not sure you do," Paula said desperately, wishing they'd never gotten into this. "Russ, you don't like to talk about yourself," she told him bluntly. "You might realize that it's not easy for me either."

He considered this for what seemed a very long moment to Paula. Then he said, "You're right," and the distance between them began to dissipate.

Paula waved vaguely toward the objects scattered all over the table. "Could we get back to these?" she suggested.

"Yes," he said quickly, and she sensed that he was as relieved as she was to change the subject, to get on to easier ground.

They got down to basics at that point. Time passed quickly and they were almost through with the flea-market items when Paula said suddenly, "There's something missing."

Russ looked up swiftly. "What?"

"The coin silver teaspoon that belonged to my great-aunt Harriet," Paula said. "It has the initial *W* for Winslow on it."

Russ scanned the table. "I don't see it," he told her.

"It has to be around somewhere," Paula retorted, and started searching. But the coin silver spoon was not to be found.

By then it was lunchtime, and Paula suggested that Russ share a sandwich with her. But as they walked out to the kitchen together, she was perturbed.

Leaning against the kitchen wall, his arms folded, Russ watched her open a can of tuna then asked, "Are you sure you didn't sell the spoon?"

"Positive," Paula told him, spreading mayonnaise on slices of bread.

"Maybe you put it in your handbag?"

She shook her head. "No."

"Stop worrying about it," Russ advised. "Either it's gone, or it will show up."

"Gone?"

"Someone could have filched it, Paula."

She turned to him, shocked. "You think it might have been *stolen?*" she demanded.

"Don't look like that." He was walking toward her as he spoke, and he reached out to touch her chin with the tip of his index finger. "The world's full of thieves, honey," he said softly. "Old coin silver spoons are nice things to have, and they're small, easily stashed away in a tote bag or a pocket."

"Damn it," Paula protested. "I hate the thought of someone stealing from me. Especially at the flea market."

"Is thievery at a flea market any worse than thievery anywhere else?" he asked her.

"Yes, it is. You don't expect crooks to operate out in the fresh air and sunshine. At least I don't," Paula admitted miserably.

"You're a funny girl," Russ said. But there was an odd note in his voice as he said it and slowly he reached out to her, drawing her close to him.

Paula, on the verge of tears because the results of her first day at the flea market had been enough of a bummer without having someone steal from her in the bargain, instinctively began to pull away from him. But Russ's grip became firmer, and she looked up to see a warmth in his green eyes that made her feel she was going to melt right in front of him.

She swayed toward him, mesmerized. Their kiss became a mutual coming together, their lips merging, this initial touch of Russ's mouth coming against hers evoking a rush of such unprecedented feeling that Paula clung to him, drawing from his strength because hers was draining away.

She felt the thrust of his tongue and she parted her lips to receive his first offering on the road to ecstasy. Her hands brushed across the nape of his neck, her fingers settling into his thick hair, the touch of it evoking still other feelings because they involved yet another sense. She was using all five of her senses with this man, Paula discovered, and she was thinking about him in a way that was new to her. She wanted to explore Russ, she wanted to learn all there was about him. And she wanted to share herself with him. She knew that she'd never given a man even a fraction of what she had to offer, she'd always held back. There'd always been a large part of her that belonged solely to Paula. Now she wanted to let Russ know that secret part of her, to let him discover her.

She was pressed so close to him that she could hear his pulse thumping. And she knew she had aroused him, the evidence was telltale, burgeoning hard against her. Such a rush of yearning, such a distillation of pure desire, flooded through Paula's veins that it was as if she'd been given a sudden, miraculous transfusion.

Russ's breathing was coming faster and his hands were molding her hips, their motion slow, steady, and infinitely erotic. Had it not been for the tea kettle this would have been *it,* Paula told herself a second later. But she'd put on the kettle so she could make a fresh pot of coffee, and—with consummate irony—it chose that emotion-fraught minute in which to start whistling, the whistle screeching louder and louder as a spiral of steam snaked toward the ceiling.

Russ muttered something under his breath and let her go. Shaken, Paula navigated the space to the stove and pulled the kettle off the burner. But the spell was broken.

As the afternoon passed, Paula's problems receded further and further into the background. There was a quiet enjoyment in working with Russ. They'd moved on, after lunch, past the things she'd already displayed at the flea market to some new boxes filled with all sorts of antiques. Now Russ, studying a Burmese cracker jar, said, "This is the real thing. You shouldn't sell it for less than six hundred dollars," he added, fingering the lovely glass, which was two-toned, shading from peach to yellow. "Actually, I think you should keep it."

The Burmese jar was another of the treasures that had always been kept on Gram's sideboard here in the old Cape Cod house. Paula said reluctantly, "If it's worth that much, I'm going to have to sell it, Russ."

"Then let me take it back to New York," he suggested. "I'm going to have to go down for a couple of days before long. This will certainly bring more on the market there than it would in the flea market."

She considered this. Then she said, "I'll do that if you'll agree to take a commission."

"A commission?" He didn't bother to try to conceal his irritation. "Paula, for God's sake . . ."

"I'm serious, Russ. I don't believe in letting people do favors without rewarding them."

He stared at her with an expression of total disbelief. Then a grin that she could only call wicked spread across his face, and he said, "I can think of a few ways you could reward me for any favors I might do for you."

She didn't know whether to cut him off sharply or to laugh. Her sense of humor won. Russ, when he grinned like that, had a devilish look so out of keeping with his usual urbanity that she couldn't help but find it funny.

Russ put the Burmese jar back and, watching him, Paula asked, "Do you do all the buying for your New York shop?"

He didn't answer at once. He reached for an old brass ladle and studied it before saying, "No, I don't do all the buying. I'd say this ladle dates back to the mid-eighteenth century, incidentally. It's a nice one, in excellent condition. I think you could easily get seventy-five dollars for it."

As he put the ladle down and reached for a little wooden heart-shaped box, their hands brushed, as they had on a number of occasions by now. But this time Russ closed his fingers over Paula's wrist and she looked up to see that his green eyes were ocean deep. He said, his voice husky, "Paula . . ."

How could there be so much in a single name?

"Paula," he repeated, "I—I can't hold back a third time. Look," he continued, "I know I'm the one who's done most of the talking about rushing things. But this is so special, Paula. Do you know what I'm saying?"

She knew.

This moment between us is like a small and beautiful bird, she found herself thinking. *And sometimes if you let a bird fly away, it never comes back again.*

Russ stood slowly, and held his arms out to her. "I want you," he told her. "Oh, God, how I want you! I don't know what the hell it is you've done to me. You're not a Gypsy, woman. You're a witch."

He was trying to speak lightly, but there was a roughness to his voice, an urgency. Looking up at him, Paula saw a mixture of desire and uncertainty in his eyes, and it was a heady feeling to know that she had it within her power to do something about both of those things.

Yet, despite the headiness, or perhaps because of it, when she tried to speak she found she had no words. They'd vanished entirely, her entire vocabulary had deserted her. She could only stare at Russ mutely, but then she went into his arms and it didn't matter. Nothing mattered, except this particular moment in time.

As if they'd been programmed to march to the same drummer, they moved toward the steep old Cape Cod staircase, Russ's arms cradling Paula against him. In her bedroom, sunlight filtered through the sheer white curtains to splash across the wide pine floorboards. Her bedstead was an old brass one, kept to a beautiful polish, and her great-grandmother had crocheted the spread.

Russ's eyes were lambent, as if lit by an inner light, as

he said, "I want to see you with the sunlight shining over you." He added, that tilted smile she loved so much edging his mouth, "I want to see if you have freckles on any of the rest of you."

She didn't. Except for the spattering across her nose and cheekbones, Paula's skin was milk-white and satin-smooth.

"Live marble," Russ said. "Warm, breathing alabaster. My God, but you're beautiful."

He'd drawn off the smudged yellow T-shirt by the time he was saying this and unfastened her bra, staring first at her breasts, the nipples pink and taut, before he reached out to stroke them with an experimental finger. His touch branded Paula, setting her all the more afire. He asked, an odd, strangled quality to his voice, "Can the rest of you possibly be as perfect?" Then slowly, gently, he eased her jeans down over her hips, the brief blue satin bikini pants she was wearing underneath them soon to follow. And the sunlight did shine on her as she stood before Russ, casting gold motes over her skin that shimmered, making her even lovelier.

He said hoarsely, "I can't believe you. You're exquisite. Porcelain, pure porcelain."

His hands were moving over her skin as he spoke, and now he bent his head, trailing kisses across her throat and down the V between her breasts. Paula, always impetuous, reached out to him, tugging at his T-shirt, tugging at his belt, possessed of the urge to see him even as he was seeing her.

He was magnificent in the glow of the afternoon sunlight. She pressed herself against him with a small, piercing cry, and she barely remembered moving toward the bed with him, and sinking into its softness.

Russ's mouth began to rove over her, starting at the line where her beautiful auburn hair swept back from her forehead. Then slowly his mouth descended down across the flatness of her stomach, and while he kissed her his hands were working, moving over the contours of her body as if he were a sculptor and she was at once his model and his clay. She tensed as he touched the most intimate of all her places, remembering that sometimes this had been a prelude to a very bad time with Howie. A painful time. But then Howie was gone from her mind as Russ suffused her with his own presence slowly, insistently, coaxing her to let him bring her pleasure until her emotions crested, becoming mixed with an agony of expectation and an ecstasy that blended into one transcending element almost too powerful and too wonderful to bear.

The crescendo came, rocking her to a moment so heightened, she couldn't believe there could be another sensation in the world that could surpass it. And, in another instant, Russ set out to prove her wrong.

Wordlessly, he took her with him on a voyage of exploration. Guided by instinct alone, she found herself touching him as she'd never touched a man before, then savoring the feel and the many textured facets of him, loving her own sense of power all the while because she knew that she was bringing him pleasure, even as he'd brought it to her.

And it was he who decreed when the time was right for both of them, urging her to join him in a mutual tempo that escalated like the beat in a tribal jungle rhythm, mounting in a marvelously primitive way that knew no restraints. Only then did they reach the peak of passion, to crash at the far edge of its summit.

In the aftermath of their lovemaking, Paula felt herself drifting, floating on a cloud of utter peace. She turned to look at this wonderful man by her side, and wondered if he was sharing this beautiful, sublime feeling with her.

But Russ's eyes were closed, his profile averted, and she could not read him. Tentatively she reached out to grasp his hand, clasping her fingers through his. To her relief he responded, tightening the pressure, his hand firm and warm and strong.

Neither of them needed to say anything to know that it had been time, and that the time had been right.

The sun was almost setting when Russ left Paula's house. She watched his long black car go out of her driveway, and felt such a sharp sense of loss that it shocked her.

Russ had told her ruefully that he had a dinner engagement and he'd been as reluctant to leave as she'd been to have him go. Now her only consolation was that he'd promised to come back in the morning, ostensibly to continue with their inventory of her antiques.

Paula thought the night would never end. She had a hard time getting to sleep but when finally she did, she slept deeply. She woke up ready to face the new day with enthusiasm.

She fixed herself scrambled eggs and toast for breakfast then, after cleaning up the kitchen, brought down some boxes of glass and china from the attic and put them on the dining room table to await Russ's inspection.

The morning inched on. Paula had expected that Russ would show up around nine, so as that hour approached she made a fresh pot of coffee. When he hadn't appeared by ten, she started drinking it. When he hadn't appeared by noon she was angry—more at herself, even, than at him. Deeply chagrined, because this morning engagement with her evidently hadn't meant very much to him—even after yesterday.

Yesterday. She couldn't regret what had happened yesterday, no matter what transpired between Russ and herself from now on. Paula admitted this as she walked around the house, inspecting the few flowers that were in bloom—blue hydrangeas, some lovely white peonies, a bed of tiger lilies that had been there ever since she could remember.

She and Russ, she reflected, had gone into a realm all their own yesterday, which made getting back down to the earth all the more difficult. Something must have come up that Russ couldn't avoid. He'd have an explanation for his absence, she assured herself. But no matter how she tried to rationalize things, Paula was at the edge of a bad case of nerves as she went back into the house and she knew that what she needed was action.

She put on a slim, black maillot-type bathing suit and drove across to the bay side of the Cape, and found a parking space on Mayo Beach, overlooking Wellfleet Harbor. She swam vigorously, then floated on her back, watching gulls soar across the vivid blue sky, and some sailboats racing off Chequesset Neck. Some of the sails were white, some were in all colors of the rainbow. They billowed in the wind and made such a lovely picture, Paula wished she'd brought a camera with her.

She paused at the Wellfleet marina for a chocolate frappe, then reluctantly drove home.

After showering she slipped into a pink terry lounger and went downstairs slowly. Balking at the idea of eating dinner alone, she poured herself a glass of wine and thought about turning on TV. But she wasn't in the mood for television.

What was she in the mood for?

Russ. The answer came involuntarily. She wanted to see him, she wanted to feel his arms around her. She wanted him close to her.

Feeling very much alone, Paula poured herself a second glass of wine. And she'd just started on a third one when the doorbell rang.

Chapter Five

$\mathscr{P}$aula was feeling fuzzy from the wine and at first she had the crazy impression that the tea kettle had been whistling again. She started for the kitchen, then recognized the summons for what it was and pattered barefoot across the little entrance hall.

Opening the door, she found herself staring up into Russ's extremely annoyed face.

"Why the hell don't you have a chain on your door?" he greeted her.

"Why should I have?" she countered.

"I should think common sense would give you the answer to that," he informed her tightly. "You're out here in the boonies, all by yourself. You should have a decent lock and chain on *all* your doors. Especially—" and his gaze raked her terry robe "—when you go around dressed like that."

He strode past her as he spoke, seeming larger than life to her. But as she peered at him more closely she saw that he also looked absolutely exhausted. His eyes were red-rimmed, lines of fatigue etched his face, and he badly needed a shave.

"What . . . what's happened to you?" she asked him, the words slurring a bit, and at this he glared down at her with such a ferocious expression that she cringed.

"What the hell!" he stated. "You're drunk!"

Paula drew herself up with all the dignity she could manage under the circumstances, the effort making her nearly trip over the hem of the long robe.

Russ clutched her arm, as if he'd expected her to fall flat on her face—right at his feet—and there was no missing his exasperation as he barked, "What have you been doing with yourself?"

"I . . . went swimming," Paula said stiffly, reminding herself that it was important to be very dignified just now. Yes, *very* dignified indeed.

"I never knew that salt water had an intoxicating effect," he said nastily. "What have you been drinking?"

"Chablis," she said, piling dignity on dignity.

"Do you have anything stronger in the house?"

"I don't want anything stronger, thank you," she said politely, as if she'd authored a book on etiquette.

"I wasn't thinking about you, I was thinking about me," Russ informed her.

"There's whiskey in the kitchen cabinet," she told him frostily, aware that she couldn't possibly get it for him herself. Between the wine she'd had and just being near him she'd almost surely drop the glass.

"Thank you very much," he said, frost matching frost. "I'd suggest you go sit down while I fix myself a drink."

Paula obeyed him because she had no alternative. But she was feeling a burning sense of resentment toward him as he came into the living room with his drink to slump into an armchair.

Then she looked at him again, and her solicitude for him eclipsed everything else. "What did happen to you?" she asked him. "You look like you were up all night."

"I was up all night," he answered tersely. "Why the hell don't you have a telephone?"

"Because I didn't want to spend the money on one," she said bluntly.

His green eyes were cold as an arctic sea as he surveyed her. "Are you always such a penny-pincher, Paula?" he asked her.

That hurt. It hurt enough to wear off a good bit of the effects of the wine she'd drunk. A lump arose in her throat and she was afraid if she didn't watch it she'd start crying.

She surveyed Russ. Despite his need for a shave, despite the weariness in his face, he still had a certain look about him. A look that reeked of money, she decided, trying to build up a healthy anger so that she wouldn't break down in front of him. He couldn't possibly understand her situation.

She said quietly, "Some people have to pinch pennies, Russ. I don't think anyone enjoys doing so. But it isn't a crime, it isn't anything to be ashamed of."

She'd hit home with him. She saw his eyes flicker and he took a deep draft of his drink before he answered her. Then he said, "Forgive me, honey. I've had a hell of a time since I left here and I was frantic because there was no way I could reach you. If you'd had a blasted phone, it would have been so much easier.

"My dinner engagement last night was with old friends of my uncle's," he told her. "My host, whom I've known most of my life, had a heart attack before we reached the dessert course."

"Russ!" Shock motivated Paula to get up and move across the room to him, kneeling down on the floor at his side and touching his arm with a consoling hand.

"We called the rescue squad and got him to the hospital, but it was touch-and-go for hours," Russ said.

"His wife isn't in the best of health herself; she wasn't up to an ordeal like this. Once they'd finally told us there was a good chance he was going to make it, I was almost more worried about her than I was about him. I stayed with her until just a little while ago. Then, a niece of hers from Boston came down so I was able to leave. I came here directly."

He fixed her with a look that made her flinch. "What did you think I'd done, Paula?" he asked her.

Russ was not ready for Paula's reaction to his question. The tears started spilling down her cheeks and in an instant he was out of the chair, drawing her to her feet, holding her.

"God, honey," he protested, appalled. "Please!"

He pulled her close to him and she leaned her head against his shoulder and sobbed while he stroked her hair. He suspected that maybe the sobs were the culmination of a lot of things, the last of which was his failure to have come here today when he'd said he would.

Had she thought he'd abandoned her? Russ looked down at her soft, wavy auburn hair and shook his head ruefully. He'd been thinking about her all day, his concern for her lacing through his fears for Carleton Edgeworth and his wife, Helen. When he'd told Paula last night that he had a dinner date with old friends of his uncle's, he hadn't added that the Edgeworths were both very special people to him.

In that terrible, long-ago summer when he'd been seventeen years old and in France for a long visit with his uncle, who was in Paris for several months on a government economic mission, Carleton Edgeworth had been the American ambassador. When they'd diagnosed Russ's illness as tuberculosis, it was Carleton Edgeworth who'd seen to it that the best specialists were called in, and later he'd made arrangements with the sanatorium in the Swiss Alps to take Russ as a patient.

Russ had spent the next two years of his life in that

sanatorium. Both Carleton and Helen Edgeworth had been frequent visitors and he'd never forgotten the morale boost they'd given him.

Later, they'd continued to give him the kind of encouragement he'd needed desperately during that long, long period in his youth when, finally returning to the States, he'd spent most of his time in the Chatham house with only a staff of servants for company, as he fought his way back to health.

It had been a long fight but, thank God, it had been a successful one. Nevertheless, those years between the time when he was seventeen to the middle of his twenties represented an interval he'd never talked about to anyone. Now, looking down at the woman in his arms, he knew that if they kept on the way they were going, he'd have to tell her about the cloudy time in his life at some point. It wouldn't be fair to her not to tell her; he only hoped that she'd be able to accept the fact that he was completely cured, and posed no danger to her.

Paula was trying to control her sobs, but once she let go it was difficult to regain the reins of self-control. Also, Russ's arms were giving her sanctuary right now, and she permitted herself to take advantage of what he was offering.

He was holding her so tenderly, his hand gentle upon her hair. She sniffed, tilted her head back, and then said, "I've gotten your shirt all wet."

He smiled his twisted smile. "It'll get dry," he promised her.

"Russ . . . I'm sorry I've been such a fool," Paula said.

He was still holding her and he said, "I don't think you were being a fool, honey. You've had a lot on your mind since your grandmother died, haven't you?"

She hesitated briefly. Then she said, "Yes."

"You've a lot on your mind with this house, too." He was releasing her as he spoke.

"Yes," she admitted. "Yes, I do have." She was still

brushing the tears away from her eyes and now she noted that Russ was watching her with a strange expression, as if he wanted to say something yet was holding back.

He looked so tired. She reached out and touched his cheek, and her voice trembled slightly as she said, "You feel like sandpaper, Russ. Can I make you some coffee or something?"

He shook his head. "No, thanks. I'd better get along home. You need to get some sleep if you're going to make the flea market in the morning."

Paula yearned to ask him to stay with her, but he was already moving toward the door. She followed along, wishing that he'd never leave her again. Not ever.

"Take two aspirin before you go to bed, and drink a cup of warm milk," Russ prescribed.

"Why?" she asked suspiciously.

"So you won't have a hangover." He grinned, and a moment of brewing tension was broken.

Paula followed Russ's prescription. She expected that she'd awaken in the morning with a headache that might be classified as a hangover anyway, but when she opened her eyes to greet the daylight she was pleasantly surprised.

She'd set her alarm for six, and it was seven before she finished loading everything into her car and started out for the flea market. It wasn't until she was paying her dealer's fee at the collection booth that it dawned on her it was unlikely she'd be anywhere near Russ today. Some of the dealers who were regulars reserved specific places. Most took whatever spaces were assigned to them.

There were not as many dealers in the flea market as there had been on Sunday. Nevertheless, there were enough so that wherever Russ was he was not visible from Paula's vantage point and—with no one to watch her tables—there was no way she could go in search of him.

Once the flea market had opened to the public, Paula also began to suspect that there were not going to be as many potential customers on a Wednesday as there had been on Sunday. It was another hot and humid day, and the people wandering up and down the lanes were doing so at a desultory pace. Nor did any of them seem to be overmotivated to buy.

Midmorning, a familiar figure loomed up in front of Paula. For a moment she couldn't place the woman, she knew only that she'd seen her somewhere before. Then she recognized the stout wife of the burly man with the Florida camper who'd been in the space next to hers on Sunday.

"Hi, there," the woman said genially. "They've kind of got you stuck out in the back forties, haven't they?"

Paula had been given a place today not too far from the huge movie screen at the back of the drive-in theater, and she'd been wondering herself whether it was the best of locations. Many of the visitors wouldn't want to trudge this far on such a hot day.

"Yes," she said. "I guess you pretty much have to go where you're told to go, though."

"Unless you reserve space, and that costs a heap extra," the woman nodded. "I'm Maybelle Stevens," she said. "You were next to my husband and me last Sunday."

"Yes, I remember," Paula responded. "I'm Paula Danvers," she added.

"Pleased to meet you," Maybelle said enthusiastically, flashing a wide grin. "Going to be hot as hell again, already's getting sticky," she added with no less exuberance. "I told Cholly, he's my husband, I think it's a waste of time setting up on a day like this. So what does Cholly say to me? He says, 'What better have we got to do?' Can you beat that?" Maybelle laughed.

Paula found herself laughing with her. There was something infectious about the big woman's laughter.

"You got some nice things," Maybelle observed now. "You in the antique business?"

"No. These are just family things I want to sell," Paula said, keeping the explanation as brief as possible.

"Nice," Maybelle nodded, fingering a small blue Spode pitcher. "What have you got on this? Forty dollars?" She squinted at Paula's price label.

"Yes," Paula told her.

"Any discount for dealers?"

This was a question Paula didn't know how to answer. Was one suppose to give another dealer a discount? Another dealer? She wasn't really a dealer herself, in the strict sense of the word.

She wished Russ was around to help her. She said, not wanting to offend Maybelle Stevens, "I don't know. I—I have it priced rather low." Even Russ had agreed that forty dollars was a more than fair price for the pitcher.

"I know that, sweetie," the big woman told her. "If I was you," she added, her tone confidential, "I'd put fifty on it. Well, got to be getting back to Cholly." She waved a hand cheerily. "Come by and see us," she invited.

Sales picked up briefly after Maybelle's departure. Paula disposed of a Wedgwood bowl, a Royal Doulton Rip Van Winkle jug, an old miniature swan sadiron, and a Coca-Cola tray marked 1917, all at the prices Russ had suggested.

By noon she was beginning to feel more optimistic, but she was also missing Russ very much. She'd not realized till now how comforting having him across the lane from her had been the other day—even if he *had* started off their acquaintance by telling her that her amethyst glass bowl wasn't Tiffany. And had he ever been right!

She'd changed the label on the bowl and knocked down the price, and she sold it at exactly twelve forty-five by the watch Gram had given her as a college graduation present.

This was something she wanted to share with Russ. Also, she needed to visit the rest room. Also, she was so thirsty, she could barely swallow, her throat was so dry. When Maybelle Stevens came by to inquire, smiling, "You still stuck there? You been there all this time? Listen, I'd be glad to spell you for a while," Paula was more than eager to take a break.

She visited the rest room and the snack bar in quick succession, and then sought out Russ. It seemed forever before she spotted the cream-colored van, and saw him standing behind his tables talking to a white-haired man who'd evidently just made a purchase. He was carefully clutching something enveloped in newspaper wrapping.

She waited till the man sauntered away before she approached Russ, and was chagrined to see that he was again wearing the oversize dark glasses, so it was impossible to read his expression.

"Damn!" was his way of greeting her. He swiftly added, "I wondered if you'd manage to show up. I've been trying to figure out how I could get someone to spell me while I went to look for you. Tim Bailey promised to come over as soon as he could, and let Cora handle their space. He's the one with all the books."

He looked Paula up and down, then said, "Well, I'm glad you remembered to bring a hat along with you. How about suntan lotion?"

"I've been using it," she assured him.

"Who's minding the store for you?"

"Maybelle Stevens," she told him. "She's the one—"

"I know," he interrupted. "She and her husband are the big people with the Florida van." He let his gaze linger on her, then he asked, "How have you been doing, Paula?"

"Not sensationally, but a lot better than Sunday," she told him. "Thanks to you. Now I can honestly say the price is right."

He nodded. Then he said, "This isn't going to happen again."

"What isn't?" She was looking him over as she

spoke, trying not to be too obvious about it. She, too, had on dark glasses today. Not as oversize as his, but still they were enough of a camouflage. He looked good, very good. He had on beige slacks and a dark brown sport shirt and, as usual, everything fit him perfectly. He was wearing his Great Gatsby hat, and he looked as handsome and self-assured as ever, and, God help me, Paula found herself thinking, *I'm falling in love with him.*

This was such a revelation that she didn't hear him at first when he explained what wasn't going to happen again, and after a time he said, "Well?"

"Well, what?" Paula asked weakly.

"It's okay, isn't it?" he asked her.

"What's okay?"

"My reserving the spaces for both of us." He frowned. "You haven't heard a word I've said, have you?"

"I—I'm sorry," Paula stammered.

"You should be, woman!" His smile softened the words. "After I realized what was going to happen to us for the rest of the summer if we let things take their course, I spoke to the manager here and reserved spaces for both of us so we can be side by side. Otherwise, there's not a chance in a hundred that we'd wind up next to each other again." He hesitated when she didn't at once answer him and said, "I wanted to be next to you. I hope you feel the same way about it."

It was Paula's turn to frown. "I do," she admitted. "But—"

"Yes?"

"Well, Maybelle says that reserving a space costs extra."

She saw Russ's lips tighten and was afraid for a moment that he was going to explode or come out with another rude statement about penny-pinching. She could *feel* him counting to ten. Then he said, "Paula, just once, would you be my guest on this, please?"

She shook her head. "No. I can't do that, Russ, it wouldn't be right. How much extra was it?"

"I'm not going to tell you," he said stubbornly.

"Then I'll find out."

"Look, please," he said, and there was a new note in his voice. It was as if he were asking a favor of her rather than doing a favor for her. "Let me do this, Paula," he told her. "I really want to. It isn't *that* much, or I'd tell you. I want you next to me on all the special Sundays, and special Saturdays, and special Wednesdays, and this is the only way we can guarantee it. So, please? Okay?"

It was quite a speech. Russ Grayson, she suspected, was not in the habit of making speeches like that. He was not in the habit of pleading with anyone; she was intuitively sure of that. She could feel the tension crackling as he waited for her answer, and when she said, "Okay"—though she was still reluctant about this, much as she wanted him in the space next to hers for the rest of the summer—he made no secret about exhaling a relieved, "Whew!"

She imagined that he would have said more, but he was interrupted by a customer asking him about a beautiful cut-glass bowl, and while he was detailing its history she said softly, "See you later," and headed back to her own space.

Maybelle had made four sales for her, and was as pleased as Paula was about this. And the afternoon continued to go well.

It was fairly late when Cholly Stevens came by for a brief visit with her. Meantime, Hilda Benson—whom Russ had nicknamed Jenny Wren the other day—stopped by, looking more like a little bird than ever in a brown-and-white print dress that went almost to her ankles.

Finally, toward four o'clock, Russ appeared, and when she saw him Paula's heart left her chest to travel to her stomach, then to her head, then plummeted back into place again.

"How goes it?" he asked casually, and it took an effort to be able to answer him at all. The things this man did to her!

"Fine," she said. "I've done twice as well as I did Sunday."

Twice as well wasn't enough, she knew that. But it was a step in the right direction. Also, this was Wednesday, not Sunday. There would be a lot more business on Sunday. Probably on Saturday too. Things were looking up, and she flashed Russ an appreciative smile.

He said, "I'm about to pack up and take off. I have to get over to the hospital."

She was ashamed to realize that she'd forgotten about his old friend's illness. Well, not forgotten about it exactly. But it had gone to the back of her mind.

She asked automatically, "Is there anything I can do to help?"

Russ shook his head. "Nothing, really," he said. "Thanks for asking, though. Look, will you lock your doors tonight and at least check through a window to see who it is before you open up to anyone."

She laughed. "If you say so."

"Paula, I'm serious about this," he threatened.

"All right, Russ."

He was casting an eye over the things on her table as he spoke, and he said, "I gather you sold the Canton ginger jar?"

"No."

"I don't see it."

"I didn't bring it," she confessed.

"Oh? Then have you decided to sell it to me?"

Paula shook her head. "No."

He didn't pursue the subject. He glanced at his watch. A slim, gold digital watch. Real gold. Expensive. The loafers he was wearing were expensive, too. Gucci, she guessed, or something equally as good. She wished that she wasn't so money conscious when she was around him, but it was hard not to be.

He was so casual about something like paying an extra fee for a reserved space at the flea market. She'd gone along with him about this because of the attitude he'd taken. He'd become so serious—and it was so flattering to think that he wanted her next to him—that it would have been difficult to refuse him.

Now, though, how could she tell him that she planned to give him the ginger jar as an exchange. She'd wanted to give it to him anyway. Now she could use the ruse of offering it in lieu of paying for the flea-market reservation. But this wasn't the moment to make that kind of suggestion.

As she watched, he took off the oversize glasses and she saw that he still looked weary, but his eyes had the same effect on her they always did. *You may not know it, Russ Grayson,* she said silently, *but you could be a master hypnotist.*

He said, "I was wondering if you'd like to come out to my place in Truro tomorrow? If it's a day anything like this one, we could spend most of the time cooling off in the bay."

"I'd love to," she said without pausing to think. But then she did think, and she asked cautiously, "If you're sure it would be all right, that is?"

"Why wouldn't it be all right?"

Paula had just thought of something, a something that had motivated her question. She asked carefully, "Do you live by yourself, Russ?"

The green eyes flared. "Who the hell did you think I live with, Paula?"

"No one," she said. "Someone. How do I know?"

"I live alone in Truro," he said a bit coldly. "Otherwise, I would certainly have told you so. I even do my own housekeeping and my own cooking. I'll even fix your dinner for you tomorrow night. How about that?"

She couldn't repress a grin. "You mean you can cook?"

"Damned well," he assured her succinctly. "Very

haute cuisine, mind you, like hamburgers or canned corned beef hash. I hope your digestion can tolerate rich food.''

He was smiling his tilted smile as he spoke, and Paula corrected her previous discovery. No, she wasn't falling in love with him. She *was* in love with him. And she drew in her breath sharply as the full realization of this knocked her both in the head and in the heart.

She became busy this time around, and Russ drifted off with a farewell wave. Her customer was a man in search of a fifth-anniversary present for his wife who, he confided, liked "old things, though I'm not that much for them myself.''

Unfortunately, his looks, his attitude, and this statement reminded Paula of Howie. She had to force herself to remember that business was business, and to deal with him.

He seemed happy, though, with the Limoges chocolate set he selected, and paid her a good price for it. This brought her day's tally to quite a decent figure, and she wished she could share her satisfaction with Russ. But he, she imagined, was on his way to Cape Cod Hospital by now.

He'd warned her that he couldn't tell her what time, exactly, he could stop and pick her up the next day. Probably in mid-afternoon, he said, earlier if possible. This time it was she, rather than he, who bemoaned her lack of a telephone.

Home, she looked at the near empty Chablis bottle sitting on the kitchen sink, grimaced, and made herself a cup of tea. After she'd showered, she slipped into the pink terry robe again then, as if Russ were looking over her shoulder, dutifully went around and locked all exterior doors.

Next she went over the list of things she'd sold today at the flea market, but as she did so something was nagging at the back of her mind. She couldn't remember packing up the little blue Spode pitcher that

Maybelle Stevens had admired, yet she was sure she hadn't sold it.

Had Maybelle sold it? Maybelle had written down the objects she'd dispensed with while Paula was visiting Russ, and rechecking the list, Paula saw that the Spode pitcher wasn't among them.

The last thing in the world she wanted to do tonight was to go through cartons of flea-market merchandise. Yet she knew she couldn't rest until she found out whether or not she was mistaken about the little pitcher. Maybe she had packed it after all. There were so many items, and she recalled that as she'd started to pack up, Tim Bailey, the man who had the book display, had stopped by to introduce himself and to suggest she pay his wife and him a visit on Saturday, if time permitted.

There was a friendliness about the flea-market dealers, Paula was discovering. They were like members of the same, exclusive club. It was fun, in fact the whole thing was fun. If it could be profitable as well, this would be a summer well spent.

Most important of all, it had brought Russ to her. Paula forced herself to continue unpacking glass and china and putting the things out on the dining room table again as she thought this. She missed him far too much. She loved him. And though she tried to tell herself—as he undoubtedly would have agreed—that it was too soon for any of that, she still wasn't listening to what she was saying to herself.

Tomorrow seemed years away. Was every hour of her life going to seem forever unless Russ was sharing it with her? How many hours of her life could she hope to have him share with her? She was aware that she intrigued him, attracted him, and they were wonderful in bed together. But love, well, love was on an entirely different plane.

She sighed, unwrapping the last of the items she'd had at the flea market, and looked with dismay at the clutter she'd made. She'd created all this mess only to learn what she'd really known in the first place. The blue Spode pitcher was missing, just as was the coin silver spoon that had vanished last Sunday.

Two such disappearances couldn't be coincidence. The Spode pitcher was about four inches high, not big but certainly not small enough to simply disappear. The spoon had been a shining silver. If she'd dropped it, certainly she would have seen it gleaming.

"Someone could have filched it, you know," Russ had said of the spoon. Well, someone also could have filched the pitcher.

She couldn't let herself think that Maybelle Stevens was the only person who'd had a real opportunity. Maybe, she conjectured, the flea market had a klepto-maniac as a regular visitor, or just a plain thief who managed to drop items into a tote bag or something equally capacious.

That was possible. The flea market was big and open, lots of people around, lots of eyes watching. Yet because of the bigness and camaraderie and the near-carnival atmosphere, it would be a relatively easy place in which someone with a little expertise might make out very well.

Too well, Paula thought gloomily. It wasn't the idea of losing money on the missing objects that bothered her, but rather the unhappy realization that from now on she'd have to be more cautious about what she did, more careful, more watchful over her wares.

She didn't like the thought of this at all.

Chapter Six

$\mathcal{R}$uss's house was a shock to Paula.

It was strikingly attractive, but it was not at all the kind of place she'd thought he'd own. High atop a wide stretch of moor, it looked down on Cape Cod Bay, the beautiful private beach beneath the outdoor deck reachable by a long flight of weathered gray steps.

The house, too, was weathered, but it was silver-toned rather than merely gray. The wood looked like driftwood caressed to a soft patina by the sea. It was a long house, long and low, everything on one level.

Russ was watching her closely as he opened the door and then ushered her into the large central room that ran from the front to the back of the house, ending on the water side with a floor-to-ceiling glass window-wall framed by oyster-colored drapes.

The colors in the room were cool—tones of white, off

white, and the oyster gray, with touches of a deeper charcoal. There was an occasional hint of yellow in a modern Chinese vase, some couch pillows, and the candles in the Scandinavian pewter holders on the teak dining room table. And there was not an antique in the place.

Viewing all of this, Paula swung to face Russ, unable to conceal her amazement, and he asked quizzically, "Well? Does it or doesn't it meet with your approval?"

"It's terrific," Paula said. "But it isn't you," she concluded, then wished she'd curtailed her usual bluntness.

"Isn't it?" he asked, a curious note to his voice.

He was carrying the tote bag into which she'd put her bathing suit and he tossed it on the low, off-white couch as he spoke. It was an enormous couch, Paula noted, long and deep with wide cushions. Like everything else in this place, it looked new and expensive.

"I'd think that your furniture would show the dirt very easily," she said, looking at the pale upholstery covering not only the couch but the wide, deep armchairs as well. "How do you keep everything so clean?"

Russ's laugh rang out, and she saw that his startling green eyes were sparkling with amusement. The lines of fatigue that had marked his face yesterday were gone, and he looked young and vibrant and very healthy.

"Things stay clean out here because I don't use them much," he confessed.

"What do you mean?" she asked curiously.

"Well, I don't use this room very much. Most of the time when I'm out here I'm either on the deck or else in the bedroom. It's sort of a combined bedroom-study." He hesitated. "You'll think I'm some kind of an eccentric," he said then, "but do you know you're just about the first person beside myself who's ever been in this house?"

She'd been searching the room with her eyes as he spoke, looking for a sign of something that was Russ.

There were no photos, family or otherwise, no pictures on the wall, no bric-a-brac except for the candlesticks and the modern Oriental vase. It was almost as if Russ had been trying to obliterate every trace of his past . . . or of his personality.

As if in answer to her pondering about this, he said, "It's only the second summer I've owned the place, Paula. It was built by an artist, but he lived here very briefly. It wasn't even completely finished when I bought it."

"But you furnished it?"

"Yes," he said. His eyes narrowed slightly. "I take it you don't approve of my taste?"

"Oh, I approve of it," she said. "It's not necessarily my taste, but I approve of it. It's . . . striking."

She'd moved to the window and was looking out as she replied. The view was spectacular. The beach was deserted, and she watched sandpipers scampering busily at the edge of the tide line. The water was a deep blue-green today, and white cloud puffs hovered lazily in the paler blue sky. The outdoors was inviting, the deck, with its comfortable lounge chairs was *very* inviting. She could understand why Russ spent most of his time on it when he was here.

She felt his hands on her shoulders, and he said, "Sweetheart, I don't think you really heard me. Except for the builders and an occasional repairman, you're the only person who's ever come here."

Still staring out at the water, Paula asked, "Why?"

"Because you're the only person I've ever wanted here," Russ told her, a huskiness creeping into his voice. "I know the place must look kind of . . . sterile, to you. But I haven't wanted to clutter it up, can you understand that? All my life I've lived in places that were cluttered with *things*. I wanted to start out with some basics and add a few things very slowly and judiciously."

"Like the blue Canton jar?" she asked him.

"Yes. I thought it would look great on the side-board," he admitted.

The sideboard he was referring to was Scandinavian in design, its lines simple and functional and, looking at it, Paula could see what he was driving at. "No curlicues," she said aloud.

He laughed. "I guess you could put it that way."

She didn't doubt that there were other ways of putting it. The thought was nagging that what Russ had really been trying to do in this house was to sweep out his past, to close the door on everything gone by and to start out with a very new broom. And Paula wasn't sure that a person could do that successfully. She wasn't even sure that it would be a good idea to do it. What had gone before was as much a part of one's life as the present and the future. She didn't believe in dwelling on the past, especially negative aspects of it, but neither did she believe it should be obliterated.

If I were to give up everything that had happened before today, a lot of me would go with it, she found herself thinking. How could it be otherwise with Russ?

She wished she could talk to him about things like this, but she had a feeling that Russ would shut her out if she tried. And this wasn't the time to get into philosophical discussions anyway. It was a beautiful afternoon, and it was only half over.

Russ had released his hold on her shoulders, but he was still standing just behind her, and Paula knew that it would take only a simple movement on her part to plunge both of them into that vortex from which desire springs. If she were just to touch Russ with her bare hands, her own passion would begin to spiral. But she didn't want that yet. Not yet.

"Doesn't anyone else use the beach?" she asked Russ, watching the sandpipers and a couple of gulls who'd landed, and were poking around a clump of seawood.

"No," he said. And added, "I own it."

This did make her turn around to face him. "You *own* the beach?" she asked incredulously.

"No one literally owns a beach, Paula," he answered rather shortly. "I own to the high-water mark."

"All of it?" she asked him, waving an expansive hand.

"No. I think I own about two hundred feet of it," he said. "The reason there's seldom anyone else on it is because you'd have to come over private roads to get to it."

They'd gone off the highway onto a fairly narrow side road to get here, Paula recalled, and then they'd branched off onto a series of hard-packed sandy lanes.

"Very exclusive," she murmured.

"What?"

"Very exclusive," she repeated. "Private. Isolated. You do have a telephone, don't you?"

"Of course I have a telephone," he told her impatiently. "What are you driving at, Paula?"

"Well, if you didn't have a phone, you could keep completely out of contact with the outside world, if you wanted to, in a place like this. *Is* that what you wanted, Russ, when you bought it?"

"My telephone has an unlisted number that I very seldom give out," he said, making no effort to mask his annoyance. "Does that answer your question?"

"I'm sorry," Paula said. "I wasn't trying to be . . . snide." She added, almost helplessly, "I guess I'm just trying to get to know you better."

The mantle of aloofness he'd donned disappeared. He smiled his wonderful smile and he said, "That puts a different complexion on things. Hey, look, we're getting much too serious. How about a swim?"

"The last one in's a turtle," Paula told him solemnly, and yet another moment of tension between them was broken.

Although Paula may have had reservations about Russ's rather austere living room, she loved his combination bedroom-study. It was furnished in aquatic tones, soft greens and blues and turquoise, and one whole wall was lined with bookshelves. There was a desk—again, in the Scandinavian style—a comfortable chair for reading, and an enormous, king-size bed. As she slipped into her burnt orange bikini, Paula tried not to concentrate on the bed. It was the most suggestive piece of furniture she'd ever seen.

Russ wore brief white bathing trunks, and she tried not to concentrate on *him* either. Otherwise, she knew she'd be wanting to lure him back to the spacious bed before they even made it down the stairs to the beach.

They ran across the sand like two teenagers on a holiday, and Russ, plunging into the water, turned back to call over his shoulder, "So. You're a turtle."

She streaked after him at this, moving as fast as she could with the weight of the water against her legs, and as she neared him she started to splash him vigorously. At first he threw up a defending hand, protesting. But then he began to splash her back and as they edged into deeper water they tumbled into each other's arms. Russ's usually perfectly combed hair was sleek as a seal's fur, and his smooth wet skin felt incredibly sexy to her touch. The salty taste of his mouth was even more so, and Paula let all the feelings she'd been trying to hold back surface, reveling in his kissing, his stroking, and the low, urgent murmurs he was funneling into her ear.

For a time they stood chest-deep in the water, exploring each other in a tantalizing new way, this entirely different medium giving them the capacity to evoke wonderfully provocative sensations. And then Russ said, "We could, you know."

"Right here?" Why did she feel she had to whisper?

He laughed. "There's no one around for more than far enough, sweetheart," he assured her.

"Broad daylight, in the water?"

"Can you think of a better place?"

She couldn't, yet she was suddenly surfeited with a deep shyness. "What'll we do with our bathing suits?" she asked him.

"I'll take them back to the beach and weigh them down with a rock," he told her.

"You can't be serious, Russ?"

"Can't I?" There was a devilish glint in his green eyes. "Want to try me, Paula?"

"All right. I dare you."

Before she knew what was happening he was slipping off the top of her bikini and then rocking her off balance so that she splashed backward and he quickly divested her of the bikini bottom. She was still sputtering to her feet as he started back for the beach, then she let herself sink into the water again, floating, with her hair trailing around her, and a transcendental sense of timelessness and beauty swept over her.

"You might float all the way to Boston," Russ warned huskily, and she looked up to see that he was near her, very near her, reaching out for her.

The touch of his hands on her wet skin was unbearably erotic. Her nipples, hardened first by the cool water, became focal points of ecstasy as he caressed them with his fingers, and then bent to take possession of first one, then the other, with his wet, salt-tanged mouth.

Then he was urging her backward, clasping an arm with hers, and he said softly, "Backstroke toward shore. You know how to backstroke?"

There was no need to answer. They were already doing it. Backstroking in unison, their naked bodies cutting through the water, Paula marveled that she could be so cool on the outside and as hot as a volcano in eruption on the inside.

When they were in the shallows Russ let go of her, and he meticulously began to cover every inch of her body with his caresses. After a time she laughed and said shakily, "You'd make a great marine biologist!"

"Quiet, woman," he commanded with that telltale huskiness in his voice again. "I'm immersed in a research project."

"Immersed—" she started to say. But he cut her off, bringing his mouth to hers, his tongue probing to stir her senses to the breaking point while his hands continued their invasion. Then the soft salt water splashed around them as they went past the talking point to enter a world in which there were only two people, destined to become as united as two people ever could be.

In that watery world they took possession of each other, clinging to each other and glorying in a consummation that matched the scope of the sky and the depths of the clouds. And it was only when they both were coming back to earth and nearly touching the ground that Paula said shakily, "We were so carried away, I suppose we could both have drowned."

Russ looked deep into her eyes and laughed softly. "I can't think of a better way to die," he told her.

Russ made frosty margaritas, and they drank them out on the deck, stretched out in the thickly padded lounge chairs, utterly content—for this moment at least.

After a time he asked Paula if she was hungry and she found that she was very hungry. He made a second round of margaritas and brought her crackers and cheese to munch on, and rejected her offer to help with dinner. Paula, seldom too lenient with herself, let herself luxuriate as she watched him take the lid off the round black barbecue and get the charcoal going, and by the time the sun had begun its descent to the horizon Russ was grilling steaks and foil-wrapped potatoes, and he'd put together a spinach salad with a fantastic dressing that he told her was of his own invention.

They ate on the terrace, occupying benches on either side of a picnic-type table. By then the sun had turned the water to a deep molten gold, and the sky was vibrant with the full range of afterglow colors.

Russ had opened a bottle of red wine to go with their steaks, and although Paula was not a wine connoisseur, even she knew, by its taste, that this was something of a very special vintage.

"To you," he said, lifting his glass, and she responded with the same toast. To him.

But then she asked, "Not *salud?*"

"Always *salud,*" he said rather solemnly. "That goes without saying." He took a sip of the wine before asking, "Are you warm enough?" With the sun gone, a coolness had crept into the summer night.

Paula was wearing jeans and a fleecy white sweater, and she nodded. "Just right," she said. "This food is just right, too. The steak's superlative. You really are a gourmet chef."

"Not exactly. Though I do have a couple of other *specialités de la maison* I'll have to try for you. Do you like to cook, Paula?"

"Not especially," she said frankly. "I think I would if I had someone to cook for. It's not much fun fixing food for yourself. I usually settle for the nearest can. Do you bother cooking for yourself when you're alone, Russ?"

"No," he said. "That is," he added rather vaguely, "I guess I tend to settle for the nearest can, too."

Again, Paula had the sense that he was holding something back. So often, she had this feeling about Russ and it was becoming increasingly disturbing. On one level—the physical level, admittedly—he never held back anything from her. He gave of himself, even as she'd given of herself, without any reservations. But when they reached the personal plane, Russ's reluctance to disclose very much at all about himself inevitably edged to the forefront.

Why? What did he have to hide?

Paula hated to probe. But she was coming to realize that unless she questioned Russ he was never going to

reveal anything about himself much before the past
Sunday.

She chose a logical starting point. "How did you find
your friend yesterday? And his wife?"

"Carleton?" Russ seemed to have drifted miles away
from her. He'd finished his steak, and he was holding
his wineglass, staring into its rich red depths. There
were two squatty candles in hurricane holders on the
table and, in their flickering light, the wine was a true
ruby.

"Carleton's doing even better than we'd hoped," he
said. "Helen started to relax once they told her he was
out of immediate danger, and she's been able to get
some rest. Her niece is with her, and—" he flashed
Paula a wry grin "—Helen's one of the few people who
does have my phone number, so she can reach me if she
needs to."

"These people were friends of your uncle's?"

He nodded. "Yes. And of mine, too. I've known
them most of my life as a matter of fact, and there was a
time when they were very good to me."

Was he going to tell her about that time? Paula
waited, but Russ did not pursue it.

"I'm having lunch with Helen tomorrow," he said,
"and I plan to drive her over to the hospital later to see
Carleton. We'll take it from there. It's a step-at-a-time
situation. Things like that often are."

He spoke reflectively, and again Paula sensed that
there were things he wasn't telling her. About Carleton
and his wife? Or about himself? She wished she knew.

"How about a smidgeon more salad?" Russ asked,
breaking into her train of thought.

"I couldn't," she protested. "Not another morsel."

"Okay," Russ said obligingly. "I'll manage to polish
the rest of it off myself."

"I'd say you have a very healthy appetite," Paula
observed, watching him deal with the salad and the last
of the potatoes.

"I . . ." He started to say something and then stopped abruptly, and Paula stared at him, perplexed.

"What is it, Russ?" she asked gently.

He evaded the question. "Nothing, really." He reached for the wine bottle and refilled both their glasses before she could stop him.

She tried to be light about this. "Aren't you afraid I'll have a hangover if I drink any more?" she teased.

"No. You've had a good, hearty meal," he informed her. "I'll bet the other night you drank all that wine on an empty stomach."

"I'd had a hamburger and a frappe for lunch."

"And nothing after?"

"No," she admitted.

"You need a few lessons in nutrition," he told her.

"With you as the teacher?"

"I do know something about the subject, yes." He switched the topic. "You haven't told me how you finished up at the flea market yesterday," he said. "I can't imagine how you've managed to wait this long."

"We had a few other things on our minds," she answered serenely, and he burst out laughing.

"As to how I made out," she said, "well, I did quite well. But I lost something again, Russ."

He frowned. "What are you talking about?"

"A little blue Spode pitcher I had is missing."

"Are you sure about that, Paula?"

"Absolutely. I checked and rechecked."

He considered this. "This should be reported to the management," he decided then.

"I wouldn't want to do that," she said quickly.

"Why not?"

"Two small items? I don't think it adds up to enough," she said.

"One item Sunday, one item yesterday. It spells a kind of pattern to me," Russ said. "Maybe some of the other dealers are having the same experience. Like you, maybe they've also held back from reporting small thefts. I think it might be a good idea for the management to canvass the dealers and find out if they've been missing things."

"I think you're pushing the panic button prematurely, Russ," Paula told him.

"Oh?"

"Yes. I could have dropped the spoon, and someone could have picked it up."

"You could hardly have dropped the Spode pitcher," he pointed out.

"No, that's true." Paula was remembering Maybelle Stevens fondling the little pitcher. Maybelle had seemed to genuinely like it. But Maybelle *couldn't* have taken it. Big, jovial, friendly Maybelle.

"Why would you object to alerting the management about this?" Russ asked abruptly.

"I don't know." Paula hedged. She was still thinking about Maybelle. "Look," she said, "I'm no more for encouraging thievery than you are, Russ. But let's just leave this alone for the time being, all right? If I find myself missing anything else, I'll be the first one to alert the management. I promise you that."

"Good enough," Russ said. He stood, stretching, and as she looked at him Paula forgot all about the flea market, and petty thievery in general. Silhouetted against the night he made an arresting figure, a figure she knew every inch of, she told herself, and the thought of this knowledge was more potent than the wine she'd drunk.

"How about going for a walk on the beach?" he asked her.

"Barefoot?"

He grinned. "Naturally."

They walked near the tide line, and the sand was firm and damp beneath her feet. The tide was ebbing, the water lapping gently. There was a sickle moon tonight, and Paula said lightly, "Look over your left shoulder and make a wish."

"Why?" Russ asked her.

"Because you just do, that's all, when you see a new moon," Paula told him. "Didn't you ever do that when you were a child?"

Her father had taught her to look over her left shoulder and wish on the moon, she remembered now. That had been on a long-ago night when they'd been visiting Gram, here on the Cape in summer. She and her parents had gone to walk on another Cape Cod beach, she having been given the special privilege of staying up later than usual.

Russ, she realized, hadn't answered her question. She stopped, peering up at him in the darkness. A new moon didn't do much to light one's way.

"Didn't you ever wish on the moon when you were a child?" she persisted.

"No," he said shortly.

"Didn't you have anything to wish for?" she asked, half serious, half teasing.

"I don't know, Paula." She sensed the reluctance in his words. Then he added slowly, "Sometimes I think I had everything to wish for."

"What kind of a childhood did you have, Russ?"

"I think I already told you that. My parents died, my uncle brought me up."

"Boarding schools and summer camps?"

"Didn't I tell you that, too? Anyway, yes, pretty much so."

"Then what happened, Russ?"

She could feel his stillness. "What do you mean?" he asked, but there'd been a pause first. A very significant pause. She knew that he was prepared to hedge.

She said simply, "Something happened, didn't it, Russ? Something that made you retreat inside yourself so that you still don't want to talk about anything in your past. But I don't think it was a woman."

"No," he said, "No, it wasn't a woman."

There was a certain finality to his tone, Paula felt, as

if he'd built a wall between them. She turned, walking away from it, away from him, but in a second he caught up to her.

He caught her arm, and he commanded, "Don't run away from me. You're right. Something did happen to me. I don't know what you imagine it might have been, but I doubt very much that you'd come up with the right answer, whatever you may be thinking." He drew a breath that was long and ragged, and he said, "When I was in my late teens I was sick . . . for quite a long time. That's all."

"All?" She peered up at him, wishing desperately that she could see his face more clearly. "What do you mean, you were 'sick'?" she asked him.

"I had tuberculosis, Paula," he said flatly. "I contracted it in France, when I was visiting my uncle there. I got it from a girl."

"I see."

"I don't think you do. She was sixteen. She was working as a maid in my uncle's Paris apartment. She was very pretty, we were both very young. It was . . . one of those things," Russ said, his tonelessness unnerving Paula. "If I'd kissed her once, it's doubtful I would ever have contracted TB from her. But we snitched every minute we could, the way any two kids bent on the same thing would do. It wasn't a romance, that's not what I'm saying to you," he added bluntly. "Just sex. Juvenile sex. She had a bad cough but I didn't think too much about it. She smoked a lot. Anyway . . ."

There was a hopelessness to the *anyway* and Paula said gently, "You don't have to go on about this unless you want to, Russ."

"I want to," he said, "and it's easier telling you, walking along here, than it would be sitting in the living room over a liqueur." He paused. "The time came when I was so damned tired all the time," he continued then. "And I seemed to be either burning up or so cold I was having chills. I didn't sleep well, everything irritated me, and then . . . well, then I developed a cough and—"

He broke off. "There's no point in going into all the clinical details, Paula. The diagnosis was made, and that's where Carleton Edgeworth and his wife come in. They were in Paris. Carleton was in the diplomatic service. They saw to it that the best possible doctors were called in, and they checked out the sanatorium in Switzerland to which I was sent."

"You were sent to a sanatorium?" This thought appalled her.

"Yes. I spent over two years in that sanatorium."

"I can't believe this, Russ," she said. The thought of his having been a patient in a sanatorium for two years hurt her.

"Look, Paula, I'm fine today," he said. "I swear that to you. If there'd been any danger to you I—I wouldn't have touched you," he told her. "Certainly," he added wryly, "I'd never have kissed you."

"No," she protested. "That's not what I meant at all. I was thinking about you, not about myself. I wish I'd known you then. I—"

"I'm very glad you didn't know me then," he interrupted. "Most of the time the order of my days and my nights was bed rest. For a while they contemplated surgery, but streptomycin was doing the kind of job it was supposed to do, in my case, and so that, at least, was avoided. Later, I was close to twenty by that time, I came back to the States. My uncle brought me to a house he owned in Chatham and I lived there for longer than I like to think about. That's when I became interested in antiques. I had to have something to do to keep myself from going crazy, and my activities were, of necessity, very limited. So I started studying up old things we had around the house and one thing led to another."

He had bridged so much. She could only imagine the gaps. She suggested softly, "It must have been quite a battle."

"Yes," he agreed quietly, "it was quite a battle. But I was lucky enough to win it a long time ago and . . . you're right. I don't like to talk about it."

He added, "It isn't that I intended keeping this from you, Paula. I planned to tell you, though not yet, I'll admit that."

They'd come to the foot of the steps that led up to the house. Paula posed the question she had to ask.

"What happened to the French girl?"

"She died," Russ said briefly. "Her case was too advanced by the time she got medical attention—after I'd been diagnosed. It's rare for someone to die of TB these days," he added. "A great deal of progress has been made in treating the disease, though it's still a lot more prevalent than many people think. Nevertheless, it's not quite the dreaded scourge it once was, thank God."

Paula started up the steps with Russ just behind her, and her legs felt very heavy, each foot seeming to weigh a ton. She was bogged down, mentally and emotionally, by what he'd just told her, principally because she felt so helpless about it. "I was sick," he'd said. Yes, he'd surely been sick. Very sick. She shuddered to think about it. No wonder he'd been so reticent in his answer when she'd asked him the other day if he, too, had been "mixed up" when in his teens.

As she started across the deck, she dreaded going into the house with him, facing him in the bright light. What could she say to him?

He gave her the answer to that question by posing a question of his own. Switching on a lamp, he turned to face her in its light, his eyes so deep a green they looked almost black. "Is this going to make a difference, Paula?" He asked the question almost casually, but this offhand manner of his no longer deceived her.

"No," she said, so quickly, so directly, that there could not possibly have been any subterfuge in her answer.

His voice shook very slightly as he asked, "Can I really believe that?"

For an answer she went to him and threw her arms around him, raising herself on tiptoes to bring her mouth level with his. Then she kissed him, kissed him with her heart as well as with her lips, and she could only hope her answer would convince him.

Chapter Seven

$\mathscr{B}$y the time Paula reached the flea market on Saturday, Russ had set up his tables and was already unpacking his things and putting them out.

"Well," she said, sauntering over to him once she'd parked her car, "you *are* an early bird."

"I didn't sleep too well," he confessed. "I thought I might as well get up and do something."

"Anything wrong?" she asked. "Your friend didn't have a relapse, did he?"

He shook his head. "No. Carleton's doing very well, and so is Helen, I'm glad to say. I just had a lot of things on my mind, that's all."

They'd not seen each other the day before, and Paula had missed him terribly. Thursday night he'd driven her back to her house, to kiss her good-bye at her front door. It had been an ardent enough kiss, but there'd been a terrific letdown in watching him drive away again. And yesterday had been so empty. She'd filled the hours with activity. Shopping, housecleaning, getting down a couple of boxes from the attic and assessing the contents. She had a better eye now for the kind of prices to put on things, thanks to Russ's tutelage.

"Need help putting up your tables?" he asked her.

"I think I can manage, thanks," she told him. "You evidently unloosened them that first time."

Nevertheless, he followed her across to her space and set up the tables anyway. This time she'd pressed the blue cloths she used to cover them and Russ's mouth twitched with amusement.

"Getting awfully neat about this, aren't you?" he queried.

"With such a pristine example in the next space I couldn't afford to be messy," Paula retorted.

"Pristine?" He considered this. "I'm not sure I like that adjective applied to myself," he said.

"Would you prefer fastidious?"

"Definitely not."

Saying, "Well, now, let's see . . ." as if to consider a proper adjective that would suit him, Paula took the opportunity to survey him. He was as well-dressed as ever, in brown slacks and a light apricot shirt, but he did look tired, and this worried her. She'd done a lot of thinking about what he'd told her Thursday night. She was still appalled by what he'd gone through, and she wondered if there were restrictions as to what Russ should and should not do.

"Maybe," she suggested carefully, "you should have stayed home and rested today."

His eyes seemed to darken. "What's that suppose to imply?" he asked her.

"You look tired, that's all."

"I told you I didn't sleep well, Paula," he reminded her patiently.

"I know, I know. I just wondered if you're supposed to . . . do so much."

Paula knew that this had been the wrong thing to say

the minute the words were out of her mouth. Russ's lips thinned to a narrow line, then he said tightly, "This is why I didn't want to tell you about myself, why I try to avoid telling anyone. I'm not an invalid, damn it, and I won't have you putting me in that category. That's what you're doing, isn't it?"

He'd lowered his voice, but even so Paula glanced around, not wanting the other dealers to hear what was going on between Russ and herself.

She said, keeping her voice low, too, "Obviously, you're not an invalid, Russ. I was just concerned about you, that's all."

"There's no need for you to be concerned about me, Paula," he told her abruptly.

"Isn't there? I thought it was common practice to be concerned about someone when you care about them."

Time stood still. Then Russ said very gently, "Okay. I apologize. But if you keep looking at me like that, I'm going to have to take you in my arms and kiss you until you gasp for breath. Do you understand that?" he finished with mock severity.

Her laugh was shaky. "Yes."

"Now, suppose you let me lug the cartons out of your car for you. Okay?"

"Okay," she said meekly.

"Got any new things?" he asked as she started to unpack the first of her cartons.

Paula nodded. "It was either Maybelle or one of the other dealers who told me old kitchen woodenware goes well," she said. "There was a whole box of it in the attic Gram evidently had stored away when she bought more modern things, and so I priced it and brought it along."

"And the prices are right?" he teased her.

"I think so. I used a combination of the reference guides and Russ Grayson to establish the prices."

He picked up a large wooden chopping bowl as she said this, looking it over carefully. Then he warned, "You're not following Russ Grayson's price policy on this, Paula. Take a look at it. The bowl's pierced for hanging, about fifteen inches wide, I'd say. It's an old one, and you've got only five dollars on it. You should be able to get twenty without any problem at all."

She made a face. "I just can't please you," she complained.

He laughed, but he said, "I don't want you to cheat yourself. As I told you the other day, there's a happy medium."

"All right," she conceded, picking up the wooden bowl, prepared to change the price on it. "I guess I shouldn't price anything from here on in without you at my elbow."

"An excellent idea," Russ approved. "Of course I don't know how long I'll be content to remain at your elbow," he teased. "Being near you tends to go to my head, and I can't always be responsible for my actions. Nevertheless . . ."

"I think you'd better get back to business," Paula told him, and he grinned as he moved over to his own space.

It was a cloudy day, slightly on the cool side. Tim Bailey stopped by shortly before the flea market opened to the public to say to Paula and Russ, "If the sun stays in we should do very well. It certainly won't be a beach day." He peered skyward. "I hope it doesn't rain," he added. "I think I've got the world's speed record for spreading plastic sheets over my books at the first drop, but it's still a nuisance.

"Come and see us," he invited them as he moved away. He called back over his shoulder to Paula, "Cora—my wife—wants to meet you."

"Now, why would she want to meet me?" Paula mused.

"Because I was telling her about you yesterday," Russ said. "Incidentally, if you have some old books you want to part with, I'd suggest you offer them first to Tim and Cora. They're experienced; they used to have a bookstore in Boston. This is supposed to be a retirement project, but Tim admits he's gotten so hooked on the flea-market scene, he and Cora are going to travel the Southern route this winter and take in markets all the way from Florida to Texas."

"That sounds like fun," Paula said wistfully. She could imagine Russ and herself packing up his van with their mutual antiques, then following the sun, making love all along the way. When Russ didn't respond, she said, "I do have books I plan to get rid of, and I'll show them to Tim Bailey first."

"Talk to him about it," Russ suggested. "Maybe he and Cora could stop by your house and look over what you have. Then you wouldn't have to lug a lot of stuff out here."

She nodded, the thought of following the sun with Russ still taunting her.

Many of the dealers made the rounds of the market before it opened to the public, often buying a variety of things themselves that they hoped to sell at somewhat higher prices. This was what happened to Paula's kitchenware that morning. The dealers, pausing to chat, started to buy it up, and before long she realized Russ had been right again. This time she'd priced everything too low, having changed the label only on the wooden bowl.

Midmorning, Russ spelled her while she went to the rest room. Maybelle Stevens was there, vigorously brushing her long brown hair, and she gave Paula an enthusiastic greeting.

"How's it going?" she asked.

"Fairly well," Paula said. "There've been a lot of browsers but not many buyers."

"That's the way it is, sometimes, on a day like this," Maybelle said sagely. "Cloudy weather, people can't go to the beach, so they don't know what to do with themselves. They're kind of at odds and ends, so they don't know what they want either. It'll be better in the afternoon," she promised. "A lot of people don't pay much attention to breakfast these days, they don't even know they're hungry. Once they get some food in their stomachs they kind of settle down, know what I mean? Then they can make up their minds better."

Paula liked Maybelle's homespun philosophy, though she doubted that Maybelle and Cholly themselves had ever skipped a breakfast—or any other meal—in their entire lives.

"Still got that blue Spode pitcher?" Maybelle asked suddenly.

Paula stiffened. She said very carefully, "No, matter of fact, I don't."

"Damn," Maybelle retorted. Then, shrugging her shoulders, she added, "Well, it's nobody's fault but my own. I should have bought it when I saw it instead of being so cheap about it. That's what Cholly always says, 'If you want something, get it.'" She paused. "Got anything else like that?" she asked Paula. "I'm thinking of starting a collection of little pitchers."

"I may have," Paula said cautiously. "I still have things to go through."

"I'll keep in touch," Maybelle promised. At the door she turned to say, "If you got any old jewelry, you'll do good with it. Antique jewelry's big today. Don't mark it too low."

With this final bit of advice Maybelle departed, and Paula was thoughtful as she walked back to her space a few minutes later.

Russ saw Paula making her way through the crowded lane, and his pulse quickened. Every time he saw her it was like a fresh experience. And each experience had a new impact on him.

He'd noticed the way her kitchen woodenware had sold to the other dealers, and he lamented it. From now on he *was* going to try to help her price everything. Otherwise, she'd be apt to lose too much of the money she so badly needed.

It was unfortunate that he couldn't filter a whole bunch of crisp green bills down her chimney, Russ thought ruefully. Too bad that he couldn't play Santa Claus in July. It wasn't that he had more money than he knew what to do with—he tried to share his wealth in every practical way possible—but he did have more money than he could ever possibly need, or ever possibly use, and nothing would have brought him more pleasure than to share it with Paula. What was the use of being rich, he asked himself, if you couldn't share what you had with someone you loved?

Paula, though, would never forgive him if he tried to bail her out of her present predicament. He knew that, and he respected her feelings. It would be far better to let her make what she needed herself. He only wished that she'd let him buy a few of her more expensive pieces from her, like the Burmese cracker jar. He would gladly give her six hundred dollars for it, confident that he could get more than that in his New York galleries. But he knew she'd no more sell it to him than she would the Canton ginger jar which he'd honestly wanted for himself. He liked it, it was a good piece, but he'd wanted it primarily because it belonged to Paula. He wanted something of hers near him, whatever it might be.

There was still a very major hurdle to be surmounted with Paula, and with each day that passed, Russ was more aware of the difficulties it involved. At some point he was going to have to tell her his full name, and he didn't know how she was going to react when she heard it. He was virtually certain that—unlike most of the women he'd met—her reaction was going to be far more negative than positive. She was so fiercely independent, and this, of course, was one of the things he admired most about her. And from everything she'd said, he doubted if she'd have much respect for someone who'd been given everything—in the monetary sense of the word—on a solid gold platter.

He wasn't sure that he and Paula were even over their first hurdle, for that matter. He'd faced up to telling her about his illness, but her shock had been apparent to him. Then, this morning, she'd done the one thing he'd feared the most. She'd acted as if he were still an invalid, and should be treated as such.

He'd hoped he could convince her otherwise, but he couldn't be sure. And he couldn't even think about going on to the second hurdle until he was confident they'd cleared the first one completely.

As she came up to him, beautiful in his eyes in her jeans and her old faded rose-colored T-shirt, she asked, "How's it going?"

"Not too bad," Russ said. "I've sold a couple of items, and your milk glass decanter and that little pewter creamer went."

"Good," Paula approved. "Do you want to take a break while I man your store? If you'll trust me to do so, that is."

"I'll stroll around for a while," he agreed. Was he imagining it, he asked himself, or was that anxious look back in her amber eyes again, expressing a doubt about his strength, or rather the lack of it?

"You're sure you don't mind handling both spaces?" he asked her, needing this time to just walk up and down and try to get his thoughts together.

"You didn't, did you?" she retorted promptly.

Russ laughed. "I can never win with you," he protested.

"Never?" Paula's lovely mouth curved in a smile. "I think that you've won, on several occasions," she said meaningfully, and even this oblique reference to those moments of ultimate togetherness they'd shared started a surge of need and wanting within Russ.

"Witch," he accused, shaking his head at her. Then he added, "I won't be too long."

Paula watched him go, her heart churning with love for him. He did look better; being out in the fresh air had erased some of the tiredness from his face. But now that she knew the truth about him, it was almost impossible not to worry about him. She wished she could be sure that he didn't tend to overdo, that it was all right—safe for him—to lead the kind of life he was leading.

She found herself wanting to console him, take care of him, protect him, and all at once—knowing that this was exactly what Russ would detest, what he didn't want her to do—she said aloud, "Stop!" with such fervor that a woman who was looking at a little Daisy and Button glass hat glanced up in astonishment.

"I beg your pardon," she said haughtily, putting the hat back on the table.

"I'm sorry," Paula said. "That is, I wasn't talking to you. If you'd like the hat, I think I could do a bit better on the price."

Mollified, the woman decided that she did like the hat. Then she pondered that she wasn't sure whether she should buy it or not. Her husband was always complaining that she was bringing home things she didn't need. Then she decided she had to have it, the color would match the decor in her bedroom perfectly. She parted with eight dollars—Paula had originally had ten on it—and they both were happy.

Russ came back, and there was a brief surge of activity not long after that. In a lull that followed, Paula asked, "Is it customary to give dealers a lower price on things?"

"Dealers usually do get a discount." he told her. "But in your case, I'd say that doesn't apply to you. You're not a dealer per se, you're just here to get rid of some of your household effects. I don't think you have any obligation to anyone. Why? Has someone been asking you to cut-rate for them?"

"Hilda Benson's interested in my porcelain pancake server," Paula admitted. "It's Austrian, and the book values it at forty-five dollars. I've got thirty-five on it, and she offered me twenty. Do you think I should have let her have it?"

"No," Russ said. "Offer to strike a bargain at thirty. If she doesn't accept that, forget it."

Paula was about to tell him that the same thing had happened with Maybelle Stevens, and the blue Spode pitcher. But she didn't want to reopen the matter of the missing items, so she kept silent on that. Instead, she said, "Why don't you let me cook dinner for you tonight, Russ?"

They were both in their own spaces as she issued the invitation, but standing close enough to each other's "boundaries" so that they could easily converse.

He grinned. "I thought you said you couldn't cook," he reminded her.

"I told you I'm an expert at opening cans."

"Well, I'd take you up on that except that I think I should go over to the hospital and check on Carleton after I get out of here," he told her. "Look, why don't you come along with me?"

"To see your friend?" She shied back from the idea of this.

He shook his head. "No. Carleton's still in the coronary care unit, so his visitor list is limited at the moment. I was going to suggest that you drive over with me and wait while I run in. I'll be only a few minutes. Then we could have dinner somewhere in the Hyannis area."

"That would be nice," Paula said. "I'd have to go home first and change, though."

"And leave your antiques behind you? I have to do the same thing. I'd rather take the Porsche than the van, anyway. Let's say that I meet you at your house around six. Would that give you time enough?"

She nodded. "Will I need to dress up?" she asked him, wondering what she could possibly find to wear if he said yes. Her summer wardrobe was down to the basics.

"No," he said. "Just about every place is casual on the Cape this time of year."

What was "casual" to Russ Grayson when it came to a matter of dress, and probably a lot of other things as well? Paula wasn't sure she wanted to know. She wasn't sure she could live up to his standards. She liked good clothes, it would have been interesting—and quite an experience for her, she conceded—to have a big, new, expensive wardrobe. But she was used to making do, to being content with what she had, and there were other things in life far more important to her than material things. People. Friends. Caring. Loving.

She looked at Russ and trembled inwardly at the thought of how much she'd come to love him in such a short time.

There was a misty rain falling as Russ and Paula started out to Hyannis that night. She'd dug her old raincoat out of a closet as a result, and old it was. And threadbare at the elbows, and missing a couple of buttons that she'd probably lost on the way to school last spring.

Russ, on the other hand, was wearing a classic London Fog that looked as crisp as if he'd stopped to buy it on his way to meet her.

Under the raincoat Paula was wearing a pleated white skirt and a turquoise blouse that was pretty, but not in the league with the dress she'd worn to dinner with him the previous Sunday. However, she had very little that was in that category, and had decided to save "the rest of her best" for future occasions, since he'd said that tonight was to be casual.

She felt a bit shabby sitting next to Russ in his sleek car, and so she was quieter than she was ordinarily. After a time he glanced across at her to say, "You have something on your mind. What is it?"

"Nothing, really," she answered.

"Are you borrowing my line, Paula?" he queried suspiciously. "Come out with it!"

"I wish I'd dressed up a bit more, that's all," she said honestly. "Also, that I'd taken the time to buy myself a new raincoat before I came down to the Cape."

"Come off it," he said amiably. "You look great."

The crazy thing about it was that he sounded so

absolutely sincere. Paula peered at him doubtfully, but his attention was back on the road again and she knew it would be belaboring the matter to go into it further.

"I've been meaning to ask you," he said. "Did you check your inventory when you got back?"

She nodded reluctantly. "Yes."

"You're not missing something else, are you?" he asked quickly.

She was. She hadn't wanted to tell him about it, afraid that it would spoil their evening together, but the fact was that when she'd gone through her things upon getting home—something she was making a practice of doing now in view of the missing spoon and pitcher—she'd discovered yet another loss.

"What was it?" Russ asked without waiting for her affirmative answer.

"A small amberina goblet," she said reluctantly.

"How small?"

"Oh, I'd guess it was about four inches high, maybe a little less. It was ribbed," she added unhappily.

"Hell!" Russ exploded. "Can you describe the colors?"

She nodded slowly. "Yes. The glass shaded from amber to fuchsia."

"I don't remember pricing that with you."

"You didn't," she said. "It was one of the things I priced myself at the same time I was pricing the kitchen woodenware."

"What did you put on it?"

"Well, it was listed in the book at ninety-five dollars," Paula said. "I put seventy-five on it."

"In New York it might have brought close to a hundred, if it was in top condition," Russ informed her.

"It was."

"Damn it, Paula, now can you see that you've got to report what's going on to the management?" he asked her.

"I suppose so," she agreed dully.

"What are you so hesitant about?"

"I just dislike the thought of pointing my finger at people, that's all. It seems to me unlikely that an outside thief—even an outside kleptomaniac—would visit the same person three times in succession, especially when I've been in a different location each time," she pointed out.

"You're saying that someone's aiming at you, specifically?"

"I guess that's what I'm afraid of," she admitted.

"Why 'afraid,' Paula?" he asked her.

"Because it seems to me it must be one of the dealers and I hate the thought of that," she confessed. "They've all been so friendly, generous, always willing to share a drink of something or half a sandwich or some fruit. I've liked all of them. It's not a pleasant idea to think one of them could be stealing from me. But I am inexperienced; I know that. I suppose I'd be an easy mark."

"This could have happened while I was manning your table, you know," he reminded her. "Or while Maybelle Stevens was, on Wednesday."

"I'll bet it didn't," she told him. "I'll bet it was when I was there myself. But I agree with you, it doesn't seem possible that three things could simply disappear in such quick succession. So it does seem likely that someone stole them."

"I'd say it's as obvious as anything could be," Russ pronounced firmly. "Look, I plan to get over there early in the morning, anyway. I'll speak to the manager on your behalf, if you like."

She shook her head. "Thank you, Russ, but I can do my own talking."

The lights from the dashboard plainly revealed his scowl. "Miss Independence," he said in a tone that was anything but pleased. "Good God, Paula, can't you ever let anyone help you?"

"It's not that," she said. "It's just that I'm perfectly capable of going to the manager myself and explaining what's happened. What can be done about it is something else again. I have no idea what can be done about it."

"Well, maybe the manager will have some ideas," he said.

They fell silent, a silence with a slight constraint to it, and Paula knew there were two reasons for the constraint. Russ was resenting the fact that she didn't want him to speak for her, to take on her burden, and also she didn't think that he understood her reluctance to take up the matter with the management in the first place.

She supposed that it all stemmed back to Maybelle. If Maybelle hadn't been interested in the blue Spode pitcher, it would be different. She had been, though, and this gave Paula a funny feeling. On the other hand, would Maybelle have come back to filch something she'd expressed an interest in? Maybe if she was a kleptomaniac she would have. Kleptomania was not that uncommon. Paula just wished that she could recognize the symptoms before anything else happened. Whoever had been stealing her things was skillful at it. They'd taken the objects right under her nose, which was disconcerting at the very least. She'd been on her guard today, after the first two incidents. Nevertheless, the valuable little amberina tumbler was missing. So much for her detective ability, Paula thought wryly.

At the hospital Russ found a place in the parking lot, then, promising he'd be back as quickly as possible, made for the entrance hastily, since the rain was coming down heavier.

Paula watched his long, rapid strides cover the ground to the lighted building, and she sighed deeply. As far as she was concerned, the flea-market thefts were just one more thorn in her side, a thorn that pricked especially because she and Russ were really not in accord on this.

She would go to the management in the morning, though. It would be idiotic not to report the thefts, especially now that she'd missed something three times in a row.

Russ was longer than he'd expected to be. Carleton Edgeworth was so much improved that he was permitted to chat for a few minutes, and he was pathetically eager to do so. After that Helen Edgeworth stopped Russ as he was on his way to the elevator, having been waiting in an upstairs lounge until she could see her husband again, since he was permitted to have only one visitor at a time.

"Could you spare a minute?" Helen asked him.

He thought of Paula, waiting out in the car, but he couldn't refuse Helen such a simple request. She was a tall woman, slim, with lovely white hair and beautiful aristocratic features. She was old enough to be Russ's mother, and he'd often wished that she *were* his mother.

He found himself wishing now that she could know Paula. Like Paula, Helen was a direct person, forthright, there was no pretense about her. But just now Helen was completely involved with Carleton. It wasn't a moment to even think about bringing anyone else into her life.

Russ moved with her into the lounge, and they sat side by side on a big, soft sofa. Helen, folding her hands in her lap, said, "At some point in the future this is probably going to involve a coronary bypass, Russell."

"I understand that coronary bypasses are among the most effective and successful surgical procedures performed today, Helen," Russ told her gently.

"Yes, that's what Carleton's doctors have told me," Helen agreed. "Fortunately, there's no rush about it. He'll have time to rest up at home first. Maybe in the fall . . ."

She looked up at him, smiling slightly. "Any chance you'll be around?" she asked him. "It will be done in Boston."

"Wherever it's done, whenever it's done, I'll be around," Russ told her with an answering smile. "You can be sure of that."

She squeezed his hand, then she said unexpectedly, "There's something different about you, Russell."

He was startled. "In what way?" he hedged.

"If you were older, I'd say it's a spark in your eyes and a spring in your step," she told him. "But you're not that old, so I'll call it . . . a special sort of vitality. Have you met someone special, my dear?"

"Someone very special," he said a bit unsteadily. "I think you're going to like her, Helen."

"When am I to meet her?" Helen demanded eagerly, and he laughed. Women were astonishing! With all her problems, Helen was still an incurable romantic. He knew that for years she'd hoped he'd "meet someone," as she always had put it. Now there was a shining light in her eyes at the thought that this had happened.

"Once Carleton is out of here and at home convalescing I want you both to meet her," Russ said, and Helen glowed.

It was only when he was going down in the hospital elevator, then crossing the wide lobby, that it came to Russ that there was no way he could introduce Helen and Carleton Edgeworth to Paula. There was no way she could possibly meet them until she'd first learned who Russell Grayson really was and—hopefully—had come to terms with his other identity.

Chapter Eight

$\mathcal{P}$aula hesitated before taking a box full of Gram's jewelry to the flea market Sunday morning. Russ and Maybelle had both told her that antique jewelry sold well, and the pieces she'd chosen were things she was sure she'd never wear herself. Yet, jewelry would be especially easy to steal, she thought uncomfortably, wishing that she didn't have to consider that.

She made a separate listing for the pendants, earrings, pins, and rings she was taking, and arranged the pieces in one large compartmentalized box. She'd keep it toward the back of one of her tables, she decided, so it would be especially easy to keep an eye on it.

She was still feeling uncomfortable about last night, and the final episode between Russ and herself, as she drove over to the flea market. It wasn't that she'd minded waiting for him outside the hospital, though he'd been longer than he'd thought he'd be. Rather, she'd grown annoyed with him because he'd been so completely preoccupied when he returned to her that she'd felt as if she was out with a stranger.

Now she reminded herself that Russ had been in her life exactly one week. It seemed impossible that this could be so, but the fact was that she could still count the days they'd known each other without even using all her fingers.

Paula knew that if anyone had told her it was possible to fall in love with someone so totally and so completely within the space of a week, she would never have believed them. Nor could she ever have accepted the suggestion that she, of all people—having been burned as she had by Howie—could possibly give herself to someone within a couple of days of their meeting. This was so totally and completely out of character for her. But it had happened.

She loved Russ. She'd given herself to him. The love had already become a part of her, and she didn't regret the giving. She never could. But last night he'd distanced himself, and it had hurt very much.

He'd taken her to an Italian restaurant in Hyannis. It had a lot of atmosphere and very good food, and under ordinary circumstances she would have enjoyed herself thoroughly—especially with Russ as her escort. As it was, he had been polite, almost too polite. After a time his meticulous courtesy had become unnerving. As a result, she'd become somewhat waspish. By the time they'd started home, she'd begun to wonder if something had happened to Russ while he was in the hospital to make him change so.

At her door he'd looked down and asked, "Truce?"

"I don't know," she'd told him. "I don't know what happened to cause us to need a truce."

"Paula . . ."

"Yes," she'd said when after a moment he didn't continue.

"Look, have a little patience, will you? I can't explain everything to you, not yet," he'd added, and she'd sensed that he was picking his words very carefully. "I have to ask you to give me time," he'd finished.

Well, she'd agreed to give him time. Once more he'd left her at the door, merely brushing her lips with his, and once more she'd watched him drive away, but last night there'd been more than a sense of emptiness. There'd been a kind of defeat. She'd thought that she and Russ had cleared things between them when he'd told her of his illness. Now it appeared that there definitely was something more. And having awakened a half-dozen times during the night, wondering consciously—as she'd evidently been doing subconsciously—what it might be had not put her in the best of mood for facing him again.

As she drove into the space Russ had reserved for her, Paula saw that she wasn't going to have to face him immediately. Though he'd mentioned that he'd intended to get to the flea market early, this morning she was first.

She parked her car, then sat at the wheel trying to decide what her next move should be. First, she should probably seek out the manager. If she'd had any sense, she told herself ruefully, she would have paused at the entrance booth and asked for the manager. As it was, she hated to leave her car unguarded before she unloaded it.

Then she spied Hilda Benson setting up in the space on the other side of her, and decided that her problem could easily be solved.

Hilda was fluttering around one long table and two card tables like a little brown bird, humming to herself as she set out a variety of everything from genuine antiques to plain, homemade bric-a-brac.

"It's going to be a good day, lovey," she greeted Paula. "Not too hot, not too cold, not too sunny, not too cloudy. Have you met Percy?"

Percy Benson was almost as small as his wife, with a shock of white hair and eagle-black eyes. "Howdy," he said cheerfully.

"Mrs. Benson," Paula began, to be quickly interrupted.

"Hilda," the little woman said. "Everyone calls me Hilda, lovey."

"Well, then, Hilda. Would you mind watching my car for just a few minutes. I need to go speak to the manager."

"Of course not," Hilda Benson retorted promptly. "Go right along."

Paula trudged back half the length of the flea market to the entrance booth, only to be told that the manager was somewhere "out there," the attendant waving vaguely toward the big drive-in theater lot. Paula could do little but nod and say she'd check again later.

Russ still hadn't arrived when she got back to her space. After thanking Hilda Benson, she hauled out her tables and set them up, covered them with the blue cloths, and then dragged out the cartons, one by one, and unpacked them. She'd finished, and it was only fifteen minutes or so before the market was due to open, when Russ drove in.

She'd begun to think he wasn't coming, and this was giving her a very strange feeling. It was such a relief to see him that she was sure she was showing it, and wished she could borrow some of the veneer he seemed to be able to cover himself with so easily.

"Would you believe it?" he greeted her. "I overslept."

Paula had experienced a miserable night's sleep, so this didn't go over too well with her. Nevertheless, she was glad to see that he did look rested and seemed his usual vibrant, healthy self again.

"I brought us something," he told her. "It's in the trunk."

"What is it?" she asked.

"I'm going to keep you in suspense." He looked at her tables, everything nicely spaced on them. "You really do have your act together," he approved. "You're not putting out any new things that you should have consulted me on about prices, are you?"

"No," she said rather shortly.

"I suppose I'd better get a move on or the paying customers will be here before I'm ready for them," he decided. As he opened the van, bending over to take out his tables, he said, flinging the words over his shoulder just loud enough so that only she could hear them, "Did I happen to mention that you look exceptionally beautiful today? That bright shade of blue is very becoming to you. But then, what isn't?"

She could feel color rushing into her face, stinging her cheeks as she absorbed this simple statement. The T-shirt she was wearing was an old one. She'd come close to deciding to use it as a cleaning rag, and then had decided to wear it just one more time. But the color was a lovely sky blue, and hearing his compliment raised her sagging spirits.

It was a busy morning, so busy that Paula didn't have time to think about getting back to the manager about the things that were missing. At the lunch hour there was a lull, and it was then that Russ came over to her to say, "It's time for the surprise. Come on across to the van."

She followed him while keeping an eye on her table. She was determined to be observant today, to let nothing escape her. But when he reached into a cooler in the back of the van and brought forth a frosty green bottle, she couldn't help but stare at it, murmuring, "Am I seeing champagne?"

"That you are," he said. "We don't want to advertise the fact that we're drinking on the premises, so we'll use a couple of paper cups, okay?" As he spoke, he popped the champagne cork with an expert gesture and then poured, and next he was holding a paper cup out to Paula.

"To our anniversary," he said.

She couldn't believe what she was hearing. "Our anniversary?" she echoed.

"A week ago today," he said. "The most memorable week of my life, I might add. I'll never forget it." He went on softly. "Can you say the same, Paula?"

"Yes," she told him, tears misting her eyes. "Of course I can say the same." She raised her cup. "To you, Russ."

He smiled. "I think I'd like it better if we said, 'To us,'" he told her, and her pulse went through a whole dance routine.

Paula was on a high as she went back to her table clutching her cup of champagne. She'd done her share of thinking about the fact they'd only known each other a week. Russ had approached it in a different way.

"The most memorable week of my life," he'd told her. And she felt warm as she thought of his words. His words, and his gesture. Bringing out the champagne had been a lovely touch to commemorate what had been a very special Sunday.

Time passed, and it was mid-afternoon when a customer stopped by who seemed genuinely interested in some of the things in Gram's jewelry box. She was a chic red-haired woman who said she was from New York, on the Cape for a week's vacation. "And I already know how much I'm going to hate to leave," she moaned.

Paula commiserated with her, then helped her look through the assortment of antique jewelry. The woman decided upon an old filigree pin and some gold and pearl earrings, and then she asked, "You don't have anything with garnets, do you? I was born in January, so garnets are my birthstone."

It was an odd quirk of fate, Paula decided later. She knew that she'd had a garnet ring in the box, quite a lovely old piece. But now she couldn't find it.

Her search intensified, finally extending to the entire tabletop, but still the ring didn't show up.

"I'm so sorry," she told the woman apologetically after she'd uncovered everything there was to uncover. "Either I left the ring home, or I've dropped it somewhere."

"Well, maybe next summer," the woman said vaguely and, at Paula's puzzled look, "I hope to be back here then."

She paid for her purchases and trailed away, and once again—although she was sure she wasn't about to find the ring in it—Paula went through the jewelry box. There was no doubt about it. The ring was gone. Missing. And she had the sick feeling that it had followed in the way of the pewter spoon, the Spode pitcher, and the amberina tumbler.

She looked up to meet Russ's eyes, and he asked perceptively, "Same problem?"

"Yes," she admitted.

"What is it this time?"

"An old garnet ring of Gram's."

"Genuine?"

"The stones. Yes."

"What kind of a setting was it in?"

"Gold. Quite a pretty setting, actually. It's an old one," she added reluctantly.

"What did you have it priced?" she was asked.

"Forty-five dollars."

"Fair enough. Paula, have you spoken to the manager?"

"Damn it, Russ," she exploded, "I tried to, this morning, but she was busy. I haven't had a chance since then."

"Then why don't you make the chance right now. I'll watch your things."

She shook her head. "No. I can't handle it right now. The ring could have fallen into one of my cartons. I want to look first before I say anything."

"The jewel box has a sturdy clasp on it, Paula," Russ said. "I doubt anything fell out of it."

"I don't know that," she insisted.

"Have it your own way," he said, "but I think you're being foolish. Again, I'd be happy to do it for you. But if you don't want me to . . ."

"It really isn't a matter of wanting, Russ," she began, only to be interrupted.

She'd noticed the tall blond man approaching their tables. He was wearing white shorts, a black Izod shirt, and a yachtsman's cap, placed at a jaunty angle. Cool blue eyes assessed her, but it was Russ the man was addressing.

"Parkhurst," he boomed genially, and Russ swung around as if he'd been shot.

"Gerald," he said. And the very blankness of his tone conveyed to Paula how taken off guard he'd been.

"Out slumming with the rest of us?" Gerald whoever-he-was inquired smilingly. "Lydia?" He beckoned to a woman who was browsing at Hilda Benson's table and she sauntered over, a stunning brunette who looked as if she'd stepped out of a fashion magazine. "Lydia, this is Russell Parkhurst," Paula heard. "Lydia Barrington, Russell. We both came up on the Peters' yacht, Bill and Amy Peters are around here somewhere. We're berthed over in the marina," Gerald continued.

But Paula barely heard the rest of his words.

What had he called Russ? Russell Parkhurst? Russ Grayson? Russell Parkhurst. Russell Grayson Parkhurst III?

Paula had never been interested in gossip columns, personality pieces, or scandal stories, but one would have to have lived in a shell all their lives not to be familiar with the name of one of the world's wealthiest and, allegedly, most eligible bachelors.

Russ *couldn't* be Russell Grayson Parkhurst III, she told herself, and was afraid she was going to be sick.

Russ was drawing Gerald and his friend Lydia away from the table, and all at once this action struck home to Paula.

He hadn't introduced her to them. He wasn't about to introduce her to them. Why, unless he had something to hide? Why, unless he'd been going along under an assumed identity all this time, living a lie with her?

Nothing had ever hit her quite so hard.

The impulse to flee came naturally, and was so strong she could not possibly have resisted it. She knocked over a carton stashed next to her car as she slipped out of the space behind her tables. She heard the sound of breaking glass coming from the upturned carton, but she couldn't have cared less. She was already striding past Hilda and Percy Benson's space, trying not to run. But once she'd gotten past them, she began to walk faster and faster until she was breaking into a trot, not caring any longer if people were looking at her curiously as she ran along the fence that formed a boundary between the flea market and a side road. Finding an opening in the fence used by the drive-in theater as an exit at night, she tore through it, intent upon one thing only. Escape.

Finally she slowed to a reasonable pace, but still she kept going. She was walking aimlessly, paying no attention to direction, the hurt still suffocating. She struck a road that led down to the bay, and by the time she reached the beach at the end of it she was exhausted, physically, mentally, and emotionally. She slumped down in the shadow of a low sandy cliff, and stared dully out at the iron-gray water. It was totally overcast at this point and the sky was as leaden as Paula's spirits. Staring at the pewter water, she felt a deep sense of despondency, of dejection—and rejection—that was soul-sapping.

Far up the beach she saw two people strolling along the tide line. A man and a woman. She was so sharply reminded of Russ and herself that the memory became a steel-edged knife, cutting deep and hurting terribly.

Why had he done this to her? Why had he pretended to be someone he wasn't at all? Above all else, why had he made love to her? Why had he let her believe that a miracle had happened to both of them, something so special that it was to be guarded, cherished, protected?

Hot tears scalded Paula, but they didn't reach her eyes. They burned, repressed, refusing to be shed. Paula drew herself together, the movement a physical huddling, a clenching of her arms, her legs, as if she were drawing herself into the smallest space possible. As if she needed to make herself small, in order to keep what she had left.

And what did she have left? She shook her head, miserable and unable to assess anything. And, at her side, she heard a taut, familiar voice, the anger tightly controlled.

"Just what the hell do you think you're doing," Russ asked her.

She squinched her eyes shut, knowing that she was behaving like a child but she didn't want to look at him. She couldn't *bear* to look at him.

He dropped to his knees beside her, and she felt his hands, one on either side of her face, cupping her chin between them.

She tried to shrug away from his touch, but it only tightened. And his voice tightened, too, as he said, "Answer me, damn it!"

She shook her head back and forth, side to side, the motion hurting. She felt him drop his hands, and she heard the raw agony in his voice as he said, "Paula, even a condemned man usually gets a chance to say something."

Slowly, slowly, she opened her eyes, to find his face so close that she automatically flinched back from him. The gesture registered with him, she saw his jaw clench, and he, too, rocked back on his heels, then positioned himself a good two feet away from her.

He kept his eyes fixed upon the water as he spoke to

her, his profile rigid. He said, "I can imagine how you must feel."

A stab of anger broke through Paula's pain. How could Russell Grayson Parkhurst III understand how any ordinary mortal could feel about anything? He moved in his own world, a world completely unrelated to the world in which *she'd* always lived.

She said coldly, "I doubt that very much."

"On the contrary," he said, his gaze still fixed on Cape Cod Bay. "I *do* know how you feel, but I think a more pertinent question is whether there's a chance that maybe you can imagine how *I* feel?"

"No," Paula said, making a small ice cube of the word.

"In other words, you've no intention of trying to understand my side of things, is that it?" he demanded.

Paula addressed a profile that could have been carved from granite. "Why should you care?" she accused.

At this he turned to face her, and she shrank from the bleakness of his expression. If she was hurting, he was hurting, too. She couldn't deny this.

"Please," Russ said, his words dropping into the silence between them, "just *listen* to me, will you? I never meant to deceive you."

The edge of his voice was ragged, a fabric torn, threatening to shred. "Perhaps," he told her, "if you can bring yourself to believe *that,* we can go on from there."

Could she believe him? At this moment Paula was too spent, too confused, to believe anything. She stood and walked to the water's edge. Stooping, she picked up a little stone, part of the rubble left behind thousands of years ago by the last of the glaciers as they crossed Cape Cod, and she rubbed its smoothness, finding comfort in the solid, hard touch of something that had endured so long.

Russ, at her shoulder, said, "It's a lucky stone."

She turned to see him looking at the small stone in her hand, black with a wide band of white quartz running around its middle. "What do you mean?" she asked him.

"Banded stones like that are lucky stones. Didn't your grandmother ever tell you that?" he asked her, his voice not sounding like Russ's at all. If she hadn't known better, she would have said he was suffering from a bad cold. "The white ring represents the luck involved," he continued. "The broader the band the more good luck the stone has to offer you—especially if it goes all the way around."

He reached out to gently take the stone out of her fingers, then he turned it over, holding it out to her in his palm. "This band is wide," he said, "and it goes all the way around. It should be very lucky for you, Paula. So—" he closed her fingers over the stone "—keep it. Keep it." He looked down at her, and all of a sudden his voice broke. "Oh honey, honey," he said, "for God's sake, don't you think I feel rotten? Don't you think I damned near died when Gerald Van Ness came up like that and blurted out my name?"

The hurt was still too strong, the memory still too raw. She didn't answer him.

"I could have strangled him," Russ went on desperately, "even though common sense told me it wasn't *his* fault. It was mine, don't you think I know that? But can't you *try* to understand why I didn't tell you my whole name that first day we met, Paula?"

He'd wounded her; she wanted to retaliate. It was an instinct as old as the first encounter between a man and a woman.

"I suppose," she said, "that you were sure I'd be just another fortune hunter."

He closed his eyes tightly, and he looked so agonized, it was all Paula could do to keep her hands at her sides. She wanted to throw her arms around him, she wanted to somehow wash out everything that had happened since that terrible moment when the big, hearty, blond man had come up and greeted Russ.

Thinking about this made her remember the flea market. How long had she been gone? She had no idea, she'd completely lost track of time, but now she asked Russ, "How did you find me here?"

"I followed you," he said, his voice sounding ages old. "I asked Perry Benson to keep an eye on our tables, and I borrowed Cora Bailey's car because there was no way I could have gotten my van out. The Baileys always take two cars, because usually Cora goes home first."

Russ spoke tonelessly, as though all this were something he'd learned by rote.

"I figured you'd gone out the back way," he told her. "I tore like hell up the road in one direction and when I didn't see you I turned around and headed the other way just in time to glimpse you turning down the side road to the beach. So I kept my distance till you'd gotten down here."

Paula had the funny feeling that Russ was summoning up some deeply hidden reserves as he spoke, putting the brakes on his emotions from long practice. And she could have been gazing into a stranger's face as he said, "We'd better get back. It's nearly four, some of the dealers will already be packing up."

"Yes." She nodded, disturbed by the change in him. Only that brief but intense way he'd closed his eyes had given any clue to his feelings about her comment that probably he'd feared she was another fortune hunter.

It came to her that this was something Russell Grayson Parkhurst III must have had to fear—or consider, at the very least—in regard to every woman he'd ever met, despite his own attractiveness. And, thinking this, she had a faint glimpse of what it must be like to be in his position. But it wasn't enough of a glimpse to counteract what had happened to her this afternoon. She was silent on the ride back to the flea market, and still silent as they walked across the asphalt

WIN The Silhouette Diamond Collection

Treasure the romance of diamonds.
Imagine yourself the proud owner of
$50,000 worth of exquisite diamond jewelry.

*GLAMOROUS
DIAMOND
PENDANT*

*PRECIOUS
DIAMOND
EARRINGS*

*EXOTIC
DIAMOND
RING*

*CAPTIVATING
DIAMOND
BRACELET*

*Silhouette
Diamond
Sweepstakes*

Rules and Regulations plus
entry form at back of this book.

to their spaces and Russ thanked Perry Benson for holding their respective forts for them.

Once Perry had gone back to his own tables, Paula hissed in Russ's ears, "What did you tell him when you left here?"

"That we'd had a lover's spat, and I wanted to go after you," he reported in a monotone.

She glared at him, but Russ had turned away from her and without following after him there was no chance of pursuing this. There was no chance of pursuing anything, as it developed, because late-afternoon customers began reaching their section of the flea market, keeping both Paula and Russ busy, and by the time the last of them had sauntered away she'd made several sales.

It was only when she started to pack her remaining stock back into cartons that she remembered hearing the sound of something breaking as she'd exited, earlier, intent only on getting away from this scene. Now she investigated, to find that several pieces of glass and china had been broken in the course of that hasty exit. Had this happened yesterday, it would have bothered her very much, because a hasty glimpse showed her that some of the pieces were good ones. But this was another day, a day in which her whole world had come to an end, so things like Limoges china and Waterford glass really didn't seem all that important.

She packed quickly, intent only on getting out of here. Later she could go over the broken things and see if there was any hope of salvaging them; later she could go over records of what had been sold and what hadn't been sold. Later. Later. She was going to have a lot of time for things "later," Paula thought bitterly.

She stashed the cartons into her car and folded up the tables. Then she climbed into the car herself and eased out of the parking space, driving away without a backward glance at Russ.

She knew she was being childish, reacting in a very

immature way, but she couldn't help herself. She needed to put space between them, she needed time to get her thoughts together before she could face him again and even begin to keep her wits about her.

That was, if she ever *could* face him again . . . and keep her wits about her!

Chapter Nine

$\mathcal{I}$t was raining Monday, one of those sodden days that made everything indoors—as well as out—seem damp to the touch.

Paula spent the morning going over her flea-market merchandise and straightening out her records. It had been impossible for her to approach these things last night; she hadn't been able to do much of anything last night except wallow in her own misery.

All the way to midnight she'd hoped that Russ might come to ring her doorbell, but he hadn't. And by the time this day had aged to mid-afternoon, she was sure he wasn't coming.

Meantime, she'd gotten her things in order, to discover that the garnet ring was the only item missing from yesterday's inventory. All the sales were accounted for, the receipts matched the amount of cash in the old white leather purse she used exclusively for

flea-market money. Nor had there been as much broken in the box of Limoges and Waterford as she'd at
first feared. She'd lost three good pieces, but at that
she'd been lucky. The damage could have been a lot
greater. But even that was not a real consolation.

Nothing, nothing, could matter very much to her
unless she could find a way to make peace with Russ.
She was discovering that more and more with each
passing hour. But how was it going to be possible to
ever make peace with Russ, let alone continue in any
sort of a relationship with him? The Russ she had
known had ceased to exist. Her flea-market colleague,
the man who'd so bewitched her, entranced her, lured
her to fall in love with him, was gone, as ephemeral
now as the proverbial will o' the wisp.

He'd never *been*, she told herself achingly. She'd
fallen in love with a myth. No, she corrected herself. A
myth had become reality, and the man she'd loved had
vanished in the strength of its aura.

Russell Grayson Parkhurst III had been the myth as
far as she was concerned, and she didn't like the reality.
She didn't even want to know Russell Grayson
Parkhurst III. She had no place in his life, nor did he
have any place in hers.

At least I have the sense to realize that, she told
herself, but such wisdom, such knowledge, did nothing
toward cheering her up.

She'd made herself a cup of herbal tea when the
doorbell finally rang, late in the afternoon. Hearing it,
Paula worked her way through a whole gamut of
emotions. None of them made any particular sense, but
all of them waged quite a war within her, and as she
went to answer the bell's summons she was wondering
desperately how she was going to handle this and keep
herself, and her dignity, intact in the process.

She soon discovered that she needn't have worried.
It was not Russ by any name standing on her doorstep.
Rather, she confronted Tim and Cora Bailey, both of
them wearing cheery smiles and bright yellow foul-

weather gear on which the raindrops sounded in a steady patter.

She scarcely knew them, but Paula was overwhelmingly glad to see them. She welcomed them into her home, let them hang the dripping raincoats out in the pantry where they could dry, and then suggested that Tim start a fire in the living room, which seemed ridiculous in July, but would take the damp chill off.

Tim obliged while Paula made bourbon and sodas for all three of them. Cora helped her get out some cheese and crackers, meanwhile telling her that they'd stopped by because Russ Grayson had mentioned she had some old books she might want them to take a look at.

Just hearing the name—that part of his name she'd known—was enough to twist the knife in Paula's heart and she winced. But Cora, intent on her task of arranging the crackers on a plate around squares of cheese, didn't notice that her hostess had paused suddenly, her hand trembling as she held the bourbon bottle, a stricken look passing across her lovely face.

They talked and drank and snacked for a while before Paula brought any books out. She discovered that Tim had taught English at Boston University and had taken early retirement because he wanted to do other things. Books had always been a first love with him and Cora was an ex-librarian, so it was natural they should have gravitated toward amassing old books, first as a hobby and now as a combined hobby and business interest.

They had one daughter, married and living in Texas, so what they planned to do in winter, Cora said, was to travel the Florida flea markets, following the sun—as Russ had mentioned—and then continue on, pausing in Texas for a long visit with their daughter before starting the trek back North.

"It should be a lot of fun," Cora said, and Tim nodded enthusiastic agreement.

Pure envy struck at Paula. Why couldn't Russ have been poor? Or, at least, not so devastastingly rich and famous? Why couldn't he have been an English teacher, or something akin to it, and in time the two of them could have retired like Cora and Tim, and followed the sun.

Why, instead, had he turned out not to be merely "Russ" at all, but a liar and a snob and a cheat and . . .

Heaping nasty words on Russ's head in absentia did no good at all, Paula discovered.

She suggested another drink and the Baileys accepted, once she'd assured them that they weren't keeping her from anything. She was tempted to say, *On the contrary you're saving my life,* but she knew that would sound a bit strange to a couple of intelligent, well-organized individuals who'd clearly gotten their acts together a long time ago.

She got out a few old books after a time, and by mutual consent she and the Baileys decided to spread them out on the rug in front of the fireplace to look them over. It was this cozy scene upon which Russell Parkhurst stumbled.

Russ had been trying desperately to stay away from Paula, and he'd succeeded for twenty-four hours. But the moment came when he knew he couldn't get through another night without first talking to her.

Even having her throw him out of her house would be *something.* As it was, he couldn't stand the separation. Today he'd faced the serious, awesome fact that he loved her even more than he'd realized. He loved her so much that he doubted he could ever again know a moment of anything even touching upon happiness without her.

He'd been tempted to go to Helen Edgeworth today and blurt out his whole story to her, and ask Helen to meet Paula and maybe try to make a few explanations on his behalf. Helen, he knew, would have found time for this despite her own problems. But it was a task he had no right to inflict on her and, anyway, to do so would have been a cop-out. He'd also thought of enlisting Tim and Cora Bailey's help, because they knew him very well. But the same thing applied.

By the time twenty-four hours had passed since Paula had driven her car out of the flea market, Russ had faced up to the fact that he was going to have to see her and speak for himself. He only hoped his vocabulary and his eloquence were in good enough shape to make her understand and, more than anything else, to believe him.

His never *had* been a case of deception. Rather, he'd been motivated by fear all along. Fear that once she found out who he was, Paula wouldn't see beyond the name. She wouldn't see *him*.

As he dashed out through the rain to his Porsche, Russ was more apprehensive about facing Paula than he'd been about almost anything else in his entire life. He was very much afraid that his worst fears already had been realized.

Paula became like a tree rooted to the spot when she looked up and saw Russ standing in her living room doorway.

He said apologetically, "I'm sorry. It's raining like hell out, so I barged right in. The door wasn't locked," he added as an afterthought.

Paula bristled, though there was nothing accusatory about his tone. And she had people with her, anyway. There'd been no reason to make sure her front door was locked. Nor was it any of Russell Grayson Parkhurst III's business whether she kept her door locked or not.

"Hi, there, Russ," Tim said genially, and Cora echoed the greeting. Only Paula remained mute, and she was conscious of emerald fire scorching her face.

"Shall I put my raincoat in the kitchen?" Russ asked her politely. "It's dripping on the rug."

"The pantry," she managed, and he nodded and strode away. But long before she was ready for him he was back in the room, holding a highball glass.

Nodding toward it, he said, "I hope you don't mind? I fixed myself a drink."

At the least, this implied a certain familiarity with the premises. She wasn't sure she wanted the Baileys to know she knew him that well. She wasn't sure she wanted anyone to know she knew him at all. She *didn't* know him at all, damn it!

She looked up and had the misfortune to meet his green eyes head-on. They held her by sheer force. She felt as if Russ had set up a magnetic field, binding her so she couldn't wrest her eyes away from him.

He asked, "May I join you?"

Paula nodded, still unable to speak, but she was appalled when he dropped into place at her side, stretching out his long length so that, in the process, his thigh brushed hers and she was at once struck by a bolt of lightning.

He picked up one of the books nearby, which happened to be an old copy of *Robinson Crusoe*.

"I used to love to read this when I was a kid," he said. "Rainy-day reading. I used to wish I could be shipwrecked on a desert island. I guess every kid wishes he could be shipwrecked on a desert island."

"I did," Tim confessed. "When I got somewhat older, though, I decided I'd rather be shipwrecked with a beautiful woman—a mermaid, perhaps—than with a man Friday."

"I pictured a siren with reddish hair and amber eyes," Russ said. "Just the two of us in our tropical paradise, subsisting on coconuts and mangoes and breadfruit. Each morning I'd pick her a fresh hibiscus to tuck into her hair."

Cora Bailey laughed. "What a romantic you are, Russ," she teased him.

"How about Tim?" Russ countered.

"Well, I've always known about Tim," Cora said, and she and Tim and Russ joined in a laughter Paula couldn't take part in.

"I have another copy of *Robinson Crusoe*," she said

hastily, feeling that she had to say something or the Baileys would begin to notice that she was acting strangely.

"Oh?" Tim queried, having already picked up another volume, a leather-bound copy of some of Emerson's works.

"It's not as old as that one, I don't think," Paula continued, nodding at the book Russ was still holding. "It's illustrated, though."

"By N. C. Wyeth by any chance?" Russ asked her.

"I don't know."

"You'll have a nice find, if it is," Tim told her. "N. C. Wyeth was Andrew Wyeth's father. He illustrated a number of children's books back in the earlier years of this century, when books were profusely illustrated, and many of the illustrations could honestly be called works of art. If your book is illustrated by Wyeth, you'll have no problem at all in selling it for a good price."

"I collect Wyeth illustrated books," Russ said, and it was all Paula could do not to glare at him. Did he seriously think, at this point, that she'd sell him anything she had, no matter what price he offered? Didn't the man know anything at all about a person's pride?

Probably not, she decided. The rich didn't have to give thought to things like pride or self-esteem or an idea of personal worth.

Tim, unaware of her reaction, said cheerfully, "See? An instant buyer, Paula."

Paula saw that Russ was about to say something, in fact she could actually watch him biting the words back. And, with a small burst of clairvoyance, she had a good idea of what it had been he'd almost told Tim. That she wouldn't sell him the book, having already refused to sell him a couple of other things.

Well, the other refusals had come in an entirely different era in their relationship.

There was a huge bookcase filled with old books in a small backroom that had been used as a study, at one point, and in later years had become a makeshift downstairs bedroom when extra sleeping space was needed. In an effort to break up the fireside tête-à-tête, Paula suggested that Tim might like to see it, and he agreed amiably.

To her relief, Russ stayed by the fire with Cora, so for the next twenty minutes she had the chance to regroup a bit as Tim thumbed through the volumes, telling her in the process that she had some very nice books.

"You should catalog all of them," he suggested. "You don't have to do a formal job of it, just list the title, author, publisher, date of publication, and any information about the specific edition, if you have it. You might list the condition as well, though I'd say most of these are in very good condition. If you could make a Xerox copy of the list, I'd be glad to go over it and make you an offer for what you want to sell, Paula. In all fairness, though, you might be able to get better prices elsewhere. I'm not in a position to pay top dollar."

It was a relief to be speaking to someone who wasn't in a position to pay top dollar for anything in the world. Paula said quickly, "I'll do as you say, Tim, and I'll be glad to let you have any of the books you're interested in, once I've decided what I want to keep."

He smiled. "Fair enough."

They went back to the living room, and as soon as Cora saw her husband she stood up. "We must be getting along, Tim," she told him.

"Oh, no," Paula protested, horrified at the thought of their leaving her alone with Russ. "Look," she said hurriedly, "I have plenty of things in the larder. I can fix us up something for supper. Nothing fancy, but—"

"We really can't, my dear," Cora said firmly, and Paula noticed that she glanced toward Russ, smiling slightly as she said this.

Had he actually had the effrontery to indicate to Cora that he'd like to be alone with her, and so would appreciate it if the Baileys left? Suspecting this, Paula was both angry and frustrated.

She didn't want to be alone with Russ. She wasn't up to being alone with him.

But the Baileys took their leave, with no dawdling on the doorstep because it was still raining hard. Paula turned back into the living room to see Russ standing in front of the fire, which was dying down now, only a few embers still glowing.

Hearing her footsteps, he swung around to face her, and Paula's resolve nearly faltered. Never in her life had she met a man who could attract her, as Russ did, simply by looking at her.

He was looking at her now, and she'd seldom seen him so serious. He said, "I'm going to ask you to let me make us both another drink, and then to sit down in here and let me talk to you for a while. After that, if you want me to go I'll go."

She latched on to the first part of what he'd said. "I don't want another drink, thank you, I've had two," she informed him sedately.

"Weak ones, I daresay, and spaced widely apart," he came back. "I'll make you another weak one, because to say what I have to say I'd like to have a drink, and I don't want to drink alone."

She nodded. "All right." But she didn't follow him into the kitchen. Instead, she sank into an armchair fairly near the fireplace, and stared at the dying embers. She'd seldom felt weaker, insofar as willpower was concerned, and she was very aware of the way Russ could weave a spell with words.

Well, she mustn't let him weave a spell, not this time. She mustn't let him make an entire web out of his charm, and then proceed to ensnare her in it. She'd been that route before.

When he came back with drinks for both of them, he

surprised her by not saying anything at all. He sat down in an armchair that was at a discreet distance from hers, and the silence between them finally became so stretched that she asked, "Shall we put another log on the fire?"

He turned to face her. "Do you want to?"

She shook her head. "No. I guess it's warm enough in here."

It was, in fact, too warm.

Russ nodded, and returned to his drink, and for a while Paula thought he was going to continue to remain silent. But after a time he admitted, "The fact is, I don't know where to begin."

There was a flatness to this statement that had its own eloquence about it, knowing Russ as she knew him.

She didn't answer, there was nothing she could answer, and he said, "Ever since yesterday afternoon I've been thinking of any number of approaches to try to use to you. Because . . . well, making you understand why I hedged with you is more important to me than almost anything in my life has ever been, Paula. Don't answer that. I don't even expect you to believe it. Just go along with me, will you?"

His use of the word *hedge* was a bit too casual for Paula's taste. As far as she was concerned, he'd done a lot more than hedge with her. Nevertheless, she sat back and waited for him to continue.

"Almost anything I can say is going to come out poorly." Russ told her after a time. "Like a play for your sympathy, and that's not what I want. What I do want is your understanding, Paula, and that's a lot to expect of anyone. Not too many people have had to live in the same kind of circumstances I've had to live in."

She couldn't resist the retort. "I would think that a majority of the people in the world would envy you your circumstances, Russ," she told him.

"Yes," he admitted quietly, "and not without reason. They're looking only at the wealth. At what it buys. They don't pause to consider what it takes away."

He was staring at the darkened fireplace as he spoke, and he said, "I'm not denying that poverty is a scourge. I only wish I, personally, could eradicate it from the world, and with it disease, famine, and all the other terrible things it brings. I'm not denying that a person who has the money to get what he needs, what he wants, is fortunate. I'm not denying that I've always been fortunate in that respect. But I *am* saying that the Parkhurst fortune has in its way created a monster for anyone who's had to live with it. The problem, you see, is that very few people in my life have ever known me."

"I would think that you'd know hundreds of people," Paula said. "Thousands of people."

"Are you deliberately misunderstanding me, Paula?" Russ asked her. "I'm speaking of *me*. How many people, do you think, have ever looked past the name and what it implies?"

"Perhaps you're suffering from a complex about that," she suggested. "You're . . . a very attractive man, Russ. You would be equally attractive without the Parkhurst name, or the Parkhurst wealth."

"Would I?" he asked, an odd note in his voice. "I've never been sure, Paula. I've never had the chance to be sure. That was the main reason for my experiment at the flea market. I wanted to see how I could relate to people just as me. I wanted to see how people would react to me, how they'd feel about me. I never anticipated anything happening like . . . meeting you," he finished, and his voice faltered as he said it.

Paula felt something stir inside her in an area she thought had become permanently frozen since yesterday. She had the crazy idea that right now Russ was speaking to her with his heart, and she knew that if she glanced in his direction at all, she'd surrender.

She kept her eyes on the darkened fireplace by sheer force of will, and heard him say, "When I saw you, well, I could use all the clichés in the world in describing how it was when I first saw you, Paula. Or, if I had the words, the talent, I could write the greatest poems ever penned about it. Initially, it was just a wonderful experience. To know someone like you, with no restrictions, no barriers between us. You were responding to me only as *me* and it gave me the greatest sense of freedom I've ever felt.

"I'd already decided I'd be Russ Grayson at the flea market," he said, "so I wasn't singling you out when I gave you that name. And there has never been a week in my life like this past week, Paula. When I told you that yesterday, when we toasted our anniversary with champagne, I meant it.

"I'd already realized there were two things you'd have to know about me. My illness, first, because it colored my life so much. Then, my total identity. I wanted to believe you already knew the most important part of that identity, in the real sense. The rest was just window dressing. At least, that's the way I tried to put it to myself. But—"

He paused, and she couldn't help but prod, "Yes?"

"Well, I *knew* you by then. I had a good idea of how you'd feel about it when you found out all about me. I dreaded it, I don't deny that. I don't deny, either, that I would have put off making *that* certain revelation as long as possible. As it was, Gerald Van Ness blundered in—"

Yes. Gerald Van Ness had blundered in.

"If it hadn't been for your friend Gerald—or someone else who knew you—how long do you think it would have been before you told me about yourself, Russ?" she asked him.

"I don't know, Paula," he said. "I'll be honest with you. I don't know."

"I see," she said, almost wishing he'd fib about this.

"You don't see," he contradicted her. "Frankly, I would have gone on without telling you forever if I could have gotten away with it, because I knew that once you found out, it would change our relationship. As it has."

She shook her head. "Our relationship has changed because you lied to me, Russ," she told him. But even as she said this she knew it wasn't the whole truth. Russ was right. It was impossible to know who he was without having things altered.

He said quietly, "I'm sorry, Paula. I'd give anything if I could go back and start all over again and try to make it different. But no matter what I'd done in the beginning, the ending would have been the same. I'm right about that, am I not? Once you found out about me, you'd have stopped seeing *me*. It would have been unavoidable and I can't even blame you for it." He shrugged slightly. "It's the story of my life," he told her, and tried to smile, but it was a poor attempt.

He stood—tall, dark, handsome, rich. What more could a man be given? Yet, looking at him, Paula decided she'd never seen anyone who looked more alone, and all of her love for him simmered to the surface and then overflowed.

"Oh, Russ," she moaned, and she started to her feet, but he shook his head.

"Please don't," he said. "I don't think I could bear it if you came back to me now because you're sorry for me." It was a very crooked grin. "Crazy, isn't it?" he asked her. "Feeling sorry for one of the richest guys in the country? Would anyone believe it?"

The bitterness in his voice was so acid it burned. But it was the kind of cauterization Paula needed. She went to him and placed her hands on his shoulders, and she shook her head when he said, "No, Paula." She reached on tiptoes to bring her mouth level with his. At first she could feel him stiffen, and then all at once he capitulated, so suddenly and with such intensity that Paula literally was swept off her feet. Russ clutched her, holding her so close to him she felt sure flesh would bruise flesh, even through their intervening layers of clothing.

"Oh, my God, sweetheart," he breathed, and there was nothing of the proper autocrat about Russ at that moment. He'd tossed all of his reserve and most of his control to whatever wind wanted to whisk it away. "I can't stand this, I can't stand being without you. I love you," Russ said, so close to her ear, so hoarsely, that she wasn't sure she'd heard him at first, and then she wasn't sure she'd heard him correctly.

"I love you," he repeated in that second before he kissed her as if he were about to devour her entirely, and the echo of those three magic words resounded, swirling out into space.

I love you . . . I love you . . . I love you. . . .

Hungry with her own desire, with a need for him she could not suppress, Paula kept hearing those three words echoing and only wished, to the depth of her being, that she could believe them.

Chapter Ten

$\mathscr{P}$aula and Russ made love that rainy summer night, finding each other in the darkness as if theirs had been a search of centuries only just now terminated.

There was a blessed velvet cloak to darkness, Paula discovered. In the aftermath of their lovemaking, secure in the sanctuary of his arms, she felt as if they were on a planet inhabited by just the two of them. But in the morning the world intruded again.

Paula fried sausages and made scrambled eggs for their breakfast, but Russ was uncommunicative as they ate. It was only as they were lingering over a second cup of coffee that he said, "I have to go down to New York today."

It was an abrupt announcement. She remembered that he'd mentioned earlier that he was going to need to go to New York, on business, she surmised. But this seemed a poor choice of times.

Last night he'd told her he loved her. The magic words still spun around in her mind, yet her belief in them remained sadly lacking, and Russ wasn't helping in that respect. If he loved her, how could he think of leaving her just now? She'd not gotten over Sunday's revelation, she was only beginning to come to terms with it. After Russ's plea for understanding last night, she was prepared to try as hard as she could to get back on their former footing.

Now, with the world intruding, she was remembering anew who this man sitting at her breakfast table really was. And because she wanted so much to keep things as they were—no, as they had been, she corrected—the question came involuntarily. "Must you go?"

She saw his frown, and wondered if she was always going to have to wish she'd curbed her tongue when it came to dealing with Russ.

He said, still frowning, "Yes. Yes, I must." He added, more gently, "I wouldn't leave now unless I had to, Paula. I've been putting off some things that must be attended to. But, also, Carleton's asked me to look after a couple of matters in the city for him, as well."

He finished his coffee, got up, and carried the empty mug over to the sink. Paula smiled a wry little smile. Russell Grayson Parkhurst III washing out his own coffee mug?

He said, his back to her as he rinsed the mug and turned it upside down on the sink apron to dry, "I should be back by the end of the week, Paula."

Paula found herself saying something stupid again. "You'll miss the flea market tomorrow."

"Yes, I'll miss the flea market." She heard the note of irritation in his voice and couldn't blame him. It had been a silly thing to say. What did a day in the flea market mean to him? He could buy out the damned flea market if he wanted to.

He turned to her, his green eyes brooding. "You'll be going tomorrow, won't you?" he asked her.

"Yes, I suppose so."

"You could park your car in the center of the two spaces and use both of them, if you like," he suggested. "You could take my tables."

"Thanks, but I don't think so," she said. "It would be a lot to handle. I think I'll stick with what I have."

He nodded without bothering to comment on this, and Paula felt a sense of hopelessness wash over her. They were speaking like two people who'd been married twenty years, should never have gotten married in the first place, and were bored with each other. There was a dullness to what they were saying, and she hated it.

Russ was washing out her coffee mug, she saw, then attacking the dishes they'd used for the sausages and eggs.

She said, "Don't bother with those things. I can do them later."

"It's no bother," he told her evenly, "and they're nearly done."

"Are you driving to New York?" she asked him.

He shook his head. "I'm going to leave my car in Hyannis and fly down."

"Do you keep your own plane in Hyannis?" She was unprepared for the scorching gaze he leveled at her.

"No," he said, his voice even as ever, only those eyes giving him away. "I don't always go cavorting around the countryside in a private jet, Paula. I'm flying to New York commercially."

It was a reproof. She didn't know why he should be reproving her, but he was. It was natural to assume that he might keep a plane in Hyannis or a yacht in Lewis Bay or both, and God knows what else. Natural? Was that what it was?

Russ was wiping his hands on a paper towel. He crumpled up the paper and tossed it into the wastebasket and then he said with more decisiveness than would ordinarily have been called for, "I'd better get going."

She trailed to the door after him, feeling that she'd done something wrong. It was as if she'd been given a test and had flunked it. But she didn't know what the questions in the test had been, so how could she have answered them satisfactorily?

Only at the last second did Russ show any emotion. Then his voice grew slightly husky as he said, "Keep the doors locked at night, will you?"

She nodded, not trusting herself to speak. She felt his lips brush her forehead and realized she'd closed her eyes without even knowing it. She opened them to watch him get into the Porsche and she blinked away sudden tears.

She could have offered to drive him to the airport. She could have met him whenever he decided to come back. She could have told him she loved him. She hadn't. Those were words she'd never said to him. Now it seemed almost too late.

The flea market wasn't the same without Russ. Paula found that it was possible to be alone in the middle of a crowd of people.

It was busy for a Wednesday, and she made a number of good sales. Nevertheless, she was dispirited as she drove home that night.

Despite the upsurge in sales, she wasn't making nearly as much money as she'd hoped to make.

After dinner she forced herself to sit down at the dining room table with a supply of paper, pencils, and a calculator, and she tried to make some sort of projection as to where she stood, and where she could hope to stand by the Labor Day weekend.

It was almost the first of August, so she had just a little over a month left before it would be time to get back to Acton and start teaching school again.

This was something she dreaded, not because she disliked her job, but because it would be so different living in Acton this year. Gram wouldn't be there. Even though Gram had been in a nursing home she'd been *there*, always willing to listen, always ready to give good, sound, practical advice when she was asked for it. But only when she was asked for it.

Paula wished, fervently, that Gram were here right now so she could talk to her about Russ. What would Gram say? Would she advise Paula to concentrate on the man she loved and to forget his alter ego?

That would be something much easier said than done. At least thus far she'd found it impossible to shut off thoughts of Russ's alter ego, except during those torrid moments when they'd been making love. And then the world, as such, had ceased to exist for her anyway. She'd been transported way beyond it.

But now in the fading light of a summer night her logic told her that she'd never be able to divorce Russ from Russell Parkhurst, and as this conviction crystallized into fact her heart became lead-heavy.

It took effort to concentrate on business. Paula worked over figures and tabulations and projections until midnight. She'd never liked math especially, so this was a chore rather than a pleasure. And the results of her figurings were no pleasure at all.

She'd already realized that she was not going to get the kind of prices she should get on her most precious things, at the flea market. The Burmese cracker jar Russ had offered to buy from her, for one thing. At the time, she hadn't wanted to sell it to him because she hadn't wanted to *sell* him anything. Now that she knew he could easily afford the jar, she wanted to sell it to him less than ever.

That seemed a paradox, Paula knew. She couldn't even fully rationalize her own feelings, she just knew that she didn't want to deal with Russ in anything that involved money. Money was a subject she didn't ever again want to touch upon with him. Not ever, she thought fiercely.

Nevertheless, she needed to find a reputable dealer who'd give her a fair price if she was going to keep the house. It was that simple. Or maybe, she thought, an auctioneer. As she understood it, auctioneers got the best prices they possibly could for things, and were interested in the sales value of the items in question because they received commissions on the sales.

Paula knew nothing about auctioneers on the Cape, and even less about reputable antique dealers. But these were things she could learn. Tim Bailey would be one person who could help her. She decided to ask his advice when she went to the flea market on Saturday.

As it happened, she didn't have to wait till Saturday. Tim and Cora appeared at the house Friday evening, apologizing because they'd come unannounced.

"We couldn't get a phone number for you," Tim told Paula.

She was chagrined by this. "I don't have a phone," she confessed. "I should have had one installed when I first came down to the Cape, but I didn't. Now it's late in the day. I'll only be here a month or so longer."

Again, she'd been going over accounts at the dining room table when the Baileys arrived, including tabulating up her flea-market sales from the previous day. And, again, when she'd gone through her inventory and then examined the contents of all her cartons, she'd had to come to the reluctant conclusion that there was something else missing. This time it was a carnival glass hatpin holder listed in the antiques price guide at one hundred and twenty-five dollars. Paula had put a seventy-five-dollar price on it, and Russ had approved this.

"It's the sort of thing only a collector is apt to buy," he told her. "And they'll be getting a good bargain at that figure."

The Baileys arrived not long after Paula had discovered this latest loss, and she was tempted to tell them about it. But she was diverted when Tim said, "I have a buyer for your N. C. Wyeth illustrated books, if you want to sell them, Paula."

Paula felt a twinge at this. Russ had said he collected books illustrated by N. C. Wyeth; he'd offered to buy

hers from her. But, again, she'd never have agreed to
have sold one to him. She'd wanted to make him a gift
of the books, and was sure he'd have refused them. Yet
she knew she couldn't bear to part with *Robinson
Crusoe*.

She felt she could hear Russ talking about being
shipwrecked on an island, and how he'd like to have an
auburn-haired girl with amber eyes with him. He'd said
he'd pick her a fresh hibiscus to tuck in her hair every
morning.

Paula blinked furiously, remembering this, then
brushed at her eye as if she'd gotten something in it.

She said, "I'd be happy to sell the books, Tim.
Frankly, I've been going over my accounts and I'd be
happy to sell anything I possibly can. I planned to talk
to you about that Saturday."

"Oh?" Tim queried.

"I thought I might put some of my better pieces with
an auctioneer if you know of a good one," Paula said.
"Or maybe you could suggest a really reputable dealer
who'd handle them for me?"

"Yes to both questions," Tim said promptly. "There
are a couple of very good auctioneers on the Cape. But
frankly, if I were you, I'd approach Parkhurst Galleries
in New York with anything you have that's really good.
I'm surprised you haven't already done that, matter of
fact. I would have thought Russ would have suggested
it."

"Russ?" Paula echoed vaguely.

Tim smiled. "I know I'm not letting any secrets out
of the bag, because Russ stopped by yesterday and had
a bite of lunch with us before he took off for New York,
and he told us you know who he is," Tim said.

Paula stared at Tim, astonished. "You knew that
Russ is the owner of the Parkhurst Galleries?" she
demanded.

"We've known Russ for years, my dear," Cora said.
"Tim used to tutor him summers when he was recuperating from a long illness at his uncle's place in Chat-

ham. Russ was unable to attend school in those years. He finished high school and got his college degree as well via tutoring. It was a year-round affair, but because of his own commitments at Boston University, Tim was only able to work with Russ in the summers."

"He was the best student I ever had," Tim said reflectively. He added, "I was in on the beginning of Russ's idea to start an antique shop. He expanded soon after that to include paintings and other art objects, and I guess there are few people interested in such things today who aren't familiar with the Parkhurst Galleries. Russ was a student of art, and he has an exceptional eye for quality and design and color as well. He is also," Tim added softly, "a terrific guy."

He was looking right at Paula as he said this, and she nearly flinched visibly. Tim was making her feel oddly ashamed of herself. Had she ever doubted that Russ—by any name—was a terrific guy? It wasn't that; her problem was that he revolved in a completely different orbit from hers.

From my own mundane little world, Paula thought.

Later, she was sure that Cora hadn't intended to make things worse. Cora hadn't merely been expressing a few of her own thoughts about Russ out loud when she said, "It's too bad people can't see him for what he is."

This was hitting the nail so uncomfortably close to the head that Paula could make no immediate answer. Then, before she could form any words, Cora continued. "Sometimes I think half the women in the world are after him, or have been. Fortune hunters, most of them. Russ admitted to Tim, once, that he doubted he'd ever be able to believe in any woman, because all his life every time a girl has looked at him he's had the feeling she was seeing dollar signs. And that," Cora said firmly, "is a pity."

Did Cora think *she'd* seen dollar signs when she'd

looked at Russ? This was negated when Cora said, unexpectedly, "The best thing that's ever happened to Russ was meeting you, Paula. Tim's the one who urged him to try the flea market just for the fun of it. Russ had seen a poster about the flea market, he knew we'd gotten involved with our books, and he asked Tim what he thought of his trying it out himself. Tim told Russ he thought he needed some fun at this point in time, and Russ agreed. Then you came along."

Russ hadn't mentioned that Tim Bailey had had anything to do with his going to the flea market. But then, he couldn't have, Paula realized. To have told her this would have risked revealing that—that damnable identity of his.

Cora was wandering around the room as she spoke. She picked up a cloisonné inkwell Paula kept on a side table and said, "This is a lovely piece, dear. Old, isn't it?"

"Yes," Paula said, overwhelmingly glad to change the subject. "My great-grandfather brought it from China."

She took advantage of Cora's absorption in the cloisonné to say to Tim, "Do want me to get the Wyeth books?"

"If you're sure you want to sell them, Paula," he told her. "Also, if you're willing to accept the price I get for them. I promise to do my best."

"You'll take a commission, of course?" she asked him.

"Very well. I think that way we'll both be inclined to continue doing business with each other," he said frankly.

Paula, on the verge of leaving the room, turned at the doorway. "Just one thing," she told Tim.

"Yes?" he asked.

"I can't sell *Robinson Crusoe*," she said.

Was it her imagination, she wondered later, or had

an expression of intense satisfaction crossed Tim Bailey's face as she said that?

Russ did not appear at the flea market on Saturday, and as the day passed, Paula began to have the terrible feeling that she was never going to see him again.

He'd gone back to New York, and his own world had swallowed him up, she decided irrationally.

By the time she got home that afternoon, Paula was so tired she went into her house, marched up the stairs, slumped down on her bed, and promptly fell asleep.

She awakened with the spine-tingling realization that she was not alone in the room. She could feel another presence and she shivered. She'd forgotten to lock the door after her—she could imagine Russ's wrath at this—and so she had no one but herself to blame for whatever was about to happen.

Slowly, cautiously, she opened her eyes and Russ, sitting on the small rocking chair by the window, burst out laughing when he saw her expression.

"Just what were you expecting, Miss Danvers?" he asked her.

She smiled weakly. "Let's not even go into it," she said, not caring this time whether or not he knew how relieved she was. Nor how happy to see him.

She feasted her eyes on him. He was wearing sand-colored slacks and a dark green shirt, and he'd never looked more handsome. Paula forgot about everything except her love for him, and she held her arms out to him with the innocence of a child, waiting to be cuddled.

She saw his hesitation, but then he asked, his voice husky, "Is that an invitation?"

"I want you to hold me," she confessed.

He'd gotten up, he was approaching the bed, and he asked, "Only to hold you?"

Paula's reserve cracked, and until this happened she didn't realize how carefully she'd been holding herself together ever since last Sunday. "Oh, Russ, Russ," she said, "I've missed you so much."

In another instant she was in his arms. He pressed her close, and his hands began to rove all over her while he nibbled at her ear, then kissed the tender spot just below it, his mouth brushing on across the line of her jaw and down to the hollow of her throat before it returned to claim her lips.

She drowned in his kiss, giving herself up to everything she felt for him. She heard him whisper, "Oh, God, sweetheart, I don't think I could have lived another day without you." Then desire's own magic began to take over and, as the summer sun bathed Paula's bedroom with gold before keeping its rendezvous with night, she and Russ, caught by its fire, made love as they'd never made love before.

It was the best of all times. That's what Paula was thinking as she slowly came back to reality to find tears stinging her eyes. She turned toward Russ, lying by her side, to see that he was watching her intently, his eyes green as rare emeralds, a small, tender smile curving his lips.

"Did I ever happen to mention that I love you?" he asked her.

She pretended to consider this. She saids judiciously, "Well, yes, I think so—" And he stopped her with a kiss.

"Witch!" he said then. "My Gypsy witch. Oh . . ."

"What is it?"

"That reminds me of something," Russ said. He edged off the bed and she watched him walk to the window. He didn't have a stitch on, and the sun's afterglow highlighted his body, converting it into living sculpture more beautiful than anything ever executed by the great masters, in Paula's eyes.

She watched him pick up his shirt from the chair where he'd tossed it. He took something out of its pocket and came back to her, holding a small white box.

"For you," he said.

She was almost afraid to open the box. She didn't want an expensive gift from Russ. She didn't want him to think he needed to buy her anything. But he cajoled, "Go ahead," and so she lifted the lid to discover a square of cotton.

Her fingers were shaking by the time she removed the cotton, and then she saw the gold hoop earrings nestled against an inner cotton lining.

Gypsy earrings.

"I nearly bought you a red skirt to go with them," Russ said unsteadily, "but I wasn't sure of your size."

Their eyes meshed, and he said, "Keep them always, will you, Paula? In memory of that special Sunday?"

"Always," she promised him. "Oh, yes. Always and always and always."

Russ insisted on cooking that night. He found an assortment of leftovers in Paula's fridge, fried some rice, added everything possible to it, and came up with a dish he called "mock paella" that turned out to be delicious.

They opened a bottle of white wine to go with it, and decided to eat at the dining room table for a change. Paula slipped into a pale yellow caftan that matched the candles on the dining room table, and she wore the gold hoop earrings.

They gave her a carefree feeling. She almost felt like a Gypsy princess. Beautiful and alluring and disdainful of ordinary convention. Was that what Gypsy princesses were? Paula wasn't sure, but she hoped so.

Russ also concocted a dessert out of canned pears, ice cream, and chocolate sauce, and as they ate it Paula told him about Tim's visit and confessed that she'd let Tim take the N. C. Wyeth books.

"Good," Russ said noncommittally. "He'll get you the best possible price for them. How's everything else been going?"

Paula started to answer this question, then stopped

short. She'd been about to tell him that she'd discussed getting either an auctioneer or a reputable dealer to take over some of her better things. With the words on the tip of her tongue, she remembered that Tim had suggested she deal with the Parkhurst Galleries. Just in time, Paula bit those words back, but not before Russ had taken note of what was happening.

"Is it the nonexistent cat who's captured your tongue?" he asked her. "Or?"

He left the question up in the air, so up in the air that Paula couldn't ignore it.

"Tim's been very helpful to me," she managed.

"Aside from the books?" Russ asked, picking up on this when she'd hoped he wouldn't.

"Well, he's learned a fair bit about the antique business," she temporized.

"The antique business? I'd say that Tim has devoted himself solely to books. Cora has an interest in antiques, yes, especially the Oriental things. But she'd be the first to admit she's still in the learning process." Russ's green gaze pinned her down directly. "What was Tim helpful about, Paula?" he queried.

"I asked if he could suggest an auctioneer or a dealer to handle some of my things," she admitted, hating this.

"And?"

"He suggested your galleries," she told him reluctantly.

She saw the flash of anger before he suppressed it. But there was no hint of it in his voice as he said levelly, "And you, of course, told him thank you but no thank you."

"Russ—"

"I honestly can't understand why you're so averse to selling to Parkhurst Galleries," Russ said, as if Parkhurst Galleries had nothing at all to do with him personally. "You'd get a fair market price for anything that was bought. I think you'd be thoroughly satisfied with any dealings you had with the galleries."

"It's not that," Paula began, but he cut her off.

"All right," he said, and there was an edge to his voice now. "Then just what the hell is it, Paula?"

"I simply don't want to do business with—" Paula paused. She'd been about to say, *with the Parkhurst Galleries,* but she dismissed this vague phrase in favor of the truth. "I simply don't want to do business with you," she told him flatly.

"Why?" Russ asked. "Do you think I'd cheat you? Or," he added bluntly, "are you afraid I'd try to pay you more for your things than they're worth?"

He'd hit upon one of her fears. An even greater one was that if she started to sell things to him, it would further cement the differences between them. But that was an area she was not about to get into. She'd been trying not to think about those differences.

"I wouldn't do that, because I know you," Russ told her. "I'm fully aware of how much you'd resent anything you might consider generosity on my part.

"Also," he went on, "I've tremendously admired your spirit, your independence, your fairness. But, you know, a person can have too much pride. Pride isn't a very commendable character trait at all when it's misguided. And it can go before a fall, to quote the old cliché. You'd better watch out for that, Paula," Russ finished softly.

Chapter Eleven

At the middle of August, Paula added up her assets. Then, one day, she made an appointment with a local builder to come over and take a look at her house with the view toward telling her what had to be done to it in the way of priority first aid.

Horace Pearce was a man she'd known ever since she could remember. He'd done work for Gram many times, and he was also a friend of the family. Paula trusted him, she knew he'd be fair with her. But she still was dismayed when she heard what he had to tell her.

He sprinkled around a lot of building terms that were unfamiliar, but in translation they added up to the fact that the old house needed a lot of first aid, and most of it came under a priority heading.

"Some of the things you can put off until another season," Horace Pearce allowed. "But I'd hate to think what's going to happen if you don't get a new roof on this place pretty soon. That's something your grandmother's been planning to get around to ever since I can remember. It can't wait much longer, Paula, or you're going to have a bundle more interior renovation to deal with."

Paula knew he was speaking the truth. The last time it had rained a leak had appeared, insidiously, in the corner of her bedroom ceiling and there was now a nasty brown stain on the wallpaper.

They'd done their tour of the house and were sitting at the kitchen table drinking coffee when Horace Pearce imparted this information. The next logical step was for Paula to ask him how much it would cost, and she did so with considerable trepidation. He spent the next few minutes "figuring," and the sum he came up with was so staggering to her she couldn't immediately assimilate it.

When the figures finally did register, she stared at him, appalled. The roof alone would cost thousands of dollars. About twice as much as she'd thought it would cost. Or, had hoped it would cost, she amended.

She tried to conceal her dismay from Howard Pearce, but she was sure she hadn't succeeded when he left her, with a compassionate pat on the shoulder. "Get in touch, Paula," he advised, "and we'll see what we can work out."

Paula sat down with her paper, pencils, and calculator again that night, hoping that when she put all the figures together they'd present a better picture. But they didn't.

Common sense had warned her all along that she couldn't hope to make enough money at the flea market to attend to the house's basic needs and also pay the taxes, which would be due come November.

Tim Bailey had sold the books with the N. C. Wyeth illustrations and Paula had been pleased with the price he'd realized for them. But it had been little more than a drop in the financial bucket.

As she worked on the facts and figures, she kept remembering what Russ had said that night about pride. She knew that she had only to go to him and he'd buy her Burmese jar and a lot of other treasures. And there were enough other things, good things, so that the tally could be considerable. But she couldn't bring herself to approach Russ, not after the case she'd made.

Anyway, there was an uneasy truce between Russ and herself these days. As if by unspoken consent, they hadn't talked very much about anything. Three times, since that first trip to New York that had distressed her so much, he'd gone back to the city. He'd usually waited till late in the day to make an announcement about his going, as if trying to forestall any protests on her part. But she hadn't been about to protest. She'd protested once. She wasn't going to make the same mistake twice.

She'd not asked Russ what it was that was taking him to New York. Sometimes, alone in the house, she'd wondered if maybe it was a woman rather than business. But she doubted this very much. It wasn't that she was so certain that Russ really loved her. She wasn't. But there was no doubting the potency of the physical attraction they had for each other. She doubted if right now Russ wanted another woman any more than she wanted another man.

Many nights during August Russ stayed over in the old Danvers homestead, and these were times that Paula knew she'd always cherish. It came to her one day that she was storing them up, as animals store up food against a harsh winter. The conclusion to be drawn from this was all too obvious. She had a growing conviction that, come fall, her relationship with Russ would end as surely as the leaves were going to drop off the maple tree in her side yard once they'd gone through their range of glorious color.

She'd become almost fatalistic about this. It was something she was conditioning herself to accept, because it seemed so inevitable to her. And each time Russ went off to New York on one of his trips, that inevitability became more certain to her.

She would go back to Acton. He would go back to New York. There was no reason to think that they'd meet again in another summer, at the flea market or anywhere else. They'd return to their own worlds, and that would be that.

Russ didn't speak of the future, and privately Paula was relieved that he didn't. The last gift she wanted bestowed upon her was one of false hope.

But in this intervening time before Labor Day, she gave all she could of herself to Russ whenever they were together. If love could have been spelled out in purely physical language, hers would have carried with it an eloquence he could not have failed to recognize.

As it was, their lovemaking was a blend of many things, primitive in the straight line of its simplicity at some moments, complicated as a maze at others, tender sometimes, almost savage other times. But always there was a rare togetherness about it. Russ was an ardent and considerate lover. Paula had learned a great deal from him about sharing oneself with another person. The sorry part of it was that she knew this was a lesson she'd never want to repeat with anyone else.

They shared spaces at the flea market except at those times when Russ was in New York, and then Paula went alone. By now she knew most of the dealers and she liked most of them, and this hurt because the small thieveries were continuing. There were few days when something did not disappear from her table, something small, and usually something valuable.

She'd mentioned the thefts to the manager, and the manager had deplored them. But there obviously was little that could be done about circumventing them, from a practical viewpoint, except by Paula herself. There were security people circulating in the area, but it was a big one. They couldn't be everywhere at once.

The only solution would be to catch the culprit in the

act, and as time passed Paula actually came to dread having this happen. Suppose she discovered that it was Maybelle Stevens, for instance, who was stealing her things? Maybelle had shared everything with her, at this point, from a peanut butter and jelly sandwich to homemade chocolate fudge. One blazingly hot sunny day, when Paula had left her hat at home, Maybelle had even insisted that Paula use the old straw hat she usually carried with her.

"My skin can take it," she'd said firmly. "Yours can't."

Paula had downplayed the thefts to Russ because she knew he wouldn't understand her viewpoint. Had it been his table that was robbed, she told herself, he'd probably have stood a day-long guard over his things to catch the thief. But then, he could afford to hire a guard. Or a whole team of guards.

It was unfortunate, but anytime anything came up about *anything* where Russ was concerned, the thought of money reared its ugly head. It was becoming increasingly difficult to forget that she was dealing with one of the wealthiest young men in the country.

One Friday morning Paula kept an appointment she'd made at a bank in Wellfleet to talk about taking a mortgage on the house. She'd gone over her situation thoroughly with Horace Pearce after a rainstorm had caused a new series of leaks upstairs, and this was a course of action he'd suggested to her.

Again, she was due for a letdown. She was not refused by the bank, but she was left with the impression that she wasn't the best possible candidate for a mortgage of any real size. Also, she soon realized that the monthly payments on a mortgage—if she *were* able to get one big enough to cover everything it would need to cover—would be staggering on her teacher's salary. She had to live, she had her own apartment rent to pay, her clothes to buy. Another year, if she had the house fixed up so that she could rent it for the summer season, when she could get a hefty amount for it, paying off a mortgage might not present such a problem. But right now it would be taking on a financial burden she really couldn't assume.

Paula called Horace Pearce that Friday night and asked him frankly if the house could possibly go without a roof until the next spring, or maybe even summer.

"Look, child," he told her, "if you can't manage it you can't manage it. I'll get over one day and see if we can make a few temporary repairs to see you through the winter. Okay?"

It really wasn't okay. But she was grateful to Gram's old friend for his consideration, and sincere in her thanks to him.

Still, she was preoccupied when she went to the flea market the next day, and every time she looked up it seemed as if Russ were watching her.

At noon he strolled over to her with a hot dog and some lemonade and said, "Take a break. Sit in the car, so you'll get a little shade. Where did you ever get that hat?"

The hat was a floppy straw creation with a bunch of plastic fruit on top of it. "It's Maybelle's," Paula told him. Once again, she'd forgotten her own hat. She was forgetting too many things these days.

"I thought it was a French designer model," Russ said with that twisted smile of his. "Look, get in the car and eat, will you? Did you realize you've been losing weight lately?"

She shook her head. "No," she said. "But I could afford to lose a few pounds."

"That's your opinion," he told her, and added succinctly, "I like you exactly as you are."

She gave him a baleful glance. It was a hot day, and she felt grimy and sweaty. Her jeans were damp, and her pink T-shirt was sticking to her skin. She couldn't imagine how anyone could possibly like her as she was.

She wanted to tell him that she wasn't hungry, but

he'd gone to the trouble of getting the hot dog for her, so it seemed as if the least she could do was eat it. It was good, too, she discovered. Russ had adorned it with mustard and ketchup and relish in exactly the right proportions.

The lemonade was tangy and refreshing. She hadn't realized how parched her throat had gotten over the morning, and she'd forgotten to bring her usual thermos of ice water.

She remembered Gram saying sometimes, "You'd forget your head if it wasn't screwed on your shoulders," and she smiled. But then she sobered. Her head wasn't screwed all that securely on her shoulders, or she would never have let herself fall in love with Russell Parkhurst.

Russ was keeping an eye on both their spaces while she ate, and Paula watched him smile his most charming smile at a woman who'd just bought a camphorglass perfume bottle.

"I let her have it for two dollars off because she says she collects them," he reported to Paula, coming over to her car and leaning down to peer in the window.

He was so close she could smell that soap and water and shaving lotion aroma of his she loved so well. She was wearing dark glasses, so she let her love for him shine in her eyes. He couldn't see through the smoky lenses.

He was wearing those oversize sunglasses of his, so he was equally inscrutable. For a second, Paula felt as if they were back to that first, special Sunday, as if they were just beginning to know each other. As if they could start all over again.

If only that were so, she thought sadly.

Russ always went back to Truro after the flea market, even if he later joined Paula. Usually, he left his flea-market merchandise locked in his van and used the Porsche when he went out.

That August Sunday he followed his routine, and as he entered his house he heard the telephone ringing. Answering it, he recognized Helen Edgeworth's voice at the other end of the line.

"I was about to give up," she told him.

"I just got back from Wellfleet," he answered.

"The flea market again? You've become quite an aficionado, Russell," she teased.

"It gets in your blood," he said. Which, actually, was true. He began to think about Tim and Cora Bailey following the sun this winter, going from flea market to flea market, and he felt a pang of envy.

Helen was not one to waste words when she wanted to come to a point. She said now, "Don't you think it's about time I meet your Paula? The next thing we know, the summer will be over."

The words struck at Russ. The summer would be over, of course. He just hadn't let himself think about it. He wanted August to last forever this year.

"I've been intending to arrange something," Russ said, "but I wasn't sure Carleton would be up to it yet."

"Carleton's bored to death at the moment, and meeting a lovely girl would be a pleasant diversion for him," Helen informed him. "How about drinks around five tomorrow afternoon? Is that too short a notice?"

"No," Russ said. "It would be fine, Helen. If, by any chance, Paula is already tied up, I'll get back to you."

"Wonderful. Otherwise, we'll see you here at five," Helen said.

As he hung up the phone, Russ was picturing the Edgeworths' home in Chatham. It was a beautiful house overlooking Pleasant Bay, and from the upstairs deck one could see across a rim of outer beach to the Atlantic.

His uncle's house, the house in which he'd spent such a portion of his youth more or less in exile, was only a quarter mile away. It was even larger and more imposing, and Russ had never regretted selling it.

The Edgeworth home was furnished with choice antiques that were each perfection in itself. It wasn't that Helen was fussy, nor was Carleton for that matter. They were simply people who'd been born to wealth, and had always been accustomed to the very best. Helen's taste was exquisite, and though a professional decorator had been called in when they'd moved to Chatham on a year-round basis after Carleton's retirement, it was her color sense and her choices that were reflected in her home.

It was a rather austere house, though, because there'd always been a certain formality to the way Helen and Carleton lived. Russ was used to that formality. He'd grown up with it, he'd never in his life met anyone more proper than his late uncle. But Paula had been raised in an entirely different environment. The house in which she lived was a home, not merely a house, and certainly not a showplace. Russ had envied her that the very first time he'd visited her.

True, he'd gone to the far end of the spectrum when he'd bought his place in Truro. But this had been primarily because he'd wanted to make it something entirely his own. He'd realized, the first day he'd taken Paula to Truro, that the place was not to her taste. Since then, he felt she'd mellowed a bit in that respect. They'd spent some wonderful times in Truro, times he'd never forget.

Why was he talking as if his time with Paula were going to come to an end?

Russ asked himself this as he walked out on his deck and looked out over Cape Cod Bay. There was a windsurfer off shore, and he watched the yellow-and-red striped sail billowing in the breeze, wishing that Paula were here by his side. He wanted to touch her. He wanted to know that she was near him. He wished that he could always have her near him. But he was afraid, bleakly, that this was not going to come to pass.

Paula had changed toward him once she'd found out

who he was. He knew that over the intervening weeks, since that awful day when Gerald Van Ness had visited the flea market, she'd tried to get back to their old relationship, just as he had. But despite her best efforts—and he'd sensed that effort—she had failed. As had he.

There was a constraint between them these days except when they were making love. Only then did they seem able to erase this invisible barrier that had crept between them so insidiously.

Unfortunately, Russ thought wryly, two people couldn't make love all the time. And it was in those other hours that the problems arose.

It was strange, but Russ, who in the eyes of most people would have appeared to have so much to give, sometimes felt that he had nothing to offer her at all.

Paula was dismayed when Russ told her they'd been invited to have drinks at the Edgeworths. She tried to think of an excuse not to go that would be convincing, but knew she couldn't possibly hope to fool him.

Finally, she came out with the truth. "I really don't want to go, Russ," she told him.

"Helen and Carleton are my two oldest friends," he said. "Helen wants very much to meet you. I've told her about you."

Does she think I'm just another fortune hunter? The question came before Paula was even aware she was posing it to herself, and it made her sick at heart. Every time something like this happened, it intensified her feeling of helplessness about the relationship between Russ and herself, much as she loved him.

There were moments when she asked herself why she couldn't simply accept his wealth. Why she couldn't take it as much for granted as she did the fact that he had incredible green eyes, and was one of the handsomest men she'd ever seen. But it didn't work that way.

It would be so much easier if you were poor, darling, she thought silently.

"I appreciate Mrs. Edgeworth's invitation," she said now, stiffly. "I just can't go, that's all."

"May I ask why not?" Russ's tone was surprisingly gentle. Paula wouldn't have blamed him for being really annoyed with her.

"I don't have anything suitable to wear, for one thing," Paula said. "And I need a haircut. And—"

"You do not need a haircut," he said firmly. "I love your hair exactly the way it is. Don't ever change it. As far as something suitable to wear, Helen won't care what you wear, Paula."

Paula smiled because this was so like a man. And Russ, seeing the smile, nodded ruefully and said, "Okay. Look, every time we've gone out anywhere you've looked terrific. Just wear an outfit you've worn before."

Paula mentally reviewed her wardrobe and found it seriously lacking. The dress she'd worn on her first dinner date with him was too fussy, she decided. Everything else she had suddenly seemed too plain.

She supposed she could try to buy something, but in her experience, last-minute clothes purchases had usually turned out to be disasters.

"Please, Paula," Russ said suddenly. "Don't let something that doesn't matter interfere."

Looking at him, she capitulated. But as she dressed for their engagement all of her previous doubts and more assailed her.

Everything seemed to go wrong, too. She chipped a fingernail at the last minute; she discovered that the beige leather pumps she'd planned to wear had a bad scuff mark in a highly visible place along one side; she couldn't find one of her copper leaf-shaped earrings.

Her hair refused to behave, her lipstick smudged, and as she touched a bit of mascara to her lashes some of it got in her eye, the resulting sting making her look as if she'd been crying.

She was wearing a simple taupe skirt with a taupe-and-beige vertical-striped top, cinched at the waist with a wide black leather belt. But she'd forgotten that the linenlike material crumpled easily, and by the time Russ called for her she felt she already looked bedraggled.

Russ's approving eye did nothing much to help. Paula was fully aware that Russ tended to be blind when it came to certain things that concerned her.

It was a beautiful late summer afternoon, and Paula knew she should be enjoying the drive over to Chatham, but her nervousness increased with every mile until she felt as if a permanent knot had been tied in her stomach.

The first sight of the Edgeworth home did nothing to allay her fears. Russ drove up a long, curving driveway to come to a stop in front of the beautifully proportioned door that marked the front entrance to this huge house, and at once that door was opened by an honest-to-goodness butler.

"Mr. Parkhurst, sir," the man said with just the right degree of enthusiasm, and Russ nodded perfunctorily.

"Good to see you, Andrews," he returned, and the dialogue struck Paula's ear like something out of an English drawing room comedy.

The scene into which she and Russ walked was very much like something out of a drawing room comedy too. They were ushered into a bona fide drawing room, as a matter of fact, the tall French windows looking out over the beautiful expanse of Pleasant Bay. The woman who crossed the exquisite Aubusson rug to greet them was a regal figure, tall, graceful, her beautiful white hair a true crowning glory. She was dressed simply in a blue silk sheath that had probably cost as much as Paula spent on clothes in a year. It was so understated, Paula thought distractedly, it had to have cost a fortune.

The dress also matched Helen Edgeworth's eyes. They were the bluest eyes Paula had ever seen. But when the older woman held out her hand and said, "You must be Paula," with genuine warmth in her well-modulated voice, some of the icicles that had formed in Paula's blood began to dissolve, and she decided that maybe some day she'd be warm again after all.

Helen was a gracious hostess, and Carleton was a gracious host. He was still convalescent, and obviously his wife was watching what he did and didn't do carefully, but there was a twinkle in his eyes that Paula liked very much.

Paula chose to stick to white wine when she was asked what she'd like to drink, as did Helen. The men chose Scotch, and a maid in a traditional black uniform, with a frilly white apron, passed hors d'oeuvres that looked delicious and undoubtedly were, but everything tasted like sawdust to Paula.

They stayed about an hour, and then Russ made the move to leave. As he lingered behind for a moment to speak to Carleton, Helen took the opportunity to lock Paula's arm in hers, sauntering toward the front door with her.

Her voice soft, she said, "I'm so very glad to meet you, my dear. Russell has been almost like a son to Carleton and me. So . . ."

She would have said more, but at that moment Russ caught up with them, and Helen had to be satisfied with giving Paula a rather conspiratorial smile.

As they were driving along Route 28 once again, Russ asked, "Was that so bad?"

"No, of course not," Paula said quickly. "It wasn't *bad* at all. They are charming people, Russ."

"Helen liked you," Russ told her.

"Mrs. Edgeworth is so polite, she'd make anyone feel she liked them," Paula retorted.

"I know Helen too well to be fooled," Russ said. He paused. "Carleton will be going in for bypass surgery in October," he said.

Paula frowned. "He looks so frail."

"I know. But he's tougher than he looks. So is

Helen. They've had their share, Paula. Their only child died when she was sixteen. Everything hasn't always been the way it looks on the surface."

"Is it ever for anyone?" she asked him.

"No, I suppose not." He lapsed into silence until they were rounding the traffic rotary in Orleans. Then he asked, "Would you like to go out to dinner somewhere? In the mood for Portuguese food? We could go out to Provincetown."

"Why don't we go home, and I'll make us cheese omelettes," Paula suggested.

"That's an invitation I can't refuse," Russ said, but not before darting a quizzical look at her first.

She loved to go out to Provincetown at the tip of the Cape, she knew he knew that. Normally, she would have been quick to agree to his suggestion because it was always fun to wander along the narrow main street with Russ, to poke around the jumbled-up little stores, and to stop somewhere for fish and chips Portuguese-style. But tonight, well, tonight she wasn't in the mood for it. Rather, she was in the mood for reflection.

Twice, now, people who'd known Russ for a long time had indicated that they were happy he'd met her.

It gave her something to think about.

Chapter Twelve

The last weekend in August was late summer at its best. But as Paula drove to the flea market on Saturday morning she was oblivious to the weather. Not only summer, but just about everything else was coming to an end, she thought ruefully.

A week from now she'd be back in Acton, getting ready for school, which was due to open the day after Labor Day. She'd be going to the flea market just three more times—today, tomorrow, and on Wednesday— she reminded herself. Not that she needed reminding.

She couldn't help but feel that she had just three more chances left with Russ, and she had no idea how to go about using any of them, let alone taking advantage of them.

As it was, she'd been living every day to its fullest, trying not to think about the future. Again, she and Russ had shared golden times in Truro, swimming in the bay, sunning on the beach, making love in his huge, super-size bed. On other occasions he'd come to her house, and she'd fixed old New England dishes—clam chowder made with milk and laced with cubes of crisp, fried-out salt pork, the traditional "boiled dinner," delicate broiled scallops. She'd never thought she was much of a cook, but these were recipes Gram had taught her. "Any human being, male or female, should know how to prepare a meal," Gram had said firmly.

Once in a while they'd driven to the Double Dragon in Orleans for a Chinese dinner, this usually on the late side. Occasionally, they'd gone somewhere for a pizza. But, mostly, they'd eaten in either his house or hers, only wanting to be together, and preferably alone.

Mid-morning on that last Saturday, though, Russ asked Paula if she'd like to go for dinner at the lovely inn where they'd had their first date, and she had a funny feeling as she accepted his invitation. There was a significance to their ending their summer together in the same place where they'd begun it.

Don't get your hopes up, Paula cautioned herself as she rearranged a few of her glass and china items to make a better display. *From all the road signs, Russell Parkhurst isn't about to commit himself to anything or anybody. By this time Russ might have, yes. But not Russell Grayson Parkhurst III.*

She couldn't pin a label on Russ's double identity—which is how she thought of it—like Dr. Jekyll and Mr. Hyde. But how she hated it.

In the early afternoon she took a break to go to the rest room, leaving Russ to look after her tables as well as his own.

"Take your time," he told her. "Browse around a bit if you want to. It isn't all that busy today."

It wasn't. There was a steady stream of customers but—because it was getting toward the end of the season and was a good beach day they weren't coming in droves, as they sometimes did.

Paula decided to take advantage of his offer, and she toured up and down some of the lanes, chatting with the other dealers. It wasn't always possible to touch bases with them on a busy day.

Tim Bailey had taken a number of her old books on consignment and now, as she stopped by to see him, she was pleased to find that he'd made several sales for her.

"I can figure out what you have coming now, or we can get to it later," he said.

"Later will be fine," she told him.

Cora appeared around the edge of their van to say, "I just opened a thermos of coffee, and it's still steaming hot. How about joining me for a cup?"

"I'd love one," Paula admitted, and she and Cora went to sit in the front seat of the van while they drank the coffee and munched on some homemade cookies Cora had brought along.

After a time Cora said perceptively, "You seem pensive today, Paula. Any particular reason why, if I'm not being too inquisitive?"

"You're not being too inquisitive," Paula said. "This is my last weekend here, that's all, and I'm going to miss it. I'll be coming next Wednesday, but that'll be my last time. I plan to drive up to Acton on Friday so I can get my apartment in shape and my clothes together before school starts. The apartment's going to be a dusty mess after being closed up all summer."

Cora said gently, "We'll miss having you around. You know, it occurs to me, couldn't you still come down weekends and do the market?"

"I thought about it," Paula confessed, "but I decided against it. I doubt I'd sell that much, probably not enough to pay for the gas and the entrance fee. And, anyway . . ."

"Yes?"

"I think there comes a time when it's wise not to try to prolong things," she said frankly.

"Ummm," Cora mused thoughtfully. "Paula, sometimes I know I tend to venture where angels fear to tread, but I have a piece of advice for you."

"Advice, Cora?"

"Yes," Cora said stubbornly. "Be patient with Russ. I've known him for years," she went on. "Tim used to take me to the house with him when he went to tutor Russ; more often than not we'd stay for dinner with him. He was thin as a rail in those days, and it was easy to tell he'd been very sick. He had little endurance, he still had to rest a great deal of the time, and you can imagine how that was for a young man just getting into his twenties. I watched him get better and better, and it was quite a moving experience, Paula. Russ was a very brave person. I admired his courage, I admired the way he accepted his illness as a challenge, and was resolved to beat it, which he did. And, during those years— there were several years—I think I came to know him very well."

Cora was staring thoughtfully at the empty coffee mug in her hand as her words trailed off. When she didn't immediately speak again, Paula prodded gently, "What are you trying to tell me, Cora?"

"He's fallen in love with you, Paula," Cora said slowly. "Oh," she went on as she saw Paula raise her hand in protest, "I know that you may have your doubts about that, and it's understandable. But I've seen the expression on his face when he looks at you and knows you're not watching him. Sometimes it tears me up because he looks so lost about it," Cora confessed. "You see, Russ is very self-confident in some ways, but in other ways he's as insecure as an abandoned child."

Paula shook her head slowly. "I know what you're saying," she admitted, "but I can't quite believe that." She turned to the older woman. "Did you know, Cora, that in the beginning I didn't know who he was. It was the better part of a month before I found out who he was, and that only by accident."

"And nothing's been the same since, has it, Paula?" Cora asked gently.

"No," she admitted. "No, nothing has."

"Don't you see?" Cora asked her. "That's the way it's always been for Russ. The whole world has focused on his name, his wealth, his reputation. He's been grist for the mills of every gossip columnist and scandal sheet in the country. He's laughed about it, saying that the only thing he's ever been successful at is dodging photographers, so at least most people who read about him don't know what he′ looks like. That's in part because he was out of circulation for so long when he was younger, and, amazingly, the press never has learned about his long illness. He drifted into real prominence only a few years ago, after his uncle died, because then he became the heir to the whole Parkhurst fortune. A financial empire, Paula. I can't even begin to comprehend the extent of it.

"The galleries in New York are just a part of it all, but that's the part Russell founded himself, and in which he's primarily interested. Nevertheless, he has to keep tabs on all the rest of it, and it's an awesome responsibility. His theory is to hire excellent people to manage things for him and to pay them top dollar. It works, but even so he has to keep his hands on the reins where his executives are concerned. Just this past month, he's had problems with a man who's been with him for years. Alcohol, a bad divorce. Russ made four trips to New York over that, and agonized about it in between. He was afraid he was going to have to let the man go; now he's hopeful that it may work out. He's persuaded the man to go into therapy."

Cora broke off. "He hasn't shared any of this with you, has he?" she asked.

"No," Paula said reluctantly. He hadn't, and this hurt, now that she was learning the reason why he'd made those trips to New York.

"He wouldn't," Cora said. "He told Tim, because somehow Russ has always been able to talk to Tim about the things that bother him. They go back a long way. But I think I know why he wouldn't have discussed any of this with you, and it's nothing for you to get your feelings hurt about, Paula."

Paula smiled weakly at this. "Why, then, Cora?" she asked.

"I think he's trying to keep a distance between anything involving the Parkhurst empire and you because he wants so much to be a person to you, not a figurehead."

"He is a person to me, Cora," Paula said, so softly that Cora had to lean closer to hear her. "He always has been. But I can't deny that it changed things when I found out who he was. For one thing, I think he should have told me from the beginning."

"Do you?" Cora challenged. "Paula, if he'd come up to you your first day at the flea market and said, 'Hi, I'm Russell Grayson Parkhurst III,' what would you have done?"

Paula laughed. "I don't know. Fainted maybe. Said, 'How do you do,' and backed away from him. Wondered if he possibly could be for real."

"See what I mean?" Cora demanded triumphantly. "Does this give you some little idea of what Russell has always had to cope with?"

Actually, it did. And Paula was thoughtful as she left the Baileys to start back toward her own space.

On the way she was intercepted by Cholly Stevens, who informed her that Maybelle was home today with a case of laryngitis. "Hell of a thing for Maybelle when she can't talk," he said.

"Tell her to mix some whiskey with hot water, lemon juice, and honey," Paula advised, "and just to sip it. That was my grandmother's treatment."

Cholly nodded cheerfully. "Maybelle'll like that prescription."

Paula smiled. "Give her my love," she said. And this was sincere. She'd come to be very fond of both

Maybelle and Cholly. "Tell her I hope she'll be well enough to come tomorrow."

"She will be," Cholly said confidently. "Maybelle's strong as a horse. She throws off most anything quickly."

The Bensons were set up in the next aisle, but as she approached them Paula was surprised to see that they were packing up. It was only two-thirty and the flea market didn't close until four. She frowned. "Aren't you leaving awfully early?" she asked them.

Percy didn't answer her, he was so busy stashing merchandise into cartons, and Hilda gave her an odd look. "I don't feel too good," Hilda said evasively. "Maybe it's the heat, or it could be my heart acting up. I got angina, the doctor tells me. Anyway, Percy thought we should call it quits."

"I'm sorry, Hilda," Paula said sympathetically. "Is there anything I can do?"

"Not a thing, lovey," Hilda said more cheerfully. "I'm bound to be good as new by tomorrow. We'll see you then."

Paula nodded, and continued on the final leg of her small safari. But as she reached the spaces she shared with Russ she got a reception she hadn't bargained for.

"Where the hell have you been?" he snapped at her.

"Just traipsing around," she said. "I stopped and had a cup of coffee with Cora. Why?"

"I could have used you here," he said tersely.

"Russ, you told me to take my time," she reminded him.

"I know, I know," he said impatiently. "The problem is I couldn't go off and leave everything unattended, and I've got to get to the manager. At least," he added levelly, "I think I'm the one who's going to have to go to the manager. I'm pretty damned sure you won't do it."

He was wearing the oversize dark glasses, and his face was inscrutable. Paula felt a spasm of fear, and her pulse began to thud. Something was wrong, something was very wrong, and she wasn't sure she wanted to know what it was.

"Well?" Russ demanded, as if he'd read her mind. "Aren't you curious?"

"Should I be?" Paula countered.

"I've discovered who your thief is," Russ said flatly.

Paula swallowed hard, dreading the revelation that she could hardly keep him from making to her. She said, staving it off, "Russ, that's an awfully serious accusation to make against anyone."

"When I saw them stealing a pendant from your grandmother's jewel box in broad daylight?" he asked roughly. "Why don't you go and ask Hilda Benson if she's got an antique moonstone pendant for sale, Paula?"

She cringed. "Oh, God, no," she protested. "Not Hilda."

"Yes, Hilda," he snapped. "I damned near caught her at it the other day, I can see that now. But when she saw me watching her she slipped the piece of jewelry she had in her hand back into the box and picked up something else, making some comment about it so I'd be thrown off guard.

"She's a damned clever thief, Paula," Russ went on angrily. "Ever noticed the way she dresses? She always wears those long cotton things that flap around her ankles, and she puts on an apron over them that ties around her waist. The apron has a big pocket that stretches all the way across the front. It could hold a hell of a lot of stolen loot, and those swishing skirts of hers are a distraction.

"She's light-fingered," Russ said distinctly. "Extremely light-fingered. I think a little investigation of the Benson domicile would show up everything you've been missing."

Paula pressed her hands to her ears, this an involuntary gesture because she didn't want to listen to him. "Russ," she said weakly, "Hilda could have taken the moonstone pendant by mistake. If she was talking to you at the time, she could have just . . . carried it off with her."

"Yes, that's exactly what she did," Russ agreed. "She carried it off with her. And this is one time when we can catch her while her act's still fresh. That's why I've been waiting for you to get back. I'm going to the manager, and we'll have the Wellfleet police cruiser waiting for the Bensons as they drive out of this place today."

As they drove out. From the speed at which Hilda and Percy Benson had been packing, Paula suspected that they'd already driven out. But even if they hadn't, she couldn't stand the thought of the police coming, of an accusatory scene . . .

"What's going on in your mind, Paula?" Russ asked her suspiciously.

"I—I don't want you to do anything about this," she told him.

"What the hell are you saying?" he demanded. "The woman's a *thief*, Paula. Are you telling me you plan to let her get away with it?"

"Maybe . . . maybe she's sick," Paula suggested.

"*Sick?* Are you out of your mind? She's about as sick as you are. Come on, Paula."

She faced him defiantly. "Russ," she said, "I happen to know that Hilda has angina."

"Who says so?" he interrupted.

"She told me so. But that's not what I'm talking about."

"Then exactly what *are* you talking about?" On this warm, beautiful summer day he was iceberg-cold, Paula saw.

"It occurs to me that if Hilda really did steal anything—"

Again, he cut in. "Do you doubt me?" he asked, and she decided he was even colder than an iceberg.

"No, it isn't that I doubt you, Russ," she said desperately. "Though, I still think slipping the pendant into her apron pocket could have been a kind of . . . reflex action. Chances are she'll bring it back tomorrow."

"Do you really think so?" he asked, with excruciating politeness.

She didn't think so. That was the worst of it, and she knew her expression was giving her away.

There'd been something definitely furtive about the way Hilda and Percy had acted this afternoon. Percy hadn't even looked at her, he'd refused to meet her eyes at all. And Hilda, well, Hilda certainly hadn't been her chipper, birdlike self. Maybe she really *had* felt sick. On the other hand . . .

"Is it beginning to get to you, Paula?" Russ asked, his tone a definition of irony, and she bristled.

"I'm not a child, Russ," she said defiantly. "Also, I've a question to ask of you. Have any of your things been stolen?"

"No. Not that I know of, which is to say that I haven't checked out everything today. Most of the pieces I've brought out here are large, though. And breakable. That could be a factor."

"Some of the things I've missed are breakable," she reminded him.

"True. But they were small. And I daresay that apron pocket is quite soft, if you put only an item at a time in it."

She ignored this. "The fact is," she said, "none of your things are missing. Therefore, this is my problem, not yours."

"In other words, you're asking me to bug off?" he suggested.

"Yes. Yes, exactly that."

Paula didn't dare look at him as she said this. She could feel his scorn, and it was abrasive. Then he said quietly, "Okay, I'll bug off, Paula. But not until I've completed a quiet little survey of my own. I'm going to talk with every dealer in this place and learn whether or not they've been missing small items. And that, dear lady, is something you can't keep me from doing. Now, suppose *you* mind the store for a while?"

With this he stalked off, and she stared after him helplessly.

She was seeing a new side of Russ. He was hard and unyielding, cold and ruthless. She could imagine him wielding his power as the head of the kind of empire Cora had described, and ruthlessly cutting down anyone who got in his way.

A small memory crept out to dispute this. Cora had also told her that Russ had been working this entire past month with one of his executives who'd gone wrong, trying to help the man put his life together again. That didn't sound like the kind of despot whose picture she had just been painting.

On the other hand, she was very sure that Russ had no tolerance for weakness. And, in his book, she'd displayed a lamentable weakness, she knew, because she didn't want to go tearing off after the Bensons, the police in tow, and make sure Hilda was arrested.

Why? Why didn't she want to bring Hilda Benson to account if she'd really been stealing her things. Maybe, she conceded, it was because she couldn't believe that "Jenny Wren" really could be a thief.

Russ was gone so long that Paula was packing up when he returned. She saw him coming, and turned her attention to wrapping up things in newspaper and stashing them in a carton, but this ploy wasn't good enough.

"The Bensons left early," Russ reported first. "But I imagine you knew that, didn't you?"

"What makes you say that?" she evaded.

"The dealer who was next to them saw you talking to them as they were packing up," Russ reported. "So it's nice to think that you gave Hilda your blessing, Paula. I doubt if you ever see her again."

She faced him at this. "What are you saying?"

"Exactly that. There are other flea markets in New England. I think you may find the Bensons doing business at one of them come the Labor Day weekend, but not here in Wellfleet. Hilda knew I saw her take the pendant. They won't be back, Paula. Mark my words."

"All right," she said. "All right."

"Quite a few of the dealers have missed items now and then," he continued. "They consider it par for the course in any flea market. Things are out in the open, you can't keep your eye on everything, so there's bound to be some thievery. But if you consider that Hilda's been picking up a few choice things hither and yon three times a week since the beginning of summer, it adds up to a rather nice cache, wouldn't you say?"

"I'm not saying anything about this," Paula insisted stubbornly.

"Have it your way, but frankly, I don't understand you," Russ told her.

"I don't understand *you*," she retorted. "I can't understand what satisfaction you'd get persecuting a little old lady."

"Persecuting?" Russ raised a cynical eyebrow at this, and he said coldly, "Very well. If that's the way you take it. Personally, I don't think anyone should be allowed a free ride. Especially when it involves the commission of felonies."

"Isn't that putting it rather strongly, Russ?" she challenged.

"No. I don't think so."

Fortunately, things had been slow over the late afternoon, and there were only a few customers still wandering along the lanes in the flea market. Paula was oblivious to them, intent only upon Russ who, not for the first time, was coming on like a total stranger to her.

He, though, was diverted by a woman who stopped by to express interest in a Heisey punch bowl he was selling, and Paula had a minute in which to try to collect her thoughts.

She knew little about kleptomania. Yet she felt sure

that if Hilda really had taken the moonstone pendant, this could be the logical explanation for her actions.

Her reverie about this was interrupted by Tim Bailey's appearance. As she greeted him, Paula wondered if Tim was one of the people Russ had questioned about thefts, and she also wondered if Tim would share Russ's conviction that Hilda Benson should be apprehended and made to pay for what Russ considered her flagrant crime.

It was a relief when Tim didn't get into it but, instead, said, "I've been promising Cora a lobster dinner one of these nights, and we thought maybe tonight should be the time. Any chance of you and Russ joining us?"

Paula couldn't imagine sharing a lobster dinner or much of anything tonight with Russ. She was too agitated by the divergence in their viewpoints, and by his hardness. But before she could tell Tim that she didn't think she could make it, Russ loomed up at her elbow.

"Sounds like a good idea," he said amiably. "How will we handle the car situation?"

"Paula lives nearest here," Tim pointed out. "I thought maybe we could leave our vans at her place and then help her clear out her car so we could use it."

"Great," Russ applauded. "We'll pack up, and you two follow us on over."

High-handed? He was being damnably high-handed, and Paula gritted her teeth. She yearned to have a confrontation over this, to tell Russ that she was damned if she'd go out and have lobster with him, but he cheerfully forestalled her by turning his back on her and started to pack up with that smooth efficiency and economy of motion she'd always envied.

She finished her own packing and got her tables folded and stashed in her car before he could come over and offer to help her do this, as he usually did. Then, still seething, she slipped behind the wheel, wondering how she was going to handle this situation.

Russ loomed up at the car window to say unexpectedly, "Look, be careful driving back to your house, will you?"

She stared at him speechlessly, and at that he leaned over and kissed her gently.

"You tend to get rather uncoordinated when you're angry," he told her, "and I know you're extremely angry with me right now. So take it easy, all right?

"It would be a shame," he added with a wicked grin, "if you ran into something and smashed up some of those valuable antiques."

Chapter Thirteen

To Paula's chagrin, the Baileys arrived at her house before Russ did. She'd wanted the opportunity to say a few choice words to him, and also to back out of going with the others for lobster.

By the time Russ drove in, Paula had unloaded her car, with Tim and Cora's help, and they'd stored her cartons in the big closet off the dining room she'd been using for that purpose.

Russ grinned at her cheerfully as he said, "I stopped and picked up some bourbon. That's Cora's drink, and I didn't know whether you had any left, Paula."

"Cora's drink!" Cora scoffed, and Tim laughed.

"He's got your number, Cora."

Tim was following Russ out to the kitchen as he spoke, and he asked, "Need some help?"

"You can get out the ice cubes," Russ offered, and Paula glowered. He was acting as if he owned her house, damn it. She was going to have something to say about that!

"I also bought some cheese and stuff," Russ announced, delving into the paper bag that had held the bourbon and bringing up several assorted packages. "Cora, how about getting a plate out of that cabinet over there and putting these things out on it?"

Cora obliged promptly, but Paula couldn't resist asking sweetly, "Want some help, Cora?"

"No, that's fine, dear," Cora said serenely. "You just take it easy. Shall we all sit around the kitchen table to have this, Russ?"

"Why not?" he agreed.

He was acting as if nothing had happened, as if they'd never had their sharp difference of opinion about Hilda Benson, and Paula felt that she could gladly strangle him. Then, once they'd sat down, he clicked his glass first to hers, then to Cora's, then to Tim's, and he said, serious for the moment, "To three of the people in the entire world I like best to be with."

It was a highly charged moment for Paula, and she saw that she was not alone. Cora's eyes grew suspiciously moist, and she said softly, "To your happiness, Russ. And to yours, Paula."

It sounded like the kind of toast one would propose to a newly engaged couple, even to a bride and groom, and Paula looked away hastily. Nor did it help when Tim said, "I'll buy that."

As they munched on cheese, crackers, and a delicious country-style pâté Russ had bought, Russ and Tim argued amiably over the choice of restaurants for a lobster dinner, finally deciding upon the Lobster Pool in Eastham.

"Good," Cora approved. "It's a comfortable place. You can be as casual in your dress as you like, so I won't feel I should have gone home and changed."

Paula was still wearing her flea-market jeans and she said doubtfully, "Maybe I should put on something else." But Cora shook her head.

"You're fine just as you are, dear," Cora assured her.

Russ grinned. "If I told her that, I'd have an argument on my hands," he said.

"That's the way women are," Tim observed sagely.

They finished their drinks, put the rest of the snacks away, and as they walked out the door Russ asked, "Do you have your car keys, Paula?"

He held out his hand for the keys as he spoke, and she said stiffly, "I can drive, Russ."

"Yes, I know," he said. "So can I."

She groaned inwardly, but she gave him the car keys. There was no point in making a fuss over small matters. She had plenty of larger ones to deal with.

As he started up the motor, Russ leaned close to her and said, "I hope you don't mind the switch in plans."

"What switch in plans?" she asked.

"We had a dinner date, remember? No," he corrected himself, "I see you don't remember. Nevertheless, I'm offering you a raincheck. I thought the lobster dinner would be a better idea tonight," he concluded.

She did remember, now, that he'd invited her to have dinner with him at the inn where they'd had their first date. And she could well imagine why he'd thought going for lobster with the Baileys was a better idea. It was not an evening for togetherness. Not with the matter of Hilda Benson's alleged theft pending between them.

"Thanks a lot," he said under his breath, but though Paula had to strain to hear the words, the bitterness came through.

With Tim and Cora right behind them in the backseat she couldn't answer.

The restaurant was nautical in decor, a pleasant, friendly place, and the food was delicious. But much as she ordinarily liked lobster, Paula had little appetite for it tonight.

Tim, Cora, and Russ did almost all the talking. Paula was content to sit back and listen as she sipped a piña colada. The others, she noted, were keeping the conversation on an impersonal plane, this whether by accident or design she didn't know.

It wasn't until they were back at her house again—Tim and Cora having accepted the offer of a liqueur to round out the evening—that the subject of the flea-market thefts came up.

It was Russ who brought it up. He said rather abruptly, "I'm not trying to stir up trouble for myself or anyone else, but I wish you'd give Paula the benefit of your thinking about the Benson woman, Tim."

"I'm not a psychiatrist, Russ," Tim protested mildly.

"True, but you're damned well informed," Russ countered. "Maybe you can convince Paula that there's little chance of Hilda Benson being a kleptomaniac."

Paula stiffened. He was speaking to Tim as if she weren't even in the room. She wanted to tell him that she had ears, she could hear. He could talk to her directly, damn it.

She decided to speak for herself. Avoiding Russ as he'd avoided her, she addressed Tim. "I'm not trying to be stubborn," she said haughtily. "But Hilda Benson is a little old woman, Tim, and I can't believe that she'd steal the way Russ is accusing her of doing. Unless it's some kind of a psychiatric compulsion," she added, drawing upon her memories of her college psychology class.

So there, she thought defiantly, still not looking at Russ.

"Well," Tim said thoughtfully, "as I've already announced, I'm not a psychiatrist. I was a psych major, and abnormal psychology's always fascinated me. But that doesn't mean I'm an authority. However . . ."

"We're not asking for professional credentials, Tim," Russ said impatiently. "Just tell us what you think."

"I've seen Hilda flitting around the flea market all summer," Tim said, "and from what I've observed, from conversations I've had with her, I have to say she doesn't fit in with my idea of a kleptomaniac, Paula.

But that's my idea, mind you. Don't look at me like that, Russ," he added. "I just want to make it clear that if you have doubts, you should go to someone with considerable more knowledge and authority than I have. However . . ."

Tim, Paula decided, really *was* behaving like a college professor. He leaned back, considering what he was going to say next, and then stated, "I'm sure I'm not telling you anything you don't already know when I say that kleptomania is loosely defined as compulsive stealing. That's to say, a kleptomaniac steals because stealing releases an underlying tension. He's moved by neurotic impulses rather than a desire or need for economic gain.

"Kleptomaniacs usually are loaded with frustrations —often subconscious ones, to be sure—and hostilities as well. A good psychiatrist can do a lot with them. They require a great deal of understanding, and treatments designed at ferreting out their deep-seated motives for the things they do. If you think of the type of personality I'm talking about, well, I'm no expert, but I don't see Hilda Benson in that light," Tim said frankly.

"I see Hilda Benson as a con artist," Russ said bluntly. "And I don't think her husband's more than a step or two behind her. You can bet they're taking full advantage of the facts that they're little and old. Hilda's also garrulous, friendly; she works her way in with people."

"You're very harsh," Paula said into the silence that followed Russ's pronouncement. "Personally, I would hate to pass judgment on people as you seem able to do so easily. I suppose it's to be expected that someone like yourself, who's always had all the advantages, might tend to be scornful of people who aren't so physically attractive, or so successful, or so privileged. But I don't think much of your attitude. I find you arrogant and insensitive and I don't think you know the meaning of the word *compassion*."

She heard Cora Bailey draw in her breath, and knew she'd shocked her. Tim Bailey looked absolutely thunderstruck. But it was Russ whose expression drew her, and in a moment she'd never forget she saw raw pain in his green eyes, and hurt, deep hurt, etched upon his face before he drew back into his shell again.

For the millionth time Paula cursed her impulsive tongue and wished she could take back those words she'd just spoken.

Cora said, "Paula . . ." and then shook her head, losing whatever it was she'd been about to say.

"It's okay," Russ said, this remark directed to Paula. He managed to smile, and he said, "Everyone has a right to his or her opinion. Also, as Paula pointed out to me earlier in the day, she's the one whose antiques have been stolen. This is her case, not mine. If she doesn't wish to pursue it, that's her business."

He stood, putting his empty liqueur glass on the old cobbler's bench that served as a coffee table. "If you'll excuse me," he said, "I'd better be getting along."

Paula couldn't answer him. She could only murmur a stereotyped reply when he said, "Good night, Paula," and made for the door. Then she heard the door thud close, heard his van starting up, and she felt her heart begin to shatter.

The Baileys had gotten up, too. She knew they were about to leave, she knew she should see them to the door, but she couldn't move. She put her head in her hands and all that was needed to tip her over the edge was Cora saying, "Don't, dear. You shouldn't have said what you did, but Russ has broad shoulders. It will be all right."

That did it. Paula began to rock back and forth, and then the tears came. She felt Cora's arms steal around her, and Cora said, "Paula, my dear, my dear. Russ won't hold it against you. He's a forgiving person, he'll understand."

"No, he won't," Paula moaned. "There's no reason why he should." She couldn't hold back the words any longer. "Oh, Cora," she sobbed, "I love him. I love him so much!"

Paula woke up at six o'clock Sunday morning as if she'd been programmed to do exactly that. She made a face at the clock on her bedside table, turned over, and tried to go back to sleep again, but it was no use.

She'd decided last night that she wouldn't go to the flea market today. She couldn't face Russ. Not yet. She needed a little time; he also probably needed a little time.

After a while, though, she admitted to herself that she had to go. She had to see him even if he turned his back on her and refused to have anything to do with her.

What she was hoping was that Percy and Hilda Benson would be at the flea market today. That would solve everything. If they were there, Paula decided, she'd come right out and talk to them about the moonstone pendant and, depending upon what they said, she'd take it from there.

She lugged all of her things out to the car, and was at the flea market shortly after eight o'clock. Most of the dealers had already set up, and Paula was glad she had a space reserved for her. Thanks to Russ, she reminded herself.

She was first at their scene, and she wondered if Russ had overslept again. She'd had a fitful night's sleep herself. She'd missed him so terribly; she'd wanted him so much. In the middle of the night she'd been tempted to get into her car and drive out to his place in Truro. She'd wanted to beg his forgiveness for what she'd said, to plead for his understanding, to ask him to give her a little more time to get used to everything that had been happening.

She hadn't done that, though. Instead, she'd drifted back to sleep again and fallen into the clutches of a nightmare.

She felt as if the nightmare were returning as morning ended and there was still no sign of Russ. By noon she was willing to admit to herself that he wasn't coming.

It was a bad day. As Maybelle usually put it, the customers today were "browsers not buyers," and so Paula didn't even have any good sales to make her feel better.

Maybelle, still somewhat hoarse, sauntered by around noon and offered to watch Paula's tables while she went to the rest room and got herself a bite to eat. Paula took advantage of the offer, but she didn't pause to get anything to eat. The best food in the world wouldn't have tempted her today. She was too heart-sick to even think about eating.

Maybelle lingered to chat with her for a few minutes and then wandered back to join Cholly, and next it was Tim who stopped by for a visit, and she saw his eyebrows go up when he realized Russ wasn't on the premises today.

He confined his conversation to books, though. Several more of Paula's volumes had sold, and he told her he'd be having a fairly decent check for her.

Then, toward the middle of the afternoon, Paula was roused from a private reverie by the sound of her own name.

She looked up, to see Percy Benson loitering at the end of the table nearest her. He was wearing an old-fashioned Panama hat, the brim pulled low, almost as if he didn't want to be recognized, and a dark blue suit that didn't look at all like the assorted garb he usually wore to the flea market.

He glanced from side to side as Paula approached him, and she nearly smiled. She hadn't realized that Percy could be so melodramatic. Then she saw the expression on his face, and she sobered. She'd never seen a man look quite so worried.

"Here," he said, holding out his hand, and instinctively she stretched hers out to meet it. She felt something small and hard drop into her palm, and she gazed down to find, to her astonishment, that she was holding the moonstone pendant.

"I gotta trust you," Percy said urgently. "Look, you gotta swear to me you'll never tell a soul about this."

"What are you talking about, Percy?" Paula asked him.

"It's Hilda's old trouble, flared up again," Percy said, his dark, beady eyes desperate. "Paula, she's had this sickness ever since she was a kid, you understand? She's been to doctors about it. For a long time everything's been okay, but lately, well, lately it's come back on her again. Know what I mean?"

Paula shook her head. "I'm not sure I do."

"Hilda can't help herself," Percy said defensively. "She's as honest as the day is long, Paula, you know Hilda. She's got a heart like pure gold, there's nothing she wouldn't do for people. But when the sickness comes over her she, well, she steals, Paula." Percy looked so ashamed as he said this that Paula felt a wrench of pity for him.

She asked softly, "Are you saying Hilda is a kleptomaniac?"

"That's what the doctors told us," Percy nodded. "It's been that way ever since she was a kid. Hilda had a rough time when she was a kid; her parents were mean to her." Percy shook his head. "I still hate to think about the things she's told me they done to her, Paula. Anyway, she's straightened out. Most of the time now when she takes something she can't stand to face up to anybody. She was embarrassed to hell and gone when she realized she took this from you. She said to me, 'Percy, if we had a daughter, I'd like her to be just like Paula . . .'"

"Look," Paula said, "I understand. Tell Hilda I understand, will you, Percy?"

"She don't think you'll ever forgive her," Percy said.

"I will, I already have," Paula tried to assure him. "Percy, thank you for telling me this."

"It's okay, it's okay," Percy said. "When Hilda came

to her senses, she wouldn't have kept that necklace for nothing, Paula.''

Paula nodded, blinking down at the pendant she was holding, and when she looked up again Percy was gone. She marveled at how quickly he'd disappeared into the crowd. But then, he was a small man, and inconspicuous when he was dressed as conservatively as he was today.

She put the pendant into Gram's jewel box and, ironically, a woman came along fifteen minutes later and bought it.

Paula had never been so glad to wrap anything up and hand it over. This time, it wasn't because of the money she was getting. Rather, the pendant was a thorn, she knew that if she'd kept it, it would always have reminded her of the impasse it had caused between Russ and herself.

Well, she'd been right, Russ had been wrong. Hilda *was* a kleptomaniac, and so should not be condemned by anyone.

But Paula's victory about this was a hollow one. So hollow, in fact, that she decided to keep what Percy had told her about Hilda to herself, at least for the time being. She wasn't in an I-told-you-so mood. Rather, she wanted nothing so much as to make peace with Russ. She left the flea market earlier than she usually did, and as she drove across the Cape to her house she was praying, not for the first time, that Russ's car would be parked in her driveway. But it wasn't.

All that Sunday evening Paula berated herself because she'd never had a phone put in the house. She'd made it ridiculously difficult for anyone to get in touch with her.

By midnight, Paula needed action. She drove into Wellfleet Center to a public phone booth and dialed Russ's house in Truro. He'd insisted one time that she put down the number, which was unlisted, in case she ever needed him.

She let the phone ring and ring and ring, but there

was no answer. Probably, she told herself, he was with Helen and Carleton Edgeworth. Or with Tim and Cora Bailey. Or maybe he'd asked someone he knew to go out to dinner with him at the charming old inn where they'd had their first date.

She didn't want to think about that first date. She didn't want to think about anything that had happened since that special Sunday when she'd first met him. It hurt too much.

Paula went home and made herself a stiff drink with Russ's bourbon, and went to bed.

By Tuesday afternoon Paula couldn't stand it any longer. She got into her car and drove out to Truro, then concentrated on finding the right set of dirt lanes that would take her to Russ's house.

She didn't care how angry he was with her, what he'd said to her, what he'd done to her. She had to make amends.

But as she approached the sandy space at the end of his lane where he always kept his car, her heart sank. The space was vacant. Nevertheless, she parked her car and climbed up the flight of weathered steps to his house.

There was a shuttered look to it. The window blinds had all been drawn to the same level, and already it had the atmosphere of a place that wasn't lived in.

Paula moved around to the front, standing on the deck where she'd stood with Russ's arms around her. She peered at the beach where they'd walked, as if expecting to see him materialize. But the beach today was occupied by only a few terns and sea gulls. She turned to face the living room picture window, and she even went so far as to move close to it and cup her hands over her eyes as she pressed her face to the glass to look into emptiness. There was nothing out of place. Then, by the door they usually used to enter the house, she saw a small red light, and it was on.

Russ had mentioned that he'd had an alarm system installed in the place because he so seldom used it.

"Vandalism's a pain, even if nothing's stolen," he'd said.

Well, the alarm system was on, Paula thought sickly. Which meant that Russ, definitely, was no longer in residence. He was gone. Gone for good, she thought, and felt such a heaviness, it was all she could do to trudge back down the steps again.

For a time she sat on the bottom step in a state of shock. Russ was gone, and she knew deep in her heart that he wasn't coming back to her again.

She'd known that sooner or later it was going to come to an end between them. She'd known that ever since his friend Gerald Van Ness had made his ill-timed revelation. But she hadn't expected the end to come like this. Rather, she'd imagined that they would simply drift apart once the summer was over. No hard feelings. No recriminations.

Paula shook her head helplessly and stumbled back to the car like a person who's had too much to drink. She was still in a trance as she drove back to Wellfleet, and as it happened the timing was exactly right. She saw the real estate office sign in the small shopping complex at the edge of town out of the corner of her eye, and she pulled into the office parking lot as if this had been what she'd been going to do all along.

Bob Mathews had also been a friend of Gram's, and Paula had planned to approach him before she left town about renting her house next summer, provided she could do something about the roof in the meantime. But now, as he invited her into his office and she faced him across a big old mahogany desk, she knew that she'd cast her die with destiny, and was about to take an entirely different course of action.

"Bob," she said, "I've been thinking things over. I've decided to put my house up for sale."

Chapter Fourteen

The apartment in Acton was even dustier than Paula had expected it would be. It was also hot, airless, and so small—after living in a house all summer—that she felt cramped.

Cramped and frustrated. Over the Labor Day weekend she cleaned and washed and ironed clothes, trying to sweep out not only the physical cobwebs but the mental and emotional ones, which were considerably more important. But she discovered that she couldn't wrest Russell Parkhurst out of her mind.

Russ haunted her. Also, every time she drove past the nursing home where Gram had lived last year, she ached anew. If only she had Gram to turn to now! She desperately needed someone she could talk to, really talk to. Someone to whom she could pour out all her feelings about Russ, her love for him, her longings.

Although she'd always looked forward to the beginning of school, and the challenge of facing a new group of fourth-graders, school was different this year, too. Mr. Broadhurst, who'd been the principal all the time Paula had been teaching in Acton's Ellington Forest School, had retired at the end of the previous school year. His replacement was a younger man, aggressive and demanding, and he was difficult to work with. He had a habit of dropping in on the different classes unexpectedly, and it seemed to Paula that he always arrived in her classroom at the worst possible moment, when it looked as if she'd totally lost control of the reins of discipline. This wasn't so. She'd always handled her students well, but she did believe in letting them express themselves upon occasion. They were at an exuberant age; they needed outlets. She liked to challenge their imaginations, and sometimes they became pretty boisterous in the course of discussion. Mr. Broadhurst had commended this. Mr. Claxton didn't.

By the end of September, Paula felt as if she'd been back at teaching for a year instead of a month. The walls of her apartment were closing in on her, everything was closing in on her, and she nearly drove down to the Cape the first weekend in October, just to get away for a couple of days. But she knew that the Cape would be too full of memories. Every grain of sand, every blade of beach grass, would remind her of Russ.

She settled for driving up to New Hampshire, where the leaves were already beginning to take on autumn's beautiful colors. She spent the night in an old inn, and was given a room with a wood-burning fireplace. All she could think about was how Russ would have loved the place, and how wonderful it would have been to have him here with her.

New thoughts were beginning to stir in her mind about him. Thinking back to the things he'd said to her after that terrible day when she'd found out who he was, she could see that she hadn't really listened to him. She'd been too blinded by the sudden revelation of his real identity.

Cora Bailey had implored her to try to understand how the world had always been from Russ's viewpoint. She'd tried to make her see how difficult it had been for Russ to ever know anyone on a purely person-to-person plane. Russ himself had tried to make her understand that. And she hadn't.

I was as bad as all the rest of them, she told herself now. *It got to the point where all I could see was the figurehead rather than the man I'd fallen in love with.*

So, Russ had given up on her. She could hardly blame him, she admitted, as she took the cable up to the top of Cannon Mountain on a Saturday afternoon, walking along some of the trails at the top and wishing, again, that Russ was here to enjoy this with her.

Sunday, on her way back to Boston, Paula remembered that Angela Smith, one of the older teachers at the Ellington Forest School, was presently a patient at New England Medical Center. On the spur of the moment she decided to stop and visit her.

Angela was recuperating well, and would be out of the hospital in a few more days. Nevertheless, there was a lassitude to the older woman's manner that Paula found dismaying. She was pleased to discover that Angela brightened up as they talked together about the different things that had been going on at the school, and the people they knew. Finally Angela confessed that she had no family and sometimes felt herself very much alone, and Paula realized that this was the root of her problem. She determined that, come Monday, she'd tell the other teachers Angela needed a dose of caring more than anything else, and she was sure they'd come through to help pull this very nice person out of an understandable bout of depression.

Paula had skipped lunch that day and had had only tea and a single piece of toast at an early breakfast, so she paused in the coffee shop on her way out of the hospital. As she stood in the cafeteria line, she was musing about Angela, and about being well into one's fifties, and alone. It would be easy to reach a point

where you'd feel no one really cared, which very
probably wouldn't be true at all. In order to have any
kind of relationships it was necessary to communicate.
An exchange between people had to work both ways.
Recalling Angela at the school, Paula remembered that
she'd always been a bit withdrawn, even a little aloof.
Probably people stayed out of her path because they
didn't think she wanted them in it.

This conjecture made Paula vaguely uncomfortable.
Of late, she'd tended to be withdrawn as well, staying
pretty much to herself. It wasn't difficult to work up a
vision of herself thirty years down the road, alone and
lonely just as Angela was.

She was nibbling on a tuna fish sandwich as she
thought this, and she shivered. It wasn't a very pleasant
glimpse into the future.

At her elbow a hauntingly familiar voice exclaimed,
"Paula!" And she looked up into Russ Parkhurst's
unsmiling face.

She dropped the sandwich, and fortunately it landed
on the plate just under it. She began to shake inwardly,
and knew she was on the verge of coming completely
unglued. Russ was wearing a three-piece gray tweed
suit that must have been made by one of the best tailors
in the world. He'd had a haircut recently, she guessed;
his smooth dark hair was even more perfectly con-
toured than usual. But the expression in his eyes
stopped her. They looked as if they'd been glazed; she
couldn't see into them, she couldn't read them at all.

"What are you doing here?" he asked abruptly, and
she became aware of the dark shadows under his eyes,
and the taut line to his mouth. He'd lost some of his
summer tan, and he looked thinner. Fear clutched at
Paula. Was it possible that he'd had a recurrence of the
terrible disease from which he'd suffered so many years
ago? Was he ill again?

She said shakily, "I was visiting a friend. And you?"

"Carleton Edgeworth had his bypass surgery last
week," he said.

"Oh. How is he?" she asked anxiously.

"Doing very well, thank you. Helen's with him, she's going to join me here for coffee." As he spoke, Russ glanced first at his slim gold wrist watch, then toward the door.

"Ah, there she is," he said, and Paula, following his glance, saw Helen Edgeworth starting across toward them. Helen was dressed in a stunning gray designer suit. She and Russ were a perfectly matched pair, Paula thought, disheartened because she was sure she could never live up to either one of them. Helen could have been the mother, Russ the son.

But she couldn't deny the look of delight in Helen's eyes or the genuine pleasure in her voice as she said, "Paula, what a wonderful surprise!"

"Russ has been telling me your husband's doing very well, Mrs. Edgeworth," Paula said. "I'm so glad."

"We're all very happy about his progress," Helen said. She turned to Russ. "I just spoke to the surgeon, and he says Carleton's doing exceptionally well," she reported.

Russ nodded without answering her, then asked, "Would you like coffee, Helen?"

"Please."

"Can I get you anything, Paula?"

"No," Paula said. "No, thank you."

She tried not to watch him as he walked toward the cafeteria line, but it was impossible to refrain from visually following his tall, beloved figure.

Helen, at her elbow, said gently, "Your heart is in your eyes, Paula."

Paula smiled tremulously. "That's what I was afraid of," she confessed.

"Paula, you can tell me it's none of my business if you like, but why have you and Russell stopped seeing each other?" Helen queried.

"It wasn't a question of our stopping seeing each other," Paula said. "He went away. That's to say, he left the Cape suddenly."

"Because you'd had a quarrel?"

Paula nodded. "In a sense, yes. That is, we didn't actually *quarrel* but we had . . . quite a misunderstanding."

"He's coming back," Helen warned. "Please, don't leave before he does, Paula. I'd like so much to talk to you."

Paula started to say that she really had to get back to Acton, but Russ's arrival preempted this statement.

He'd brought a cup of coffee for Helen and one for himself and nothing else. He drank his coffee black, and he drank it fast. Then, with another glance at the gold watch, he said, "I'll have to grab a taxi and get out to the airport or I'll miss my flight."

Helen nodded somewhat reluctantly. "Very well, Russell."

"I'll be in touch," he promised. He turned to Paula, and she saw the muscle in the side of his jaw twitch, before he spoke. "I hope everything's going well with you," he said.

"Yes, thank you, everything's going fine," she answered, the words almost clumping together into a kind of mumble.

He nodded, then he was gone, and Paula couldn't help herself. Tears filled her eyes, and though she blinked furiously she couldn't get rid of them.

Helen said quietly, "I've a room over at the Copley Plaza, Paula. Could you come back there with me for a little while?"

Would this be wise, or wouldn't it be wise? Would it only be prolonging her agony if she went back to Helen Edgeworth's hotel with her? Helen would want to talk to her about Russ, she knew, and this would hurt. She felt as if, just now, he'd rejected her all over again.

Still, she couldn't refuse the chance to hear about him, even a little bit, from one of the few people in the world she knew who knew him.

She nodded, but managed to insert a small escape valve by saying, "I can't stay too long."

Paula had put her car in a parking garage, so she and Helen decided it would be simpler to taxi to the hotel. Helen had a beautifully furnished corner room, and to Paula's surprise the first thing she did once inside the door was to kick off her elegant leather pumps.

"They pinch," she said, and then curled up in a low armchair with a grace and agility that belied her age. And, all at once, Paula felt relaxed with her.

"All the time we were in Chatham," Helen said, "I was wishing you'd call me up, or simply come over, Paula."

Paula stared at her in astonishment, and Helen nodded wisely. "Oh, I can see why you didn't," she said. "We must have seemed quite austere to you, but we're not."

"You didn't seem austere," Paula said. "You and your husband were both warm and friendly to me. It was just—"

"I know," Helen said. "Russell has told me that the one thing he doesn't like about our house is that it reminds him of the homes where he grew up. But there is a difference. Regardless of the outward formality, which I admit to, there is a lot of love in our house. There has been a lot of warmth and laughter over the years. The same can't be said about the places Russell lived in. He had a lonely childhood, and then there were those terrible years where he was fighting for his health. He would hate hearing me make this kind of a case for him, Paula. The last thing he ever wanted from anyone—even when he was flat on his back in a Swiss sanatorium—was pity. But I think you need to know a lot about a person to fully understand them. And, you see, I want you to fully understand Russell. He needs you so much."

Paula slowly shook her head at this. Then she said, her voice thick, "I wish that was true. But I don't think Russ needs me at all, Helen. I'm sure he's doing very well without me."

"Outwardly, yes," Helen agreed. "Inwardly

. . . well, I don't think so. I've known Russell a long time, but I've never seen him react to a woman as he does to you. I think he cares very deeply about you. And from the expression on your face in the hospital cafeteria a little while ago, I'd say you return that caring. When Russell brought you to our house that night, I could see that you were very special to him. This may sound odd to you, but I sensed that he was so vulnerable where you were concerned, that my one fear was that you might hurt him. Now," Helen admitted wryly, "I'm not sure who's hurting whom. Only that it seems to me that both of you are suffering."

Paula said unsteadily, "Russ is the one who shut up his house in Truro and took off. He's the one who left."

"Yes, it's true he left physically," Helen agreed. "But you'd already left *him* in other and more important ways, wouldn't you say? Russell and I spent some anxious hours last week waiting for Carleton to come out of the recovery room. He didn't say much about you—he was very tight-lipped—but from the little he did say I received the impression that the minute you learned his last name was Parkhurst rather than Grayson, everything changed between you."

Putting it that way made it sound so simple. She'd learned his last name was Parkhurst rather than Grayson, and it had changed her world.

Paula said sadly, "Unfortunately, what you're saying is true, Mrs. Edgeworth."

"Helen, please," Helen Edgeworth urged.

"Helen, then." Paula nodded. She continued. "Yes, everything changed when I found out Russ's full name. It was such a shock. And . . . I hated it."

"You hated discovering that Russell was an extremely wealthy and eligible young man?" Helen asked, a curious note in her voice.

"Oh, very much so. I knew all along that Russ wasn't lacking money. He had expensive cars, expensive clothes, a certain air about him. But I could deal with that. I couldn't deal with the magnitude of the whole thing when I found out who he really was. Can't you understand that?"

"Not entirely," Helen confessed. "You'd already fallen in love with Russell, if I'm understanding you correctly. Wasn't that the most important thing?"

"Yes, of course it was," Paula said hastily, and then stopped short. "Yes, of course it was the most important thing," she continued more slowly. "But you see, what I discovered was that Russ wasn't . . . Russ."

"Did you?" Helen asked. "Is that really what you discovered, Paula? It seems to me that Russell didn't change because of what you learned about him. You did."

This hit home.

Helen didn't belabor the subject. She switched to talking about Paula herself, and it wasn't until later that Paula realized how skillfully she'd been questioned. Helen surely must have made an excellent diplomat's wife, she thought ruefully as she drove back to Acton. She'd literally told Helen all her troubles by the time the afternoon was over, including her decision to finally put the house up for sale.

"I think that was a wise thing for you to do," Helen had nodded. "It's been too much for you to tackle at this stage of your life. I know how difficult a decision it must have been for you," she added quickly. "But when something becomes a burden, it ceases to be enjoyable, or, sometimes, even tolerable," she finished.

Well, Helen was right. Gram's house had become too much of a burden to her at this stage of her life. To keep it would mean giving up absolutely everything else, and she wasn't sure she could do it even then.

Much as she needed to sell the house, though, Paula dreaded the day when the sale would actually take place. Among other things, she'd have to go back to clear out the furnishings, and at that point she would have to make a final decision about disposing of most of her antiques. She decided to look into some of the

Boston antique shops, and knew this was something she should do now instead of waiting till the last minute. But she couldn't bring herself to take that next step. Bob Mathews had warned her, anyway, that it was unlikely the house would sell till spring, unless it sold before the end of October. It was already close to the end of October, and as each day clicked by on the calendar Paula felt as if she'd been given a reprieve.

Then the Saturday morning came when her phone rang, and it was Bob Mathews.

"I think we've got us a sale," he announced jubilantly.

Paula knew she should be sharing his enthusiasm, but she couldn't. "That's great, Bob," she managed to say weakly.

"There's a catch, Paula, but I hope it's not going to be a serious one," he told her. "The prospective buyer wants to take possession as soon as papers can be passed. Matter of fact, the date I've been given is November fifteenth. Would that be possible for you? I know it means coming down here and looking a lot of stuff over."

November fifteenth! "That's only three weeks, Bob," Paula protested. "I don't see how I could possibly handle it."

"It would be worth an all-out effort," he said seriously. "I honestly think this may be the best offer you'll have for quite a while."

"I don't know, I don't know," Paula said, frantically trying to sort through her thoughts. "There's so much to arrange, Bob. I should have gotten to everything sooner, I know that, but at the time I listed the house with you I, well, I wasn't thinking too smartly about anything."

Only about Russ, she reminded herself silently.

"Paula, I'll do anything I can to help you," the real estate agent promised. "I know what your circumstances are; I'd hate to see you lose this chance. Odds are that if we don't make the sale now, the house'll sit idle through the winter, and that won't do anyone any good. The buyer has already spoken to me about getting someone to put on a new roof, and even with that there's been no quibbling about the price. It's a real opportunity, Paula."

She believed him. Nevertheless, now that the moment was at hand, she was finding it very hard to face up to it. The Cape had always played such an important role in her life, and Gram's house spelled stability to her.

Grow up, she told herself tersely, and spoke into the phone again. "Can you give a tentative yes?" she asked Bob Mathews.

"I imagine so."

"I'm not trying to stall, Bob," Paula told him. "I do need to make arrangements at school to take a few days off, and our new principal isn't the easiest man in the world to deal with. Let me see what I can arrange."

"Okay," he agreed. "I'll also see what I can arrange at this end."

He called again the following morning, and he was elated.

"I think we've solved the problem," he said. "Our buyer is an antique buff, and she's interested in buying the furnishings if you can agree to a price. I think the only thing to do is come down here, Paula. Mrs. Baldwin has to go back to New York this afternoon, but she says she can meet you at the house early next Saturday afternoon, if that's convenient for you. You can go over the contents together. I won't need to sit in on it."

How could she face up to this? Paula felt sick as she thought of turning over everything she owned in the world to a total stranger, even though she would be getting paid for it.

Damn money! she thought. It really *is* the root of all evil.

There was nothing logical to say to Bob Mathews, though, except yes. And the meeting was arranged for one o'clock the following Saturday afternoon.

It was a beautiful late fall day, but there was an edge of sadness to it for Paula, not only because of what she was facing but because of the weather itself. The leaves were drifting off the trees, and newly bare branches seemed to telegraph the message that winter was not far away. Usually, Paula loved winter, she loved the crisp cold air in New England and the pure whiteness of the snow. She liked to skate and to ski and normally took advantage of every opportunity that came her way to participate in winter sports. But this year there was no joy to the prospect of doing any of the things she usually did because she'd be doing them alone. Even if she were with other people, she'd be alone. She'd always be alone without Russ.

She tried to force him out of her mind as she drove toward the Cape, but the closer she got to Wellfleet the more he intruded into her thoughts, into every fiber of her being, and she felt like a woman possessed.

She drove directly to the house, as Bob Mathews had suggested, to find that the prospective buyer had gotten there ahead of her. And when she saw the blue sedan in her driveway, reality struck like an arctic wave.

Subconsciously, she'd been nurturing the crazy hope that maybe it was Russ who was buying her house. She'd fantasized that Russ somehow had been motivated to do this, to come back to her, to make a place for them in which they could live happily ever after. But the sight of the blue car convinced her, as nothing else could have, that she was dealing with life in all its grimness, and not a fairy tale.

The woman who walked around the end of the house reminded Paula of Helen Edgeworth at first glance. She was tall and slim, she had silver-gray rather than white hair, and she was beautifully dressed, her dark brown coat cut in the latest fashion.

As they introduced themselves to each other, Paula

found herself liking Martha Baldwin. Definitely, she'd been made from Helen's mold. They could have gone to the same school. She had the same grace, poise, and diction.

Paula soon found that Mrs. Baldwin was also very knowledgeable about antiques. As they moved from room to room she saw that this woman had a genuine appreciation for fine old things, and she began to feel better about her house passing into Martha Baldwin's slender white hands.

Price presented no problem. They came to a ready agreement, and the only awkward moment was when Mrs. Baldwin asked what things Paula would want to keep for herself.

She'd already taken her personal possessions to Acton, and a few odds and ends that were really dear to her. Now she hesitated and said, "I think the only two things I really must have are an old copy of *Robinson Crusoe* and a Canton ginger jar."

"That's all?" Mrs. Baldwin asked, looking at her curiously.

"Yes," Paula said firmly. "That's all, and I can take them with me today. I think you'll find everything else in order, Mrs. Baldwin. I'll leave all the kitchen things and the bed linens—not that they're all that great. But they'll give you something to start with when you move in."

As she spoke of this Paula was thinking of the meals she and Russ had eaten together in the kitchen, and the transcending times they'd shared upstairs, in her maple bed. And her composure nearly faltered.

Her nerves were stretched by the time the interview was over, even though Martha Baldwin could not have been more pleasant. She made one last check of her beloved house and its contents, trying to pretend that she was leaving it only for the weekend rather than forever. She'd thought of stopping by at Bob Mathews's office on her way out of town, but she was too upset to do so, her nerves far too frazzled. She decided it would do to call him in the morning and tell him she and Mrs. Baldwin had come to terms. Mrs. Baldwin might already have contacted him herself by then, for that matter.

As she drove over the Cape Cod Canal, Paula had the feeling that she was putting a huge chunk of her life behind her. She tried to look positively at this, tried to tell herself that now she'd have some money to do things with. She could travel. She'd always wanted to travel. She could take a short trip to the Caribbean on the February break, she could go to Europe next summer, or Alaska, or somewhere. But there was no joy in the thought of any of this.

The problem was that she'd still be alone.

It was Russ who'd turned out to be the Gypsy, she told herself. It was he who'd woven the magic spell, ensnaring her so that there was no way at all she could ever be free of him.

Chapter Fifteen

The letter was waiting in Paula's mailbox when she got home from school on an early November Wednesday afternoon. It had a Florida postmark but there was no return address on the envelope and she was curious, as she ripped it open, as to whom it might be from.

She searched for the signature first, and saw that Cora Bailey was the writer. Seeing Cora's name evoked a whole string of memories. Cora and Tim, Maybelle and Cholly, the flea market—would she ever be able to think of any of these people, or of the flea market, without suffering the kind of pain a deep loss incurs? They—and the flea market—were so tied up with Russ in her memory.

As she glanced down at Cora's letter she was almost afraid to start reading it. There was a chance the Baileys had been in touch with Russ, and she wasn't

sure she wanted to hear about it, if so. It had done her
no good at all to see him so briefly, and then to talk
about him to Helen Edgeworth. It had helped to be
able to confide in someone else, to pour out her soul.
But it had been a very temporary release.

After she'd left Helen that day, she'd realized she'd
forgotten to give the older woman her address or phone
number, and she wasn't listed in the directory. She
could, of course, undoubtedly have gotten in touch
with Helen simply by sending a letter to Mrs. Carleton Edgeworth in Chatham, Massachusetts. But she
hadn't done this, and though she'd been tempted,
she had made up her mind not to. There was no
point to deliberately inflicting pain on herself. And
that's what talking to Helen about Russ again would
do.

Now she started to read Cora's letter, then almost at
once her attention was riveted to the page because this
wasn't what she had expected at all. Cora wrote:

> Tim and I arrived in Florida last week. It's early
> in the season, but we thought we should scout
> things out before all the snowbirds arrive down
> here and I'm glad we did.
> We went to a big flea market over near Ocala
> on Sunday, and would you believe it, almost the
> first people we saw there were Maybelle and
> Cholly Stevens. Tim and I felt like we'd found a
> couple of long-lost friends.

Paula smiled as she read that. She couldn't imagine
two more different couples than the Baileys and the
Stevenses, but dealing in flea markets had a way of
injecting people with a real camaraderie. Cora went on
to write:

> After the market closed that day, we went out
> for tacos and beer, and Cholly and Maybelle told
> us quite a story. I think it's something you'll want

to know about. Matter of fact, Maybelle says she's sure she kept a clipping about it, and you'll probably get a letter from her enclosing it in a couple of days. Friends of hers who live in the area where this happened and knew that the Stevenses hit a lot of the flea markets sent the newspaper story to Maybelle.

It seems that on their annual pilgrimage south, Hilda and Percy Benson set up at a flea market in South Carolina. This time they didn't get away with the game they've evidently been playing for quit a number of years. It was a relatively small flea market, and Hilda was spotted filching an antique necklace. The flea-market operators had been having trouble with thievery, so they hired a detective in plain clothes to watch the Bensons for the next couple of days, and they struck pay dirt.

Hilda and Percy haul their own small mobile home when they travel. A warrant was obtained, the trailer was searched, and what a horde the police found! I feel sure all the things Hilda took from you must be among it. Maybe if you contacted the authorities in the town—I don't have the name of it, but it will surely be on the masthead of the clipping Maybelle sends you—something could be done about having your property returned to you.

Meantime, the South Carolina police got busy, and in contacting authorities in other states they discovered that Hilda and Percy have quite a record. Hard to believe, isn't it? It certainly proves out the old cliché that you can't tell books by their covers.

Russ had seen through the Bensons' "covers." She, on the other hand, had been duped. Paula bit her lip, pausing in her reading of Cora's letter as she remembered the last time she'd seen Percy Benson.

He'd told her such a sad tale of Hilda's miserable

youth, and the affliction that had supposedly plagued Hilda all her life. Paula had already felt certain that there had to be an explanation for Hilda's having taken the moonstone pendant aside from the obvious one that Russ had latched on to so quickly. So Percy had had no trouble at all in convincing her that Hilda's compulsion stemmed from a psychosis that had tormented her most of her life.

She'd felt so sorry for Hilda and Percy, Paula thought resentfully. And she'd turned on Russ so bitterly, convinced that he simply had no sympathy for people who'd been born less fortunate than he was.

How wrong she'd been! And she should have known better. The signposts had been there all along. Russ had been unfailingly courteous, kind, and considerate from the the very beginning of their relationship. If he'd become irked with her at times—even angry—it had been because she'd provoked him. There was nothing plastic about Russ's personality. His wealth hadn't fitted him into any mold at all. He'd had to conform to some things, true. He'd had no choice. But he'd made it so abundantly clear, time and again, that all he really wanted was to be himself. He'd wanted to share his love with her, he'd wanted to share himself with her, but once she'd found out who he really was, she'd drawn back. She hadn't wanted to . . . at moments she'd tried very hard not to. But Helen Edgeworth had been right.

It was Paula who'd changed, not Russ. Russ had been Russell Parkhurst all along. In coming to the flea market he'd changed his name, but not his identity. Basically, he'd been himself.

She hadn't been able to see that and it would still be hard, she admitted, even now when she could understand much more about Russ and his motivations than she had at the time.

Hard, but maybe not impossible.

But it was too late to conjecture about what might have been, and there was no point at all in stirring up her imagination about what might be if she and Russ were to come together again. Paula returned to her reading of Cora's letter, and the story got worse instead of better.

According to the newspaper story, Hilda and her husband have been working this scam for years. They've been stealing in the North all summer and then selling the stolen merchandise in the South come winter, and vice versa. No wonder it was so difficult to get to the root of anything, Paula. You were dealing with professional crooks. Real swindlers.

So, as it turns out, Tim and Russ were both right. I was somewhat on the fence, and you thought you were championing a falsely accused underdog. Ah, well, my dear. We learn something new every day.

With that Cora went on to say that she and Tim had decided to move on to the Gulf Coast for a while, en route to Texas, and she'd send along an address where they could be reached as soon as they had one.

Maybelle's letter came two days later. It was short—Maybelle wasn't much of a writer—and it concluded, "Can you beat it?" Then there was a hastily scrawled postscript: "Cholly sends his love."

Paula unfolded the clipping Maybelle had enclosed. Pictures of Hilda and Percy Benson stared up at her, and the account of their escapades was a long one. Paula read it once, read it again, and was tempted to read it still a third time. The newspaper story made it clear that this wouldn't be the first occasion when the Bensons had spent some time in jail. But Paula didn't doubt that they'd somehow wangle out of much of their sentence and would more than likely be back at their old flea-market stands come another summer.

She and Russ were the ones who would not be doing business at the flea market, Paula thought sadly. Remembering him in his Great Gatsby hat, with those oversize sunglasses, she felt as if she'd been hit in the chest with a hard, unyielding object that had knocked all the breath out of her and left only a dull ache.

Maybelle's letter had been in the box when Paula had gotten home from school, this time on Friday. It was late afternoon when she'd finished reading it. Restless, she put her coat on and drove over to Walden Pond, where the great naturalist Henry Thoreau had lived in another century. Parking her car, she struck out on a woodland trail. It was a raw November day, the sky overcast, only the last of the most tenacious leaves, withered and brown, still clinging to the tree branches. Paula walked and walked and walked until it became too dark to see clearly any more. Then, because she couldn't face the emptiness of her apartment, she drove to a Chinese restaurant on the Great Road and ordered a bowl of steaming, fragrant soup laden with noodles and thin slices of roast pork. It was delicious, but she couldn't finish it. Being in a Chinese restaurant reminded her too much of the times when Russ had taken her to the Double Dragon in Orleans. Once they'd drunk a rum concoction called Love Potion, and Russ had laughed and said, "Not that we need one."

As they hadn't.

When she finally did go back to her apartment, after browsing around a small shopping mall and buying a couple of paperback novels she hoped would offer escape from her problems, Paula couldn't settle down. As if for emphasis, she read both Cora's letter and Maybelle's letter over again, and then she knew what she had to do.

She owed Russ an apology. She didn't expect that making it would alter anything that had happened between them. She didn't expect a miracle just because she'd say, "You were right and I was wrong." But this was something she had to say to him anyway. She felt deeply that she owed this to him.

She wanted to reach him by phone right now before she lost her courage, but her problem was that she had no phone number for him. She tried asking Information for the number of Russell Grayson Parkhurst III in Manhattan, only to be informed politely that the number was unlisted—as she'd expected it would be. She dialed the Truro house in the event that maybe there'd be an answering machine with a referral of some sort, but there wasn't. The phone merely rang and rang and rang. Paula could picture Russ's beach house empty and in darkness, and it was a very forlorn picture.

Tim and Cora might have a number where he could be reached, but she didn't know where to get in touch with them. This left Helen Edgeworth. Once again Paula consulted Information, to be told that Carleton Edgeworth's Chatham number was, also, unlisted.

So much for the wealthy and their desire for privacy, she thought bitterly. And then she remembered that her own phone number, here in her Acton apartment, was unlisted. She'd done this because she didn't want to be bothered with solicitation calls, and similar small annoyances, and had felt that she could give her number only to the people she wanted to have it.

Had her motivation been so different from either Russ's or the Edgeworths's?

She could write Russ, of course. In the morning she could check out the address of the Parkhurst Galleries —which would be easily obtainable from the telephone directory—and then she could write him and tell him what she'd learned about the Bensons, and how sorry she was, and . . .

She shook her head. This time around, writing a letter wouldn't do. She needed to speak to him. She needed to hear his voice, to judge his reaction to what she would be saying to him. She needed a response from him.

In the morning she decided to call the Parkhurst Galleries in New York, and then had a sudden attack of cold feet. She paced her apartment, trying to get up the courage to dial the gallery's number, in the meantime asking herself why she was being such a damned fool. The worst he could do was to refuse to speak to her.

After a time she decided to do some grocery shopping first, and to make the phone call afterward. It was five minutes after twelve that Saturday when Paula finally sat down at her telephone, to be informed by a polite, recorded message that the Parkhurst Galleries closed at noon on Saturdays, but would be open again for business at ten o'clock Monday morning.

Paula gritted her teeth. Monday she'd be in school, and this was a phone call she couldn't imagine making on the school premises.

Monday turned out to be a terrible day. In the middle of the morning she was summoned to the principal's office, while a substitute came and took over her room in her absence.

Mr. Claxton was at his desk, looking especially forbidding. He was tall and thin and dark, with a parchmentlike complexion, and as far as Paula had ever been able to determine, he had no sense of humor at all.

"It would appear," he said once Paula was seated a discreet distance from his desk, "that some of our parents have issued complaints about you."

"About *me?*" She couldn't believe this. "What kind of complaints, Mr. Claxton?"

"They take exception to the type of books you've been encouraging your pupils to use for their book reports," he said sternly. "And I admit, Miss Danvers, that from what I've been told, your choice of subject matter leaves much to be desired. These are fourth-graders we are dealing with. Young, impressionable children."

"I don't choose the books they read for reports," Paula said, trying to keep her temper in check. It would be folly, and an invitation to disaster as well, to let herself flare out at this man. For one thing, he was cold as steel and just as inflexible. He would resent an outburst on her part, and would take his own kind of measures to deal with it.

Now he asked icily, "How are the books selected, Miss Danvers?"

"The children select them themselves, Mr. Claxton," she told him.

"With no supervision on your part?"

"No," she admitted.

"So they may choose books that deal with—er—with suggestive material not suitable for their age group, or, simply, trash?" he suggested.

"My students choose books that deal with subjects that interest them," Paula said, matching his coolness. "Some of the boys favor science fiction, and I can see no reason why they shouldn't. Some of the girls favor romances, but they are generally romances written for girls in their own age bracket. I can see nothing wrong with that, either."

"I note you use the word *generally*," Mr. Claxton pointed out.

"Yes."

"Then you do admit that there have been specific occasions when reports have been submitted on books that definitely were not suitable?"

"I don't know how you define *suitable*, Mr. Claxton," Paula said wearily. "One of my students submitted a report on a romance novel her mother had been reading, and she'd noted that her mother seemed to enjoy it very much. I didn't feel that I should take her to task—although the book certainly was too mature for her—because this would seem to have been casting a reflection on her mother's judgment. Do you consider me wrong about that?"

"Most certainly." Mr. Claxton said with no pause for contemplation about this at all. "The mother in the case was an adult. You certainly see the difference, don't you, Miss Danvers?"

"Yes, of course," she said. "My feeling was that the

influence should have come from the home rather than from me. That's all."

"You have an important role to perform," Mr. Claxton said, "and I sometimes think you shirk your responsibility as a teacher. You are molding young minds, Miss Danvers. Molding young minds," he repeated. "Need I say more? I suggest that you assign books for reports in the future instead of leaving the choice to your students' discretion."

"They'll still be reading the same kind of books they've been reading, if they want to," Paula could not refrain from pointing out.

"That is not your concern. Your concern is what happens here, in this school," Mr. Claxton stated firmly.

It seemed to Paula that there was a discrepancy in what he'd been saying to her, but she was not about to go into it with him. The man's whole attitude disheartened her. She'd suspected from the first time she'd had to deal with him that he was far more interested in furthering his own career—and playing politics with the School Committee in the process—than he was in his students.

I won't be coming back here next year, she told herself as she left his office. *I'll have to get another job, somehow, somewhere.*

By the time Paula left the school that Monday afternoon it had begun to rain, a cold rain that was closer to sleet. She was shivering as she let herself into the apartment. She quickly switched on lamps to help dispel the gloom, then changed into a soft wool lounger and made herself a cup of cocoa. Only then did she sit down at the phone, staring at the number of the Parkhurst Galleries she'd written down the Saturday before.

It was nearly a quarter to five. Would the galleries still be open? Would Russ be there, even if it was?

Impatient with herself because of her delaying tactics, she reached for the phone, but her fingers were trembling as she dialed the number and when she heard someone say, "Parkhurst Galleries" at the other end of the line she was momentarily tongue-tied.

It was with difficulty that she managed, "May I speak to Mr. Russell Parkhurst?"

"One moment, please," the voice answered impersonally.

Paula heard a couple of clicks at the other end of the line, and this time it was a woman who spoke. "May I help you?" she was asked politely.

"May I speak to Mr. Russell Parkhurst, please?" Paula repeated.

"May I ask who is calling?" the voice countered.

"This is Paula Danvers," Paula said, hating to give her name to this stranger. She wanted to reveal herself only to Russ, she wanted to talk only to Russ.

"I'm sorry, Ms. Danvers," the woman said smoothly, "but Mr. Parkhurst is not available. Could someone else help you?"

"May I ask to whom *I'm* speaking?" Paula queried.

"Yes, of course. I'm Eleanor Grant, Mr. Parkhurst's personal secretary. Perhaps if you could tell me what it was you wanted to discuss with him I could direct you to someone who could be of assistance."

Paula was reminded of a gate, with guards posted all the way around it. Polite guards, but still trained not to let a person through.

"This is a personal matter, Ms. Grant," she said reluctantly.

"Perhaps you could tell me the nature of the matter?" the secretary persisted urbanely.

"No, I most certainly could not," Paula said, anger flaring. She was tired, depressed, discouraged over her job, and she missed Russ desperately. "I think," she said, steadying, "that if you could relay the message to Mr. Parkhurst that I am on the phone, he'd be quite willing to speak to me."

"Mr. Parkhurst is in Europe, Ms. Danvers," Russ's secretary said. "We don't know exactly when he will return, but I'll be happy to leave your name and number with his assistant and any information you wish to give me will be relayed to him."

"There's no need," Paula said bleakly. And remembered to add, "Thank you very much," before she hung up.

In Europe. Russ was in Europe. Where in Europe? On business? For pleasure? Alone? With someone?

Questions raced through Paula's mind, and none of them could be satisfied.

Tuesday morning she was tempted to call the school and say she was sick, this a kind of subterfuge she usually detested. She didn't, but by afternoon she had a dull headache, by evening she'd developed a fever, and for the next three days she lived in solitary confinement, dosing herself with aspirin and fruit juices while she slowly recuperated from a miserable bout of some unidentified virus.

It wasn't until the weekend that she was able to get body and mind together enough to make the decision to write Russ a letter. She made eleven attempts before she was satisfied enough with what she'd written to mail it to him. Even then, she wasn't happy about writing to him at all. Though she marked the envelope "Personal," she suspected that the efficient Ms. Grant might scan all his mail anyway.

Because of this, she was more impersonal than she otherwise would have been.

"I wanted you to know that I've received word from both Cora Bailey and Maybelle Stevens about the Bensons," she wrote.

It seems you were right and I was wrong. They were arrested in South Carolina, and they evidently have a long record of thievery in a number of states.

I'm very sorry, Russ. More sorry than I can say. I was hasty, I misjudged you, and as a result things came to such an unhappy ending.

I wish you well . . . always.

You know the thrill of
escaping to a world where
Love, Romance, and
Happiness reach out
to one and all...

Escape again...with 4 FREE novels and

get more great Silhouette Special Edition novels —for a 15-day FREE examination— delivered to your door every month!

Silhouette Special Edition novels are written especially for you, someone who knows the allure, the enchantment and the power of romance. Romance *is* alive, and flourishing in these moving love stories that let you escape to exotic places with sensitive heroines and captivating men.

Written by such popular authors as Janet Daily, Donna Vitek, Diana Dixon, and others, Silhouette Special Edition novels help you reach that special world—month after month. They'll take you to that world you have always imagined, where you will live and breathe the emotions of love and the satisfaction of romance triumphant.

FREE BOOKS

Start today by taking advantage of this special offer—the 4 newest Silhouette Special Edition romances (a $10.00 Value) *absolutely FREE,* along with a Cameo Tote Bag. Just fill out and mail the attached postage-paid order card.

AT-HOME PREVIEWS, FREE DELIVERY

After you receive your 4 free books and Tote Bag, every month you'll have the opportunity to preview 6 more Silhouette Special Edition romances— *before they're available in stores!* When you decide to keep them, you'll pay just $11.70, (a $3.30 savings each month), *with never an additional charge of any kind and no risk!* You can cancel your subscription at any time simply by dropping us a note. In any case, the first 4 books, and Cameo Tote Bag are yours to keep.

EXTRA BONUS

When you take advantage of this offer, we'll also send you the Silhouette Books Newsletter free with each shipment. Every informative issue features news about upcoming titles, interviews with your favorite authors, and even their favorite recipes.

Thinking about the letter once she'd posted it, Paula wished she could assault the square mailbox on the corner and get it back. She could have phrased what she'd said so much better. She could have said so much more, regardless of his secretary's possible inspection.

She could even have had the nerve to write, at the end of her letter, "I love you, Russ."

Chapter Sixteen

$\mathcal{N}$ovember 24 was Paula's birthday. Gram had always called her a Thanksgiving-time baby, and she'd been raised with the warm, secure knowledge that her arrival had brought a lot of happiness into her parents' lives, and Gram's as well.

Her birthday had always been a very special day to her. But this year was different in so many ways, and she didn't feel like celebrating. She was glad that it was a school day, glad that she could immerse herself in her work.

When she arrived home that afternoon, though, there was a number of birthday cards from friends in her mailbox, and they only underlined her loneliness. It seemed as if her close friends had become dispersed all over the country. She got along well with the faculty at the school, though—with the exception of the principal —and she knew that if she'd let a hint slip that it was her birthday, the other teachers would have arranged a celebration for her. Now she wished she hadn't been quite so close-mouthed.

She decided to drive into Boston and treat herself to dinner out and a movie. An old friend, Ralph Emery, lived in Boston and she was tempted to give him a call. But she'd discouraged Ralph the last time she'd gone out with him, shortly before moving to Wellfleet for the summer, and this seemed the wrong time to pick up the threads of their relationship again. No, it would be better to have dinner alone and then find a really good movie to go to.

Paula was running the tub for a bath when her doorbell rang. The man standing on the threshold represented a special messenger service, and the large envelope for which he made her sign didn't look at all like a birthday greeting.

Puzzled, she opened the envelope and drew out a very legal-looking document. She quickly discovered that it wasn't merely legal-*looking,* it was legal.

A deed to Gram's house in Wellfleet, registered in the name of Paula Danvers.

She sank onto the nearest chair, stunned.

It took a while to rally. She examined the document over and over again, but there was little doubt that it was a bona fide deed, unless someone had gone to the trouble to play a very sick practical joke on her.

Paula didn't usually keep much liquor in her apartment, but she did have a bottle of sherry. She poured out a glass and sipped it, cautiously eyeing the deed, which she'd placed on her living room coffee table.

There was a catch to this. There had to be a catch to it. And there was one person who should be able to give her the answer.

On this cold, late November afternoon, Bob Mathews was in his office, and he answered cheerfully after his secretary transferred Paula's call to him.

"The frost really is on the pumpkin down here on the Cape," he told her. "How's the weather up there?"

"I haven't noticed," Paula said truthfully. "Bob, a messenger just brought something very interesting to my door."

"Hmmm," Bob said by way of answer.

"You know what I'm talking about, don't you?" she persisted.

"Yes, I guess I do," he said, his cheeriness fading.

"I think I deserve an explanation about this before I send the deed back to you," Paula told him.

"Send the deed back?" There was no concealing his consternation. "Paula, you can't do that," he insisted.

"I can't accept the gift of a *house* from anyone," Paula said.

"It's your house, Paula."

"That's the most ridiculous thing I've ever heard," she exploded. "Who's behind this, Bob?"

"The person who purchased your house decided not to retain title to it," the real estate agent explained. "It was decided that the title should revert to you. You own the property again, so I'd say you're in the driver's seat at this point, Paula. You turned a nice profit, and you've also been given back your house."

Paula counted to twenty. Then she said, "You can't be serious. I'm asking you again. Who's behind it, Bob?"

"I can't tell you that, Paula."

"You have to tell me, Bob! How do you think this makes me feel?" she implored him. "I *think* I know who's done this, but I have a right to be sure."

Who else but Russ could have done such a thing? But why would he have done it. *Why?*

"I can only tell you that your house was purchased by Mrs. Martha Baldwin," Bob said. "You met her, you talked to her, you came to terms with her about the price for the furnishings."

"And so you're saying that having bought the whole place lock, stock, and barrel, Mrs. Baldwin decided to deed it back to me approximately eight days after I

received the settlement check?" Paula demanded
scornfully.

"I can't account for people's actions, Paula," Bob
Mathews said.

She drew a deep breath. "I can't believe you," she
told him. "This isn't like you, Bob. Gram always felt
you were one of the most honest men she'd ever met.
That's why I listed the house with you."

"I don't think my honesty is at question here," he
pointed out a bit stiffly.

"Well, I do," she flared. "Where can I reach Mrs.
Baldwin? Maybe she'll have something to say about
this."

"I'm not at liberty to give you Mrs. Baldwin's
address or phone number," the realtor told her.

"That's ridiculous, Bob."

"No, it isn't. We dealt through Mrs. Baldwin's
attorneys after your meeting with her, I already told
you that. When the papers were passed, everything was
in order. The deed you have up there in your apartment also is in order."

"Then am I supposed to give the money back?"
Paula queried.

"Don't be foolish," she was told abruptly. "You sold
the house, Paula."

"We're going around in circles," she said desperately. "I sold the house, I got paid a very good sum for it,
and now the house has been given back to me. Certainly you can be direct enough about this to admit it
doesn't make sense, Bob."

"Maybe not to me and not to you," he answered
evasively. "But it makes enough sense to Mrs. Baldwin
so that this is what she wanted to do and she's done it."

"With no explanations to you for her actions?"

"No."

"Bob, will you admit that Mrs. Baldwin has been
acting as a front for someone?" Paula demanded.

"I'm not saying anything more about it," she was

told firmly. "There are ethics in every profession and I intend to uphold the ethics in mine. There are times when confidentiality has to be maintained—"

"Oh, come off it, Bob," Paula interrupted rudely. "You were representing *me* in the sale of the house."

"True," he said smoothly. "I was entrusted with acting in your best interests. And believe me, Paula, that is what I did."

She could get nothing further out of him. Frustrated, she hung up the phone and set about examining the envelope the deed had come in. The name in the upper lefthand corner was that of a prestigious Boston law firm. Glancing at the clock, Paula saw that it was after five-thirty and she was certain that there wouldn't be a prayer of reaching anyone in authority at the law firm, or, certainly, at the Parkhurst Galleries.

It didn't seem possible to her that she could wait till the next day to get to the root of all this. She gave up on the idea of going into Boston for dinner and a movie, took her bath, and then poured herself another glass of sherry and switched on the TV, trying to lose herself in a rerun of an old situation comedy she'd always enjoyed. But this proved to be a fruitless effort.

She heated up a can of chili for her birthday dinner, and was in bed by nine o'clock, hoping that she'd fall asleep fast and sleep soundly so that the night would pass.

She fell asleep fast but she didn't sleep soundly. When she awakened in the morning, Paula felt as if she'd been battered by her incessant dreams. She was in absolutely no state to go to work, and she called in to tell Mr. Claxton's secretary that urgent personal business had come up that couldn't be avoided.

If Mr. Claxton wanted to have her neck for this, she'd face his reaction to this later, when she had to.

By nine o'clock she was pacing the floor, thinking about calling the lawyers who'd evidently handled the transferral of the deed. Which of the illustrious names heading the return address on the envelope should she try to reach first?

None of them, she decided finally. Not until she'd called the Parkhurst Galleries and verified what had become a growing suspicion that wouldn't be suppressed.

Paula remembered that the galleries opened at ten o'clock. She managed to wait until nearly a quarter past the hour before dialing the New York number. Then she asked to speak to Mrs. Martha Baldwin and sat back, her pulse pounding, when she was told politely, "Just a moment, please."

The next minute a woman said, "Hello? This is Martha Baldwin," and Paula at once recognized the voice. It also could have been Helen Edgeworth's voice.

Her mind whirling chaotically, she hung up.

What role did Martha Baldwin play at the Parkhurst Galleries? Once Paula began to think coherently at all, she pondered about this. Then she remembered Russ's personal secretary saying on the phone that she'd be glad to relay a message to his assistant who would, in turn, relay it to him.

Officially, Martha Baldwin must be Russ's assistant. And she must play a very significant role in his business, he must have tremendous confidence in her, Paula mused, if he'd entrusted her to handle the matter of buying Paula's house and then returning it to her.

Paula couldn't help but feel that she'd been sabotaged by Mrs. Baldwin, and she wished she hadn't liked the woman quite so much. It was going to be difficult to confront her under the circumstances. But she'd have to do so.

Paula immediately booked an early flight to New York before she could change her mind.

The Parkhurst Galleries were located in the East Sixties, in a converted building too impressive to be called a mere town house.

A *mansion's* closer to the right word, Paula thought as she paid the cab driver and approached the massive, wrought iron and glass front door.

She stepped into a large foyer from which rooms opened out in every direction. She had the impression of room flowing into room, and she was sure without passing over another threshold that each room would be a repository for fantastic treasures.

A beautifully dressed young woman approached to ask if she could be of help. Even her voice was as modulated and perfect in tone as everything else about this place.

Paula felt awkward, actually gauche, as she requested to see Martha Baldwin.

"Do you have an appointment with Mrs. Baldwin?" she was asked gently.

"No, but I've made a special trip from the Boston area to see her," she answered. She'd deliberately not called for an appointment with Russ's assistant because she'd been afraid she'd be refused.

"If you'll make yourself comfortable," she was told now, "I'll see if Mrs. Baldwin is free."

Paula sat down on a long, low sofa. A wide tapestry had been hung on the wall over it, and she suspected the tapestry must be close to priceless.

The weather had been so uncertain when she'd left Boston that she'd put on her old raincoat, snapping in the fleece lining. Beneath it she was wearing a wool dress that was in an amber tone that almost matched her eyes. The dress was three years old, though, and while it had basically good lines it had already edged out of style.

I'm not a match for even the receptionist in this place, she thought, wishing she'd taken more pains with her hair, her makeup—everything!

From time to time other employees walked through the foyer, but although Paula suspected they must be glancing at her covertly—perhaps with curiosity, she was so out of place here—they were so discreet she couldn't be sure.

Minutes ticked by, and she got up and strolled through a door into one of the gallery rooms, and at once she was transfixed by beauty. The room was devoted entirely to American glass, including beautiful examples of glass that had been manufactured by the Sandwich Glass Company on Cape Cod. The colors glowed, the reds, the blues, the yellows, and the greens all so clear and vibrant. There was very little glass in the world more beautiful, where color was concerned, than some of the old Sandwich glass, Paula decided, going from case to case.

The displays were perfect, too. Backgrounds and lighting had been selected to enhance the glass. And this attention for detail followed through in each of the rooms Paula visited. Each room, too, had its own personality, reflecting a specific subject and period.

There were customers in the galleries, and each seemed to be attended by a courteous employee, obviously there to take care of any possible need, or to provide a potential buyer with accurate information about the object being offered for sale. Paula overheard one brief dissertation on Chinese porcelains and another on German steins, and was impressed.

The Parkhurst Galleries captivated and entranced her. She had no idea of how many rooms there were, nor how many floors in the mansion the galleries occupied. She suspected it would take days to tour the place thoroughly and take in everything. She hadn't even glimpsed the rooms where the paintings, sculptures, and similar works of art were kept.

She was staring at a display of Tiffany glass, remembering that first day at the flea market when Russ had informed her in no uncertain terms that she'd mislabeled her Imperial Jewels bowl, when the young woman who'd met her at the door returned.

"I apologize for keeping you waiting so long," she

said, accompanying the words with a lovely smile. "Mrs. Baldwin was in conference and couldn't be interrupted. If you'll follow me, please."

Paula was led back to the foyer, and then to a small elevator secreted behind the massive staircase that curved up to the second level. And it was only when the elevator started whirring upward that she came close to pushing her personal panic button.

The beautiful things in the Parkhurst Galleries had diverted her temporarily. She'd come close to forgetting her real mission here. Now, reminded of it, she had a terrible feeling of inadequacy. She was going to be facing Martha Baldwin, who was a virtual stranger to her. What was she going to say to her? Almost anything she might say would come under the category of an accusation.

I was a fool to come here, she told herself bitterly. *I should have hired a Boston lawyer myself, and let him handle this. No one can make you accept something you don't want. Especially a gift of this magnitude. But I should have let an intermediary say that for me. I shouldn't have attempted to deal with it myself.*

The elevator came to a stop, the door opened smoothly, and the receptionist said, "Come with me, please, Miss Danvers."

Here, on this upper level—it was the third floor, if she'd counted correctly—there was quite a different world. A long, vertical corridor ran straight ahead from the elevator, and a horizontal one bisected it. The thick carpeting underfoot was a deep shade of sapphire, and the walls were painted oyster white. There were paintings in rich gold frames spaced at intervals, and Paula didn't have to glance twice at them to know they were originals, as valuable as the works hung in most museums.

As she followed the receptionist, all she could see was a succession of closed doors. She felt as if she'd intruded into a highly private world, a world in which she was an interloper. Then, before they reached the end of the long vertical corridor, the receptionist opened one of the doors and said, "In here, if you please, Miss Danvers."

Paula stepped into a large room that was a combination office and a drawing room, with the drawing room atmosphere predominating. A thin woman with jet black hair and huge black eyes was sitting behind a lovely antique desk painted in tones of cream and gold. She arose swiftly, coming around the desk to offer her hand to Paula.

"I'm Eleanor Grant, Mr. Parkhurst's secretary," she introduced herself. "We spoke on the phone the other day."

"Yes," Paula said, knowing that her hands must be cold and clammy to the other woman's touch, and wishing that her pulse would stop fluttering.

"I do wish you had telephoned in advance," Russ's secretary said, but she spoke pleasantly, and there was no shade of reproof in her tone. "Then we wouldn't have had to keep you waiting. This has been quite a busy day, you see."

"That's perfectly all right, Miss Grant," Paula said swiftly. The last thing in the world she wanted to listen to was a polite but meaningless apology.

"Well, then," the secretary said. "If you'll follow me, please."

A memory of a time when *The Wizard of Oz* had been one of her favorite books flitted back to Paula. It had been necessary to follow the yellow brick road to get to Oz. Everyone had followed the yellow brick road, the Cowardly Lion and the Tin Man and the Straw Man and, of course, Dorothy.

As she started out behind Miss Grant, Paula felt that she could well be Dorothy, starting out on the yellow brick road. Except that in this case the road wasn't going to lead to Oz, and possible fulfillment. Rather, her yellow brick road was going to end in Martha Baldwin's office.

Miss Grant led the way out into the corridor, and the

carpeting was like velvet under Paula's feet. This time they went all the way to the end of the wide hall, and Miss Grant thudded twice on the door there before opening it.

Then she went inside, stating first, "Here she is, sir," before holding the door back for Paula.

The "sir" was only beginning to register as Paula stepped over the threshold. And by then it was too late.

Chapter Seventeen

$\mathscr{P}$aula heard the door close gently behind her, and she froze. The room into which she'd stepped was a large one and, like Russ's bedroom in the beach house in Truro, was decorated in aquatic tones. As the blues and greens and turquoise swam before her eyes, Paula was forcibly reminded of the bedroom in Truro, the huge super-size bed, and the bliss she'd found there with this man who was standing behind a large antique oak desk at the far end of the room, watching her.

Bookcases lined the walls of Russ's office even as they did those of his Truro bedroom, and there were comfortable couches and chairs with brightly colored scatter pillows. Some of the furnishings were old, some were new, and they made a happy melange.

She looked across at Russ curiously, noting this, and as if reading her mind he said, "I redecorated recently." Then, with no further explanation, he added, "Come sit down, Paula, will you, please?"

She moved forward slowly, her caution mounting with each step she took. She glanced at him as she lowered herself into the chair by his desk, and saw that he was again dressed in a three-piece suit, this in a heather brown shade. He looked even more tired than he had when she'd seen him at the hospital in Boston, and once again she was alarmed. She didn't think she could bear it if he were seriously ill again. He'd been through enough.

He pulled out the chair behind his desk and sat down. The silence that filled the space between them seemed to have a sound all of its own, and it hurt her ears. Into it, Russ said, "I know you asked to see Martha Baldwin. But it was my feeling that you should deal directly with me."

He sounded as formal as he looked, and it was easy for Paula to imagine that she could feel the rough abrasiveness of the wall he'd built between them.

He was waiting for her to say something, but she couldn't. After a moment he asked impatiently, "Paula?"

She swallowed hard, wishing fervently that she'd never come here. She should have mailed the damned deed back to him.

"I got your letter," he said, and at this she had to look at him. His eyes had never been more green, and today they weren't glazed. They were clear and deep and she could stare right into them.

She said tightly, "I tried to reach you by phone. I couldn't get your number. Your home number, that is. I did call the galleries, but they said you were in Europe."

He frowned slightly. "Did you leave a message?"

She shook her head. "No. There seemed no point to leaving a message."

"I wish you had." He paused. Then he said, "If I'd

known you'd tried to reach me, I would have . . . gotten back to you."

"It was just to tell you that . . . that you were right about the Bensons," she said, feeling miserable.

"Cora also wrote me about the Bensons," he said. "I'm sorry it happened that way, Paula. It must have been difficult for you."

"Yes, it was difficult for me," she agreed. "I felt like such a fool. I *feel* like such a fool. I condemned you, because I didn't want to believe that Hilda could be stealing my things. And I felt that you—"

This was getting on dangerous ground.

"I know what you felt about me," he reminded her, the impersonal tone creeping into his voice that, she'd learned, usually meant he wasn't feeling very impersonal at all.

"No," she protested, and then stopped. She'd come here to do something about the house deed, she reminded herself, she'd not expected to see Russ. She was at a terrific disadvantage, because she'd been caught completely off guard at the sight of him. The force of his attraction for her was as potent as ever. He stirred her sensually as no man ever had before or, she knew to the depths of her heart, ever would again. And she loved him so much. Still, it wouldn't do to tell him that she hadn't meant any of the terrible things she'd said to him. She'd been speaking out of anger and frustration; later she'd come to realize only too acutely how wrong she'd been. But despite this almost irresistible urge just being near him suffused her with, this was not the time to get into emotional issues. Not until they'd settled the matter of the deed once and for all . . . and maybe not even then.

Paula was carrying the legal envelope with the deed enclosed in it in a tote bag. She'd wished for a leather briefcase, which would have been more suitable, but she didn't have one.

Now she groped in the tote bag, found the envelope,

and reached out to lay it on Russ's desk. But the distance was a bit too wide, and the envelope promptly drifted to the floor.

It was a small thing, but it was enough to set Paula even further on edge than she'd been already. She had to get up to retrieve the envelope, stooping down and nearly hitting her head on the edge of Russ's desk before she straightened again. This time she kept a grip on the deed.

"I really think I'd better see Mrs. Baldwin," she said. "This involves her."

Russ was eyeing the envelope rather warily, but there was nothing hesitant about him as he said, "The hell it does! Martha was acting for me. I think you're fully aware of that."

"Regardless," Paula persisted, "she was the one I dealt with, and so did Bob Mathews. I'd prefer to settle this with her."

"She's not empowered to settle it with you, Paula," Russ said almost gently. "Martha had a call from Mr. Mathews last night, so she's aware of your feelings—"

"Traitor," Paula interrupted, feeling completely betrayed.

"What?" Russ asked, perplexed.

"Bob's been a traitor to me, everyone's been a traitor to me," she said, and glared at him. "I suppose when you have enough money you can buy anyone off," she commented bitterly. Even as she spoke, she knew she was literally forcing herself to be caustic, to be angry with him. Because her emotions were at war—and where Russ was concerned, anger was her only possible defense.

She saw his eyelids flicker ever so slightly, but that was all. His face was impassive. He said, "I'll try to disregard that crack, though I'm getting damned sick and tired of having you blame everything that happens between us on money."

"What else is there to blame it on?" she asked him.

"Your attitude, maybe," he shot back, and this time he let his irritation show through.

"I'm not here to discuss my attitude," Paula said stiffly. "If you don't like it, just kindly tell me where Mrs. Baldwin's office is and I'll take it from there." She added, "I thought you were supposed to be in Europe, anyway."

"Or you'd never have come?" he finished for her. "Oh," he said, with an eloquent lift of an eyebrow, "I can believe that. If you'd thought I was within a thousand miles of Manhattan, you wouldn't even have considered coming near this tight little island, would you? Well, no one was lying to you, Paula. I *was* in Europe."

She hesitated, wondering how he'd take this, but she had to know. She asked, "Are you all right, Russ?"

He scowled. "What's that supposed to mean?"

"You're not sick again?" she ventured. "I wondered when I heard you were in Europe. I—I thought of Switzerland. You looked tired and thinner when I saw you in Boston, and you seem even more so now."

"And this concerns you, Paula?" he asked mockingly.

"Of course it concerns me," she retorted, stung.

His voice softened as he said, "No, I'm not sick again. But yes, I am tired and yes, I've lost some weight. It's nothing to be worried about, though." His eyes lingered on her. "I've had a lot on my mind these past few weeks," he said.

He drew a deep breath. "I was in Europe on business," he said. "I got back last night, and as you can imagine, there was quite a bit to catch up with here. I've been in conference all morning, and so has Martha. Mostly about you," he added almost under his breath.

Paula had had only a glimpse of the Parkhurst Galleries, but she could imagine what running them must entail. She would have thought that the matter of the deed to her house—and her displeasure about it as relayed to Martha Baldwin from Bob Mathews—would have received the lowest priority on a very long list.

Russ said bluntly, "If you'd stop and *think* for a minute, maybe you wouldn't look quite so startled. Incidentally . . ."

"Yes?"

He shrugged. Then he said, "I had the impression that you might have a couple of presents for me."

She was astounded. "Me?" she echoed. "Me have presents for you?"

"I guess they'd come under the category of gifts that can be given to the person who has everything," Russ said, not sparing the irony. "Or, to be more accurate about it, to the person some people tend to think has everything."

She frowned. "I don't know what you're talking about," she told him.

"Don't you? Martha said that when you agreed to sell the contents of your house, you insisted that you had to keep two items. A copy of *Robinson Crusoe* and a blue Canton ginger jar. I had the probably mistaken impression that you might have meant them for me."

She didn't answer him. She couldn't answer him. She watched him pick up a millefiori paperweight from his desk, turn it over, and then set it down again.

"You said you'd redecorated," she reminded him suddenly.

"Redecorated?" He stared at her as if he hadn't heard her, then his thoughts seemed to swing back into focus. "Yes," he said, "I did. This office was done in that discreetly elegant kind of style I abhor, and once I came back to it again I couldn't stand it. So I had everything taken out and I started from scratch. This may be a decorator's nightmare, but it's my own. I've also redecorated my apartment, which is on the top floor of this building. I even think you'd approve of what I've done to it."

She sidestepped that. She said, "This building has four stories?"

"Yes," he nodded. "My apartment takes up the fourth floor. We also own the building on either side of this one, so the galleries have plenty of room to spill out. But we're digressing, aren't we, Paula?"

She nodded and, standing, reached over and laid the legal envelope neatly in the middle of his desk.

"I can't accept this," she said firmly. "You should have known that before you did such a ridiculous thing. The deed will have to be changed to your name. I can't understand why you ever made such a gesture. It was foolish and grandiose."

"And arrogant and insensitive and lacking in compassion?" he finished, and she flushed. How often she'd wished she'd never said any of those things to him!

"Yesterday was your birthday," he surprised her by saying.

"How did you know that?" she asked suspiciously.

"It was easy. I checked your driver's license one day when you were out of the room," he confessed, and she held her breath. He'd very nearly smiled as he'd said this, and suddenly she realized she'd give almost anything to see him smile again.

"I'd hoped to get back from Europe in time to fly up to Boston and deliver the deed to you personally," he went on. "But I was held up with some final business in Paris, and I couldn't leave in time. I wanted you to have the deed on the right day, so I asked the lawyers to send it over to you by messenger."

"Oh, they did, they did," Paula assured him. "Having it done that way added such a personal touch. A stark document in a legal envelope, without a single word as to who it came from or why or—"

"I planned to make the trip to Boston tonight and to storm your citadel if I had to, and to explain that, Paula."

"Even if you had, it wouldn't have mattered," she told him flatly. "As I've said, there's no way I'd ever think of letting you do this, Russ."

"And there's no way I'm going to take the deed back and have it altered," he said firmly.

"No?" Paula moved to the desk so quickly that he couldn't possibly have stopped her, and grabbed the envelope. "Then," she said, "you can just burn the damned thing up and we'll both forget about it. But as a starter—"

She wrested the deed out of the envelope and with sure fingers started to tear it up. The paper was tough, but she managed to rip it, and then to rip it again and yet again, and finally she threw the shreds that were left down in front of him.

"I know it must be easy for you to think you can do anything you want, Russ," she told him furiously. "You've been conditioned that way, I guess it really isn't your fault. I suppose your money has always let you ride roughshod over people, but you can't buy me! I never wanted your damned money, anyway. I only wanted—"

She came to a sudden halt, aghast at what she'd come so close to confessing to him. She started to retreat, the need to get out of this place and away from him overpowering her. But before she'd taken two steps he'd come around the side of the desk, and he clamped a strong hand firmly on her arm.

"Finish that sentence," he commanded, but Paula shook her head vigorously from side to side, her beautiful auburn hair rippling as she moved.

"If you have one atom of guts in your whole body, you'll finish that sentence," he threatened.

"All right," she said, challenged. With her impetuous nature she'd never been able to resist a dare. "I never wanted your money," she choked. "I only wanted . . . you."

Time stood still. Russ felt as if he'd been riveted to

the spot, clutching Paula as the magnitude of what she'd finally said to him swept over him.

He'd learned a lot about willpower a long time ago. But he'd never have been able to keep his distance from her. He'd been aching with the need just to touch her from the second she'd walked through his office door. He'd longed so desperately to take her in his arms, to feel those rebellious auburn curls against his cheek, that he'd dug dents into his palms with his fingernails.

He was fully aware that his whole caper in regard to her house had been a quixotic gesture, and he'd known from the time he'd started out on it that she'd resent it initially. He'd hoped that later he could make her understand why he'd been motivated to do what he'd done. But now he wondered if that could ever happen.

It was Helen Edgeworth who'd told him that Paula had put her house up for sale. And it was Helen who'd also told him that he was being an idiot about Paula.

"She's so much in love with you, she can hardly see straight," Helen had insisted, but he'd found it impossible to believe this.

Paula had never told him she loved him. He'd made his declaration, but she'd never returned it. That was a fact that had come back to haunt him many times over the past weeks. That, and a number of other facts.

If he could have given his fortune away, he would have done so. If he could have divested himself of all his assets and made himself poor for Paula, he would not have hesitated. But he was not in a position where he could consider himself alone. He employed hundreds of people in his far-flung business enterprises. They depended upon him, and he owed it to them and to their families to keep the Parkhurst empire on an even keel. He'd inherited obligations and responsibilities with his money that he would gladly have shed many times. But that, he'd often told himself, was part of what life had put on his particular plate and he'd learned to accept it and to deal with it in much the same fashion that he'd come to accept and then to deal with his illness.

He'd wished many times, since the end of August, that he could have explained this to Paula. He hadn't been able to bring himself to seek her out and try, perhaps because he'd known that when it came to talking about his fortune or his position, she was very unreceptive. So unreceptive, that he'd been afraid whatever genuine emotion, whatever love, she'd come to feel for him had been trampled out.

It was very difficult to believe that he'd correctly heard what she'd just said to him.

Russ moistened his dry lips, and asked huskily, "Would you repeat that, please?"

She'd turned away from him so that he couldn't see her face, but he still had his hand clamped on her arm. She shook her head. "No," she said, her voice so low he could barely make out the word.

"Paula, please. Am I dreaming, or deluding myself, or did you really just tell me that you . . . that you wanted *me*?"

She swung around to face him at this, and he saw the torment in her eyes. She said, "Oh, my God, Russ. Didn't you always know that?"

"No," he said. "No. I'm not always as sure of myself as you seem to think I am, Paula. I haven't been sure of myself at all where you've been concerned. If even once you'd told me that you loved me . . ."

"That I loved you?" Her lips curved into a bitter-sweet smile. "Oh, Russ," she said, "how I loved you!"

He thought his heart was going to stop. "Past tense?" he asked her, almost afraid to pose the question.

"Yes," she said, and he was sure his heart did stop. Then she added, "Past tense and present tense and future tense. It seems to me I've loved you forever, and

I love you now, and I'll always love you. Always and always," Paula said, the tears spilling down her cheeks. "Always and always."

Paula hadn't intended to make such a confession. She stopped, appalled, afraid to look at Russ. Then she felt his finger on her chin, tilting her head upward, and in another second their lips met. It was a kiss without a beginning and without an end. Infinite, it expressed all the kisses that ever had been or ever would be, and Paula gave herself up to it, the hurt and the pain that had been a part of her for so long beginning to dissolve.

She felt him tugging at her shoulders, and he said, "Will you kindly let me get this damned raincoat off you?"

She laughed, and then shrugged herself out of the coat, and felt Russ's hands cupping her breasts.

He said, "That's a beautiful dress, it just matches your eyes, but you might as well be encased in armor. Where the hell's the zipper?"

A beautiful dress? She looked at him to see if he could possibly be serious, and found that he was.

She touched his probing hand gently, and she said, "Your secretary might come in any minute."

"She'd better not without announcing her intentions first," he growled.

"Russ . . . stop."

"Do you really want me to stop?"

"No, of course I don't," she said, "but your secretary really might come in, or Mrs. Baldwin, or—"

"All right," he said, and gradually released his hold on her. "All right. We'll go up to my apartment."

"I suppose you have a whole staff of servants there?" she suggested.

He drew back, his eyes narrowing. "We're not about to start *that* sort of thing again, are we?" he demanded.

"No, no," she said hastily. "I just thought that you really would have a staff."

"I employ a man and his wife," he answered. "A

Scottish couple. They're pleasant people. I feel they're my friends as well as my employees. Does that answer some of the questions racing around in that suspicious mind of yours?"

"Yes," she said. "Russ, I don't mean to always be bringing things up to you. It's just that I . . ."

"I know," he said. "At least I think I know. I think maybe part of your problem is that you want to be alone with me as much as I want to be alone with you. With no attendant pomp and vanity. Am I right about that?"

"Yes," she nodded.

"That's one reason why I gave your house back to you," he said, glancing toward the remnants of the deed that lay shredded in the middle of his desk.

"Russ," she began warningly, but he chuckled.

"Maybe," he said, nodding toward the deed, "we can put it together with Scotch tape. Otherwise, we'll have to have a new one issued. If you prefer that it's in both our names, that's all right with me, but I'd honestly rather it was in your name alone. I feel it really is your house, though I hope you'll want to share that and everything else you have with me as much as I want to share everything I have with you."

She frowned at this. "What are you saying?" she asked him.

"You don't really think I ever intended you to live in Wellfleet by yourself, do you?" he asked her. "On the contrary, I felt that your grandmother's house would be a place where we could be alone when we wanted to be. The beach house in Truro is ideal for what it is, but we could spend Christmases in your house and other . . . wonderful times . . ."

Russ's voice faltered slightly, and Paula looked at him more closely. It was hard to believe, but she could definitely see a trace of moisture in his intensely green eyes.

"I'm not doing this too well," he confessed. "Believe

it or not, it's the first time I've ever proposed to a woman, and I suppose I'm scared as hell that you're going to refuse me." He shook his head, smiling at her, and the sight of his smile was dazzling to Paula. "You're such a spitfire," he accused.

"Russ," she began, beginning to feel as if someone had put her in the base of a kaleidoscope and she was turning into a mass of whirling patterns. "Please . . ."

"Paula," he said, "I was serious when I said I planned to fly to Boston tonight to storm your citadel. I would have blasted the whole building down if I'd had to to get to you. When Martha told me this morning that she suspected you were about to toss the deed back in my face, I made up my mind that we'd been apart long enough. Anyway," he added, "I was going to take a second birthday present to you."

"I don't want any birthday presents from you, Russ," she managed.

"Are you sure about that? The present I was going to offer you," he said slowly, "was . . . is . . . me." He placed a firm finger across her lips, silencing her before she could answer him. "Please," he said, "don't tear me up, Paula. And don't try to give me back to myself."

Paula felt a warm current of love for him begin to flow through her, starting at her toes and cascading upward, all the way to the crown of her head. She reached out for him, drawing him against her, and she said, "Give you back? Oh, darling, darling, this is one time when no one's going to take my gift away from me!"

For quite a long while they were both too busy to speak. Then Russ raised his head to ask, "Was I right, Paula? Were the copy of *Robinson Crusoe* and the Canton ginger jar meant for me?"

She leaned back and laughed, her amber eyes sparkling, her lips curved in a tantalizing smile that made her look like a Gypsy princess. This morning she'd put on the gold hoop earrings he'd given her as if they were talismans, and they swung as she teased, "What do you think?"

"I think I'd better find them wrapped up in silver paper and tied with white satin ribbon the day we get married," Russ warned her.

And he did.

a fabulous $50,000 diamond jewelry collection

by filling out the coupon below and mailing it by September 30, 1985

Send entries to:

U.S.
Silhouette Diamond Sweepstakes
P.O. Box 779
Madison Square Station
New York, NY 10159

Canada
Silhouette Diamond Sweepstakes
Suite 191
238 Davenport Road
Toronto, Ontario M5R 1J6

SILHOUETTE DIAMOND SWEEPSTAKES ENTRY FORM

☐ Mrs.   ☐ Miss   ☐ Ms   ☐ Mr.

NAME _____ (please print)

ADDRESS _____ APT. #

CITY _____

STATE/(PROV.) _____

ZIP/(POSTAL CODE) _____

RTD-A-1

RULES FOR SILHOUETTE DIAMOND SWEEPSTAKES

OFFICIAL RULES—NO PURCHASE NECESSARY

1. Silhouette Diamond Sweepstakes is open to Canadian (except Quebec) and United States residents 18 years or older at the time of entry. Employees and immediate families of the publishers of Silhouette, their affiliates, retailers, distributors, printers, agencies and RONALD SMILEY INC. are excluded.

2. To enter, print your name and address on the official entry form or on a 3" x 5" slip of paper. You may enter as often as you choose, but each envelope must contain only one entry. Mail entries first class in Canada to Silhouette Diamond Sweepstakes, Suite 191, 238 Davenport Road, Toronto, Ontario M5R 1J6. In the United States, mail to Silhouette Diamond Sweepstakes, P.O. Box 779, Madison Square Station, New York, NY 10159. Entries must be postmarked between February 1 and September 30, 1985. Silhouette is not responsible for lost, late or misdirected mail.

3. First Prize of diamond jewelry, consisting of a necklace, ring, bracelet and earrings will be awarded. Approximate retail value is $50,000 U.S./$62,500 Canadian. Second Prize of 100 Silhouette Home Reader Service Subscriptions will be awarded. Approximate retail value of each is $162.00 U.S./$180.00 Canadian. No substitution, duplication, cash redemption or transfer of prizes will be permitted. Odds of winning depend upon the number of valid entries received. One prize to a family or household. Income taxes, other taxes and insurance on First Prize are the sole responsibility of the winners.

4. Winners will be selected under the supervision of RONALD SMILEY INC., an independent judging organization whose decisions are final, by random drawings from valid entries postmarked by September 30, 1985, and received no later than October 7, 1985. Entry in this sweepstakes indicates your awareness of the Official Rules. Winners who are residents of Canada must answer correctly a time-related arithmetical skill-testing question to qualify. First Prize winner will be notified by certified mail and must submit an Affidavit of Compliance within 10 days of notification. Returned Affidavits or prizes that are refused or undeliverable will result in alternative names being randomly drawn. Winners may be asked for use of their name and photo at no additional compensation.

5. For a First Prize winner list, send a stamped self-addressed envelope postmarked by September 30, 1985. In Canada, mail to Silhouette Diamond Contest Winner, Suite 309, 238 Davenport Road, Toronto, Ontario M5R 1J6. In the United States, mail to Silhouette Diamond Contest Winner, P.O. Box 182, Bowling Green Station, New York, NY 10274. This offer will appear in Silhouette publications and at participating retailers. Offer void in Quebec and subject to all Federal, Provincial, State and Municipal laws and regulations and wherever prohibited or restricted by law.

SDR-A-1

Silhouette Special Edition. Romances for the woman who expects a little more out of love.

If you enjoyed this book, and you're ready for more great romance

...get 4 romance novels FREE when you become a Silhouette Special Edition home subscriber.

Act now and we'll send you four exciting Silhouette Special Edition romance novels. They're our gift to introduce you to our convenient home subscription service. Every month, we'll send you six new passion-filled Special Edition books. Look them over for 15 days. If you keep them, pay just $11.70 for all six. Or return them at no charge.

We'll mail your books to you two full months *before they are available anywhere else.* Plus, with every shipment, you'll receive the Silhouette Books Newsletter absolutely free. *And with Silhouette Special Edition there are never any shipping or handling charges.*

Mail the coupon today to get your four free books—and more romance than you ever bargained for.

Silhouette Special Edition is a service mark and a registered trademark.

She fought for a bold future
until she could no longer
ignore the...

ECHO OF THUNDER

MAURA SEGER

Author of **Eye of the Storm**

ECHO OF THUNDER is the love story of James
Callahan and Alexis Brockton, who forge a union
that must withstand the pressures of their own
desires and the challenge of building a new television
empire.

Author Maura Seger's writing has been described by
Romantic Times as having a "superb blend of
historical perspective, exciting romance and a deep
and abiding passion for the human soul."

COMING NEXT MONTH

ONE MAN'S ART—Nora Roberts
To Genevieve Grandeau, love meant giving, sharing...trusting.
Grant Campbell was a loner. Could he, would he, allow
himself to be drawn into the life of this beautiful socialite?

THE CUTTING EDGE—Linda Howard
Brett Rutland's search for an embezzler brought Tessa Conway
into his life. For the first time, Brett was falling in love...until
his heart's desire became his prime suspect.

SECOND GENERATION—Roslyn MacDonald
Hollywood had taught costume designer Deanna Monroe that
there was no such thing as instant love. But Rick seemed to
defy Hollywood law, and Deanna was too charmed to realize
she could be heading for heartbreak.

EARTH AND FIRE—Jennifer West
Chalon Karras had once fallen in love with and married a rich
older man. Now Chalon was filled with grief over his sudden
death, and guilt at her growing passion for his dangerously
handsome son.

JUST ANOTHER PRETTY FACE—Elaine Camp
They met while working together on a film shot on location in
Egypt. Among the pyramids, assistant director Savanna Collier
and actor Teague Harris discovered the passion that made
Hollywood infamous, and treacherous.

MIDNIGHT SUN—Lisa Jackson
Because of a bitter family feud Ashley Stephens and Trevor
Daniels had tried to deny the flaming passion between them for
eight long years, but even fiery hatred couldn't keep them apart
forever.

AVAILABLE THIS MONTH

ALMOST HEAVEN
Carole Halston

WATER DANCER
Jillian Blake

REMEBER THE DREAMS
Christine Flynn

SWEET BURNING
Sandi Shane

TEARS IN THE RAIN
Pamela Wallace

THAT SPECIAL SUNDAY
Maggi Charles